Praise for *Hostile Takeover: A Love Story*

"Piano has done a great job of marrying the corporate world with the complicated world of the heart. Love and business collide in this novel where the intricate dealings of business intersect with one woman's past and change everything about her future. Fun and entertaining, *Hostile Takeover* will definitely make you a believer in true love."

—Kris Radish, best-selling author
of *The Year of Necessary Lies*

"*Hostile Takeover* is touching story about love lost and found. Piano's heroine, Molly Parr, is unsinkable as she navigates stormy romances and the murky waters of the corporate world. Smart and sassy, Molly rides the waves of life, living by her motto, 'you have to love with your head and your heart.'"

—Judith Hennessy, author of *First Rodeo*
and co-owner of White Raven Productions

T0160861

hostile takeover

hostile
takeover

a love story

PHYLLIS J. PIANO

SparkPress, a BookSparks imprint
A Division of SparkPoint Studio, LLC

This book is dedicated to my mother, Marjorie,

who always wanted to be a writer.

table of contents

chapter one

Molly smoothed her skirt and straightened the jacket of her business suit, looking in the mirror for the last time before she left for work. It was early, still dark outside. Her shoulder-length, light-brown hair had the right shape and shine, her hazel eyes accented with just a touch of eyeliner. She was attractive, but not conscious of it.

The past year had been extremely difficult for her, and she knew she wasn't herself. So often, she felt she was watching herself going through the motions of life.

Molly used to relish her job as a corporate attorney and was rewarded for her hard work with a promotion to chief counsel for her company. But her life wasn't her job, and that became all too apparent over the last year.

Even though she tried to put it out of her head for *just a minute*, she couldn't. It was exactly one year ago today that he died.

Grief hit in stages, and Molly felt she'd experienced them all. Jim and Molly had decided to wait for children, as both their careers were humming along, and they took advantage of their time off by traveling the world.

They'd met in law school, and from the day they first talked, they were never apart. It had been a great love and wonderful life, and their friends and family envied them. But now it was all over.

Molly was nearing forty and would never have Jim's child, perhaps any children now. It was pancreatic cancer that took him just three months from the day they received the diagnosis.

He fought to live, participating in experimental drug trials, but it was too late. Pancreatic cancer is so scary, as there often are no symptoms. He was vibrant and healthy, and then he wasn't. Molly had little time to adjust to the possibility of his death, and then there it was. Final. Irrevocable.

While she put up a good front by forging on with her life and deeply immersing herself in her work, Molly was struggling.

Both friends and family wanted her to begin to move on, even tried to set her up on dates. But she had no interest. She continued on, but the joy was gone. There was just this eternal flatness, this living, but not really *being*. She always hoped it would get better over time, but she didn't feel it yet.

Molly grabbed her purse, settled into her car, and backed out of the garage, heading out into the rainy, early March New England morning. She gazed at the puddles alongside the road, ringed by the sprouting of new, emerald-green grass, and looked up to see the steeple of the old, white clapboard church on the corner.

She hoped the gray beauty of this day would lift her spirits. If not, she hoped her assistant, Cissy, who always seemed to find the exact right thing to say, could help pull her out of this mood. Her work was a refuge, and she could spend sixty to seventy hours a week buried in every tiny detail. It was a blessing really, but life didn't have the same purpose without Jim and their future together.

Molly arrived at her office and hadn't even taken off her coat when her assistant came in with lattes for them both.

Cissy, a petite blonde in her forties, slipped into a chair and placed the coffees in front of them. "All your appointments have been pushed back until nine thirty, so we can have a good gab. We can talk about Jim or whatever you want to talk about. It's your call."

Molly gazed at her assistant with great affection, and tears filled her eyes and spilled out onto her desk.

Cissy bounded up and grabbed some tissues. "I didn't mean to make you cry. I'm so sorry," she said, tears of her own brimming her eyelids.

Molly wiped her cheeks and smiled. "There was no way I wasn't going to shed tears today. Thanks for delaying my appointments and giving me this time to gather myself.

"I don't want anyone else to know about this or to talk to others in the office about Jim. Once I'm ready for the day, I'll be okay." She showed the same spirit she'd demonstrated time and again over the past year.

Cissy reached over and grabbed the photo of Jim and Molly from the back of her desk. Jim was tall with light-brown hair and a slim, athletic build. His smile was kind and open. "You must miss so many things about him."

Molly took the photo from her friend and colleague. "This was taken on our honeymoon in Italy. We went to Sicily after touring the Amalfi Coast and posed for this picture in Taormina among ancient ruins. So beautiful…" she murmured.

"I miss talking to him, being with him, planning all our adventures and our future… and of course, the intimacy. I miss him so much." Molly sighed. She knew she could talk to Cissy about anything.

Both women took long sips of their lattes and were silent for a moment.

"Well, Jim was the love of your life. I've never heard you talk about any other. Was he your first?"

13

Molly's face clouded, and it was difficult for Cissy to read her. "No, there was a passionate love before Jim, but it ended badly," she answered quietly, eyes downcast.

Cissy wanted to hear the whole story, but the phone rang and Molly picked up. "Yes, Ken. I'll be right there. This does sound like an outstanding opportunity." She hung up, nodded at Cissy, and moved urgently to see her boss, as he was resetting all their meetings. And just like that, the hectic day began.

The time flew by in a whirlwind of meetings, phone calls, and frantic emails, and it wasn't until six o'clock that Molly and Cissy came up for air. Their company was a conglomerate, WHK Industries, and it had quadrupled in size in the last few years through organic growth and strategic acquisitions.

Ken Squareton, the CEO, had been with the company for thirty years, waiting for his turn to lead. He was a classic CEO in so many respects: tall and handsome and a brilliant visionary who commanded respect.

He could have left the company many times to take leadership jobs elsewhere, but that wasn't Ken. He was ethical and loyal to a fault, and perhaps that's why Molly held him in such high regard.

Ken was also a mentor to Molly and helped her move up the ladder with him during her fifteen years with the company. He recently asked her to take on the company's philanthropy and foundation, as he valued the work they did in the communities in which they had a presence. Ken wanted Molly to expand their corporate citizenship programs globally.

She found this work fascinating and wished she had more time to devote to it, but her day-to-day legal work and her responsibilities with the company's board of directors kept her too busy. Nonetheless, Molly truly appreciated that Ken contin-ued to give her more responsibility and challenging work.

When Jim died, she didn't know what she would have done without her job and Ken and his wife, Jen. They took Molly out for countless dinners and events and included her in family gatherings with their three wonderful sons, as Molly's family was back in the Midwest. She knew she had an unusual situation at WHK with Ken; the rest of corporate America was another story.

Molly was energized by all the confidential meetings that day about a potential acquisition that could transform their company. There would be lots to do in the coming weeks. It was good to feel excited again and engaged with her work. *Maybe I am making a little progress with my grief,* she thought, *even on this particular day.*

As Molly was trying to get through a few more emails, Cissy came into her office with a proposal. "I say we go out for dinner. You've had a stressful day, and I know getting through this particular day must be so difficult. So let's celebrate Jim's life with a really great bottle of wine and dinner."

Molly smiled at her assistant. Cissy Slocek was so intelligent and such a great person. She found herself pregnant at seventeen while still in high school, had the baby after she graduated at eighteen, and married the father. Unfortunately, her husband became an abusive, alcoholic monster, and she left the marriage with her two kids and literally nothing else.

Cissy started working at the business as a temp when she was nineteen, working her way up over time to become a top executive assistant. If she were able to get an education and focus on her career early in her life, Molly had no doubt she could have done anything at the company, including her job.

She worked hard to give her kids all the advantages she didn't have when she was young. Her daughter, Erika, became a physician's assistant, and her son, John, was a software engineer.

Cissy had done a fantastic job of raising them on her own; she couldn't be prouder of them.

It must have been awful for her to deal with her abusive husband. Not long after they divorced, he drank himself to death, so the kids only had their mother growing up. The hardships she endured were difficult to imagine, and Molly admired her so much.

She knew it was unusual to have such a close relationship with her assistant, but Cissy was exceptional. And both women worked hard to separate their business relationship and friendship.

"Well, it sounds like an offer I can't refuse," Molly said, smiling at her friend. "I suppose you already have reservations."

Cissy laughed and nodded. "Absolutely. It's our favorite, Bellini's."

Molly shut down her computer, and the women headed out.

Bellini's Italian restaurant was decorated in a very contemporary but warm fashion. The candles created a nice, soft glow, and the small vase with fresh flowers provided a beautiful centerpiece as the women dined on expertly crafted cuisine. They ordered one of the best bottles of Barolo and didn't blink at the price, as it was a special occasion to honor Jim.

"It's nice to have such a luxurious meal today with a great bottle of wine. It makes me think of Jim and some of our very best days together," Molly said, smiling sadly.

"Let's have a toast to Jim, a fantastic man and wonderful husband," Cissy said, raising her drink.

"Cheers," they both said, clinking their glasses.

"Well, with what's going on at work, it looks like we did the right thing in having our dinner tonight. It sure seems we'll be busy for some time." Cissy knew all the confidential information at the company, and Molly trusted her implicitly.

"You're right," Molly replied, nodding. "It looks like we'll have plenty of late nights."

"Given that we'll be so busy and won't have any time to gossip, I want to hear about this 'passionate' love you brought up this morning. I've been dying to know about this all day, but we were too busy," Cissy said with keen interest.

Molly squinted at her with a frown. "It's kind of a long story…"

chapter two

Seventeen Years Earlier...

Molly couldn't believe she was about to graduate from the University of Wisconsin and then head to law school. What luck she had to be accepted at Northwestern Law School, which was several hours' drive from her Wisconsin hometown. She won a small scholarship, and her parents had saved everything to give her the kind of education they couldn't afford for themselves. She also worked up to three jobs during college to help defray the expenses. Molly never splurged on anything, but she thought graduation deserved a first-class celebration.

She had an outstanding circle of friends at school, and she knew they'd go for her idea to celebrate graduation with a party and a live band. Her roommate Ruth's parents' house would be perfect for the event.

Combing the classified section in the school's paper, she spotted the description of just the right band:

If you want a party band to get your friends moving, you need to hire Rockster Tunney. We're a four-piece rock band that can play rock classics as well as some of the most popular R&B favorites. You ask us, we'll play it. We're cheap, too, because we need the bread. Party on!

Molly dialed the number at the bottom of the ad. A deep, resonant voice said, "HEEELLLLOOOOO, this is Tunney of Rockster Tunney. What can I do for you?" Stifling a giggle, Molly explained she needed a band for a graduation party. After some haggling, they agreed on two hundred dollars and set up a time to meet at the student union to discuss the set list. He argued about this a bit, but she insisted. She had to make sure this band was presentable and up to the task. Two hundred dollars was a lot of money!

On the day of their meeting, Molly ran over to the student union bar, which was located in the basement. The students didn't seem to mind the dark setting, as the bar featured a number of excellent drafts. She looked around and saw a tall, lanky man with hair down to his shoulders, cowboy hat, and ripped jeans. It had to be Tunney.

He must have been about six three and looked to be about five years older than her. He smiled as she put out her hand to shake his. "I don't usually meet women with a handshake, if you know what I mean," he said slyly.

Molly laughed out loud as she slid into the booth.

Tunney grabbed the waitress and ordered two beers. "Hope that's okay with you, 'cause you're buying."

"I guess so," Molly answered, a bit shocked he was making her pay.

Over the next hour, they talked about the songs the band would play, both rock and R&B, and the other members of the band. Rockster Tunney was made up of Tunney's brother Tam, cousin Murph, and best friend Brett.

It sounded like the band was pretty good. They'd played at some local clubs and opened for some touring rock acts coming through town. Molly found she really liked Tunney and enjoyed talking with him.

"Why do you and your brother have such strange names?" she asked him.

He smiled and said, "Well, those are the names we've used all our lives. My mom insisted on giving us these awful, traditional family names, and my dad immediately gave us nicknames. They seem to fit us."

"But what are your real names?" Molly asked, knowing she wouldn't receive a straight answer.

"You need to know me a lot better to find that out." He laughed. "And even then, I probably wouldn't tell you."

They agreed to chat on the phone just before the party in May.

As Tunney left the student union, he called out, "It's on the calendar in ink, boss!"

The weeks after Molly met with Tunney just flew by with exams, studying, and work. She helped out at the student newspaper, served as a teaching assistant, and did some tutoring on the side. It seemed she didn't have time to breathe.

Molly dated a bit, but it was nothing serious. It felt like most guys wanted more than she was willing to give, and some of the guys she really wanted to ask her out didn't. But Molly wasn't concerned. She focused on her studies, her work, her friends, and the graduation party.

Ruth and Molly went to Ruth's parents' house the week before the party to plan everything out. The partiers were asked to bring something, mostly finger foods. The band would perform outside, near the pool. Ruth's family was the most well-to-do of their crowd of friends and lived near the school. Her parents were off on a European holiday but would return in time for the formal graduation ceremonies the following week.

After a final call with Tunney, the band agreed to arrive around eight. The music had to stop before midnight because the girls were concerned the neighbors would complain about the noise. Ruth had promised her parents they would clean the house and make sure there would be no trouble.

The night of the party, Molly took extra care in getting ready. She wore her best jeans that showed off her figure and a silky mint-green top with a beautiful patterned scarf around her shoulders. Her hair was long and feathered around her face. She was looking forward to seeing Tunney again and meeting the rest of the band.

Molly was the first to arrive, and she and Ruth rushed around to get everything ready for the party. Extra chairs were set up, snacks put out, and other food stored in the fridge to serve later.

Bobby, Ruth's boyfriend, who she met in business classes, was the leader of the crew in charge of the drinks, which included kegs of beer, soft drinks, and cheap wine. Bobby was just a fantastic guy, always helping friends with schoolwork and chores like moving.

Bobby and Ruth had been dating for over a year, and it seemed really serious. They were one of the few couples Molly knew that could make it together long term. She envied their relationship. She wanted to understand what it was like to be in love like that.

Ruth and Molly weren't really sure how many people were coming, but they thought it could be as many as a hundred. But as guests came in a steady stream, both women felt they would exceed their estimates.

Molly spotted Tunney's cowboy hat above the crowd as he sauntered into the party. She'd already had a glass of cheap wine, so she greeted him with a hug. He gave her an amused look and asked where they should set up. She led him over to the spot, and he agreed it would work, as there was easy access to power at the side of the house.

"Well, Miss Molly, let me get this band set up and then I'll introduce them to you, *boss*," he shouted as he walked toward the van. Tunney sure could make her laugh.

Molly and Ruth walked over as the band was finishing their setup, and Molly introduced Ruth to Tunney. After a few quick words, Ruth excused herself. She wanted to freshen up before she addressed the crowd and introduced the band.

Tunney grabbed the guitarist, who had his back to Molly, and spun him around. "Molly, this is our lead guitarist and my brother, Tam…"

Molly reached out her hand to Tam and faltered. He was about two inches shorter and younger than Tunney and had collar-length, dark-brown hair and steel-blue eyes. He wore a chambray shirt with jeans that fit him perfectly. Tam was gorgeous.

When their eyes met, she felt the attraction sweep through her. She'd never felt like this before. When she took his hand, she felt like she didn't want to let go.

Somehow she got her words out. "Oh…Tam, so nice to meet you." Molly finally took her hand away but couldn't stop looking at him. It was hard to tell how long they stood there, eyes locked.

Tunney eyed both Molly and Tam and said with a sly smile, "Tam, you can flirt with *the boss* later. For now, you need to help this band get set up so we can play for these kids."

Molly flushed red and told both of them she would see them during the break when they could grab some food. She looked Tam in the eyes again before she ran off, and he gave her a nod and a crooked grin.

She was so rattled that she ran away from all the others to shut herself behind the closed door of the upstairs bathroom, locking it tight. She popped the toilet lid down and sat there to gather herself.

Looking out the window, she could see Tam setting up the amps and then testing the sound. It was like he was the only person out there. Her heart beat so fast and her palms were sweaty. She needed to get ahold of herself and calm down. After all, she was the co-host of this graduation celebration.

"How in the world am I going to make it through this party?" she wondered out loud. "Stop acting like a besotted schoolgirl."

Molly gathered herself, joined the party, and got drawn into multiple conversations with friends. She relaxed for a moment, as it seemed like everyone was having a good time. She actually stopped thinking about Tam while chatting.

When Molly heard Tam singing right after Ruth's introduction and welcome, the sound of his voice jolted her. She grabbed some more cheap wine, hoping that would calm her down again.

Excusing herself from a circle of friends, she headed to the kitchen, busying herself by replenishing some snacks and bringing some finger food from the refrigerator out to the patio, where most of the partiers were gathered.

Molly went back into the kitchen and looked out the big picture window above the sink to see Tam playing the guitar and pulling the microphone closer to begin the next verse. Of course, he was singing one of her favorite songs, and she couldn't take her eyes off him.

"Don't you think you should join the party rather than watching it through the window?" Ruth teased as she came into the kitchen with empty bowls to refill.

"I was just putting more food out for our guests," Molly said, flushing again.

"You don't have to put on an act with me. I know what's going on with you. Just remember what they say about musicians…"

"That they're a bit dangerous?" Molly answered.

"Listen. They seem like great guys to me, but what I've heard from a couple of my friends who dated musicians is there are always other women and plenty of illegal substances. Maybe you should just steer clear," Ruth suggested.

"I think it may be too late for that." Molly sighed, and she went back outside.

Walking near the pool, she was corralled by a number of friends from school. She walked around, playing the host, introducing people, and continuing to replenish the snacks. She carried around her glass of wine but didn't drink much, as Molly decided she wanted to keep her wits about her. All the while, she kept tabs on Tam. She loved hearing his voice, and his guitar playing was first rate.

The whole band was really rocking, and Tunney's bass lines and vocals were fantastic, too. She edged closer to the band and stood and listened for a minute. It didn't take long for him to spot her.

As the song ended and the applause rang out, Tam stepped up to the microphone, looking straight at her.

"It's wonderful to be here tonight," he said, continuing to stare right at her as the crowd clapped and hollered their support. "It's not every day the band gets a view as beautiful as this."

Molly could feel herself heat up again… It was the strangest thing to know she and Tam were having a conversation of sorts and the crowd was oblivious.

"Y'all have been a great audience, and we'll do a couple more songs and take a short break. Here's a special one, just for you," he said, smiling right at Molly.

She was mesmerized and couldn't move her feet from her vantage point even if she tried, but she didn't *want* to move. Molly just wanted to look at him, basking in his attention. When he started to sing, she couldn't turn away.

While Molly and Tam remained in their "conversation,"

there were at least two people who noticed what was going on. Tunney glanced over at his brother and saw the way he looked at Molly and her intense gaze back.

This ain't good, Tunney thought. Tam was a real ladies' man; he had them coming and going. Looking like him and being in a band... Well, being in the company of women wasn't a problem for guys like Tam.

Tunney smiled to himself, as he did all right with the ladies too. The smile faded, though, when he thought of Molly. She wasn't like the women who usually flirted and connected with his brother.

Tunney had enjoyed his "meeting" with her at the student union very much. Molly seemed like a fantastic girl with her head on straight, destined for success. He thought she seemed sweet and a bit innocent. He didn't want to see her hurt, and if Tam's history was any indicator...

Ruth was standing on the other side of the pool and saw exactly what was going on. She didn't know Tam at all, and she couldn't judge his intentions, but she could see her friend was in deep. She made her way over to Molly.

As the song ended, Ruth grabbed Molly's arm. "Aren't they fantastic?" she shouted, leading the crowd in applauding the band.

After the applause died down, Ruth steered Molly by the arm and asked, "Can you come help me in the kitchen?"

They made their way through the crowd to the kitchen, and Ruth pulled Molly into the pantry and shut the door. "I wanted to drag you away from there before everyone saw what was going on between you and Tam. It's just so obvious," Ruth said excitedly. "So... you know Pete came here to ask you out. He's a fantastic guy, pre-med at the University of Chicago, and is a much better fit for you than some womanizing musician."

Molly flashed back and remembered Pete had come over earlier and they had a few words, but she'd excused herself to go to replenish snacks in the kitchen *and* stare out the window at Tam. She liked Pete a lot but wasn't attracted to him. *Damn.* Now, she felt embarrassed and angry.

"That's not fair. You don't know anything about Tam," Molly said. "And I think the world of Pete, but I'm not attracted to him. Sorry!"

Ruth regarded her with frustration. "Would you have said that a few hours ago before you met Mr. Hot Rock Singer? Face it. A guy like Pete is a much better match for you."

"That's not how it works. You have to feel with your head *and* your heart. I don't have that with Pete. I'm so happy you love Bobby, both with your head and heart, but please don't try and run my life and tell me who I can be with and who I can't."

With that, Molly pushed past Ruth and flung herself out of the pantry. She headed outside to where the band was playing, and her timing was perfect, as they just ended the last song before their break. She was upset with Ruth, and now Molly had missed the rest of the set while she was being lectured in the pantry.

She stopped and applauded loudly as the band took their bows. She headed directly to Tam and Tunney. "That was fantastic. Would you and the band like to have something to eat?" she asked.

Ruth quickly appeared at her elbow. "I can show you where to grab some food, and I think you've all earned a beer," she said a bit too cheerfully.

"Thanks. I think we'll take you up on that," Tunney said to Ruth. As she turned to lead them to the kitchen and the band followed, Tam stopped and gently touched Molly's arm.

"Maybe we can grab something together," he said.

"I'd really like that," she whispered.

Molly and Tam walked to the kitchen together, lagging behind Ruth, Tunney, Brett, and Murph. Tam grabbed the kitchen door and held it for her. She smiled at him as she went inside, ducking beneath his arm. She quickly assembled two plates for them, and he grabbed two beers.

"Where to?" Tam asked.

Molly tapped his arm with the edge of one of their plates and led him to the study to get some privacy. It was a nice office, with an Oriental rug, leather couch, dark wooden desk with two chairs, and tall, beautiful built-in bookshelves up to the ceiling.

She closed the French doors to the study so she had Tam to herself, avoiding potential intrusions. They sat in the desk chairs and put their drinks and plates on the table, making sure not to make any marks on the beautiful wood. Molly meant to keep her promise to Ruth's parents to keep the house pristine.

"Well, this is nice," Tam said. "Just the two of us. Gives us a chance to get to know each other. If I'm honest, I was thinking about you the whole time we were playing." He smiled, quickly taking a bite of his sandwich.

"I was, too," Molly answered quietly, a bit surprised at their candor. "I guess I'll start so you can eat, since you're the one working tonight."

She explained she was an only child with wonderful parents from a small town northeast of the university and was graduating with a degree in political science. She knew she was babbling a bit as she talked about her family, her close circle of friends, and then described her upcoming studies at Northwestern Law School in the fall. The truth was Molly really wanted to hear about him.

He seemed to be listening carefully as he finished his

sandwich and swigged his beer.

"Your turn now," Molly said, tipping her cup toward him before she took a sip.

"Well, you already know I have a brother named Tunney and a cousin named Murph, and Brett's also a good friend of mine, and we're all in a band together."

"What does Tam stand for?" Molly interrupted. "I asked Tunney what his real name is, and I didn't get very far!"

"Well, you may never know that." Tam laughed out loud. "I have another brother and a sister. My grandparents and parents were immigrants from Poland, and my last name is Rozomolski.

"But to tell you something you probably didn't expect—I'm just finishing my masters in engineering from the university this month."

Molly didn't try to hide her surprise. "You're right; I *didn't* expect that. You're such a good singer and guitar player. I thought you were probably pursuing a career in music."

"I love music and actually took some courses when I got my undergraduate degree, but the band is Tunney's," Tam answered. "Frankly, I don't think he'll ever pursue anything other than music. He loves it. I've loved it, too, but I always knew I wanted to do something else with my life. The problem is I'm not entirely sure *what* at this point." He laughed. "I can't really even tell you why I chose engineering—probably because I'm good at building things, and a close friend of the family suggested it as a good career.

"My parents didn't have much of an education, so they weren't much help directionally, other than showing us the value of hard work and encouraging us every step of the way," he added.

Molly agreed. She thought his parents sounded a lot like hers. "It's hard to know what's ahead, what the right choices are…"

"You seem to know exactly what you want," he said, pushing aside his empty plate, moving over to the couch, and patting the seat next to him.

"I'll admit the law has always been interesting to me, so I guess you're right—"

Tam interrupted her as she settled in next to him. "I wasn't talking about your career choice."

Molly flushed *again*.

"You blush quite easily," he pointed out. "When I was singing to you and when we met, you flushed red just like you are now," he said, smiling broadly. "It's really cute."

Molly's blush deepened further as she crossed her legs and turned toward him. "This is so embarrassing. I'm sorry I can't be as cool and collected as you."

Tam moved closer to her. "You don't need to be cool and collected with me," he said as he looked in her eyes, adjusted her scarf around her shoulders, and touched her cheek.

Just then, the study doors burst open and Tunney strode in, startling them both. "Tam, I warned you about flirting with the *boss*. Now get your ass back outside. We have work to do," he said sternly.

Tam rolled his eyes and rushed out, visibly upset by his brother's intrusion.

Tunney grabbed Molly's arm and said quite seriously, "Didn't your mother tell you to stay away from musicians? They may be great at a party but not so great in the long run."

Molly broke free. "Thanks for the advice," she mumbled as she headed after Tam.

The band was getting ready to start again, and Molly pulled Tam aside just before he had to go on. "Can we talk after you're done playing?"

Tam took both her arms in his hands and looked deeply into

her eyes. "Yeah, we need to finish our conversation. Please don't let others convince you otherwise."

Looking into his steel-blue irises, Molly didn't want him to let go of her, but she knew the rest were ready to start. She pulled away and nodded, letting him know they would see each other later.

The band played more classic rock and R&B, and the crowd loved it. Plenty of folks got up and danced when they starting playing Stevie Wonder's "Superstition." It was a favorite of Molly's, and she had a tough time not dancing to it, so she grabbed Ruth and they had a great dance together.

When the song was over, Ruth pulled Molly aside and asked, "Are we okay?"

Molly gave her a hug and told her, "I know you think I'm going to get hurt. *But* I need the chance to get to know Tam, and I will," she said firmly.

Her friend looked at her with great concern and nodded solemnly. "I understand."

It was time to start closing down the party, half past eleven, so Ruth asked the band to play one last song. Molly stayed out of Tam's sight. She wanted to listen to the last song on her own, focusing on him and the music. She closed her eyes, listening to his beautiful voice, and smiled to herself.

At the end of the song, she heard Tunney speak to the crowd and Ruth come to the front to thank the band and all the guests for coming out to celebrate graduation.

Molly started the kitchen cleanup to have some time on her own. In just a few minutes, she would see Tam again. What would she say? She absolutely knew what she wanted to do, but was it the right thing?

Tam, Tunney, Murph, and Brett were breaking everything down to load their instruments and equipment into the van.

Tam pulled Tunney aside because he didn't understand why his brother acted the way he did earlier.

"Why did you pull me away from Molly like that?" Tam asked, clearly irritated. "You know I would've come back on time after the break."

Tunney gave him a long look. "I did it because I've seen all the chicks you've dated and dumped. This girl is something special, and I think you could really do some damage here.

"So my advice is don't get involved unless you're serious. That's it. It's not like I should be the one giving anyone advice about women. It was never my best subject at school," Tunney said as he broke down the amps.

"I get that you and Ruth don't think this is a good idea, but there's something about this girl. You see it, too.

"I need this chance to get to know her. I'm serious about that," Tam said, just loud enough to be heard by his brother, not the other musicians or the partiers, who were still animated, laughing and talking, as they filed out to their cars.

"Okay," Tunney said. "But please, take it seriously. Molly deserves that."

Tam nodded and headed out to find her.

She was in the kitchen, putting snacks away, washing dishes, and trying to get everything back in order.

Tam came into the kitchen and walked behind her at the sink. He came so close she felt his breath as he whispered in her ear, "Do you think you could take a break?"

She spun around to face him and took him by the hand to lead him into the pantry. Shutting the door behind them, she smiled to herself about the irony that she was with Tam in the same room in which Ruth lectured her about how wrong he was for her. Things were moving fast now.

Tam pulled Molly to him and looked straight into her eyes;

she would always melt when she saw those beautiful steel-blue eyes. He touched her hair, then her cheek, and she grabbed his hand, running it over her face.

Molly reached up and felt the stubble on his cheeks and traced his soft lips with her finger. His hair was so dark and thick, and she had to touch it, feel his hair between her fingers. She felt so brazen, but she wanted to know him, touch him all over. When she looked in his eyes, she could see her abandon and passion was equally matched.

Tam kissed her gently to start, and she felt incredible electricity. She linked her arms around the back of his neck and they kissed urgently, passionately, and she didn't want it to end. The truth was he didn't either...

Molly pulled away to look him in the eyes.

"Unfortunately, I think we should leave before someone breaks in here," she said softly.

"Okay," he answered, "but not before this..." He gathered her in once more. The kiss was wonderful but different. It felt sweet and sad yet full of promise.

Molly opened the door and snuck out with Tam right behind. He headed out to help load up the band equipment, and Molly continued the cleanup, both in the kitchen and outside on the patio.

Bobby and Ruth were loading large bags into the trash container when Ruth spotted Molly on the patio and walked over. "Looks like you had a bit of an interlude in your cleanup efforts."

Molly was in no mood to pull any punches. "It was the most wonderful few minutes I've spent in my entire life. He's kind, sweet, and intelligent in addition to being gorgeous. And, oh, by the way, he didn't mention any drugs when we talked *and* is finishing his masters in engineering," she added.

Ruth cocked her head at her friend and then threw her

hands in the air. "I give up. All I want is for you to be happy. You deserve to be. I guess I get a little protective when I really care about someone."

"You're just going to have to trust me on this," Molly said, giving Ruth a hug. "I wonder if I could be released from my cleanup duties early?" she asked mischievously.

"Well, you did get a head start on us… so you're free to go. Give me a minute and I'll get the cash to pay Tunney. I know you want to thank him too," Ruth said.

Molly nodded as Ruth walked away, heading in the band's direction.

Tunney was getting ready to take the last bit of equipment to the van when Molly approached him. "Tunney, I can't thank you enough. You and the band were great. It was a magical night."

"Boss, I can't help believing I'm no longer your favorite member of the band," he said with a twinkle in his eye. "I talked to my brother about you and told him not to screw this up. I think he has a lot more experience with the opposite sex than you do, and I'm not trying to get personal…"

Molly laughed. "You may be right about that, but I'll be okay. Thanks for your concern."

Ruth walked up just then with the cash to pay the band. "Tunney, thank you for doing a great job tonight. I heard from many of our friends about how much they enjoyed the band.

"You made this a special night for all of us, and I hope you thank the entire band on behalf of Molly and myself," she said, handing him the two hundred and an extra twenty as a tip.

"Thanks for that," Tam said, joining the small group. "But I was hoping Molly would thank me herself," he said with a sly grin.

Molly reddened again and looked toward the ground, and Tunney broke the awkward silence. "Well, we've loaded the van, been properly thanked, and I have the dough, so it's time to hit the road, brother. That is, of course, unless you want to walk home."

Tam looked to Molly. "I can give him a ride," she said.

Ruth observed Tam and Molly and said, "It's a beautiful night. Why don't you two grab a drink and sit by the pool? Bobby and I are just finishing cleaning up the house."

"Thanks so much, Ruth," Molly said, beaming at her friend.

"You're kind to offer," Tam agreed, nodding his thanks.

"Well, it's time for this old rocker to hit the road," Tunney said and headed to the van.

Molly stopped him and gave him a hug.

"Darn it. Ain't I the lucky one?" Tunney laughed. "I got a hug coming in and now going out from this beautiful woman."

Molly looked up at Tunney. "Thanks for doing such a great job and for looking out for me. Thanks for everything."

"No problem, boss. Don't do anything I wouldn't do," Tunney said as he walked away.

Ruth came back out with a glass of wine for Molly and a beer for Tam. "Enjoy," she said, immediately stepping back inside the house.

Tam and Molly sat in two loungers near the pool. It was an amazingly warm May night for Wisconsin, so they didn't even feel chilled. It was dark outside now, but the pool lights were on, which created a wonderful, soft glow.

Molly turned to Tam and asked, "Where do we start?"

Tam laughed. "I kind of liked where we left off before."

"So did I, but that's too easy, isn't it?" Molly giggled.

"I'm not sure anything is easy with you."

"I have to be honest. You scare me because I want to know you so badly," Molly said, staring straight into those beautiful steel eyes, "*in every way*, but this attraction I feel for you is so intense, and our worlds are about to change so much…" Her voice trailed off.

Tam sat up straight. "You do have a tendency to analyze things."

"It's a habit of mine," Molly said, shrugging unapologetically. "You know Tunney and Ruth have some concerns about us getting together. Should I be concerned?"

"Wow, I've never had an *interrogation* to be with a woman. Maybe it's the law school thing." He laughed. When Tam saw Molly wasn't joining, he sobered and said, "Okay, I'm serious about this as well, so tell me your concerns."

"Well..." Molly started. "I'll be leaving for Northwestern at the end of the summer and will be in law school two years. You're finishing your engineering degree and don't know where you're going to be or what you're going to do. I've also been cautioned by *your own brother* and my smart and dear friend to be careful around you."

Tam frowned. "It sounds like you're trying to talk yourself out of being involved with me already."

Molly laughed and flashed her eyes at him. "I'm afraid that's not possible. Especially after our time in the pantry."

Tam put down his beer and moved over to her lounger. She scooted over to make room for him. He cupped her face and kissed her very tenderly.

When they broke apart, she whispered, "I can't really invite you home with me. I have three roommates."

"Let's go to my apartment," he offered, kissing her more urgently this time.

Molly touched his face, and she pulled away slightly. "I need to tell you something if I'm going to your apartment tonight."

Tam looked at her expectantly. "Sure, Mol, anything."

She didn't let her friends call her "Mol," as she hated it, but she loved it when Tam said it.

"I... um... I'm a virgin," she whispered unsteadily.

Tam sat up a bit straighter. "You don't pull any punches, do you?"

He knew she'd focused on her education rather than dating, but he was surprised to hear she was a virgin. Wow. *This complicates things*, he thought.

Tam knew being Molly's "first" could deepen things between them further. Damn, he'd never had to think this hard about sex. This woman really was trouble, but he felt like he already had strong feelings for her. The whole situation was new for him.

She popped up and looked into his eyes, sensing his concern and second thoughts. "You're not chickening out, are you?" she asked.

"I wouldn't say that. It's just this is a big thing in your life, and I'm not sure you're ready. We just met tonight, and I don't think you're the type of girl to sleep with a guy you've just met. I can't believe I'm saying this."

Molly lifted his face to look directly at him. "It is difficult for me to put into words how much I want you. And it's not only because I melt every time I look into your gorgeous eyes. It's what I see in you. Everyone wants to paint you as this ruthless womanizer, but that's not what I see at all."

Tam regarded her with questioning eyes and asked, "What do you see?"

Molly paused for a moment. "I see the most incredible man—intelligent, kind, talented, driven. He'll achieve a lot… be respected, revered actually. He'll have lots of loyal friends and women falling in love with him…"

"Like you?" he teased.

Molly kissed the side of his face, his neck, his nose, his eyes before bringing her lips to his. "If you're lucky," she whispered before getting lost in him. When they stopped kissing, they just stayed in the lounger, holding each other.

Tam and Molly talked for quite a while and decided they should have at least one real "date" before they took their relationship any further.

If it were up to Molly, she would have gladly gone back to his apartment the night of the party, but Tam insisted they begin their relationship differently. So instead of spending the night with him, Molly dropped Tam off at his apartment. She did her best to get him to change his mind, not letting him leave the car before their passionate kisses steamed up the inside of the windows. He stuck to his guns, however, and wished her good night.

The next morning, she sat in her bed, drinking a cup of coffee and laughing to herself, remembering the scene from the night before. Tam pressing himself against the windows and insisting he had to leave the car. What did he say?

Mol. We have got to stop before I grab you and take you into the apartment with me.

It was very difficult to let him go. Having his arms around her felt so good, and she loved kissing him, the taste of him. When she playfully unbuttoned the top two buttons on his shirt and ran her hands over his bare chest, he moaned his pleasure. She felt warm just thinking about it. Their passion for each other was evenly matched, but Tam was right for them to get to know each other. Molly couldn't wait to see him again.

She heard a knock on the door, and Ruth came in. "Well, you're in bed late this morning. Bobby just dropped me off. It's almost noon. Aren't you going to let me know what happened?"

Molly smiled. "Come on in. I'll give you the short version. No, I didn't sleep with him, but that wasn't for lack of trying. When I told him I was a virgin, he insisted we have a chance to get to know each other. We're going to have a 'real' date, and we'll go from there."

Ruth looked a bit surprised and cocked her head and said with a raised eyebrow, "*He* was the one who insisted on no sex, not you? I'm sorry, but that seems hard to believe."

Molly pointed at Ruth. "You need to give him a chance. How many times does he have to pleasantly surprise you until you realize he's a pretty great guy?"

She frowned. "Not sure yet, Molly. Now don't run out of the room and yell at me again. I'm not trying to tell you what to do. I just want you to proceed with caution."

Molly shook her head. "I'm being honest with you when I say 'caution' isn't a driving force for me right now—just the opposite. To be in Tam's arms was something I've never experienced before.

"I feel like he's just so special. I could be falling in love with him, and I'm so ready to make love with him. I dream of it."

"That's exactly what I'm afraid of," Ruth said.

chapter three

Present Day...

Tim Bart sat at his desk at TBBM Technologies and looked out the window at the beautiful view. As the CEO, he had the best office in the building. Everything was gleaming, sleek and new.

He'd started at the company after he got his MBA, and TBBM grew in leaps and bounds, in no small part due to his acumen in leading strategy and acquisitions. He was rewarded with rapid promotions and was named the youngest CEO in the company's history the year before.

Tim always credited his team for the company's—and his—success and prided himself on his ability to pick the right people, and those in his senior ranks were top rate. He preached people development to his leadership team and they took it seriously, and his firm was now a sought-after employer.

The company's results were fantastic, and its stock price was one of the best performers this year on NASDAQ. Tim's name was starting to pop up in the media in lists of young, talented CEOs. He didn't necessarily like to be in the news, but it was rewarding to him just the same.

He'd just met with a set of investment bankers to talk about launching a takeover bid for a company he felt would be a good fit for TBBM Technologies. While TBBM was more of a high-tech company than the target he hoped to acquire, Tim felt the older corporation could be a real *cash cow* to feed the growth of his faster-growing company.

Tim lost his train of thought about the acquisition as he looked over at the photo of his wife—now ex-wife—and kids. He loved his kids more than anything, and the split really hurt them badly.

Most people at the company didn't know; it wasn't anyone's business. Tim really kept to himself when it came to personal information. He had no interest in reliving his past or having anyone snooping around in his life. Business is business, and his personal life was his own. And this acquisition would provide him with a much-needed distraction.

He stared out the window at the pristine New England scenery. What *was* his personal life? It seemed like the only thing he did outside of work, business dinners, and travel was spend time with his kids. They were growing up so fast. Chad was ten and Marnie was twelve going on twenty-one. She wanted to grow up so fast... hair, makeup, boys... That really scared him, as he thought of himself as a teenager and his pursuit of girls. He grimaced.

Tim was going to have to find a way to have a chat with his daughter about boys and sex. He knew his ex-wife, Della, had already approached the subject, but perhaps the two of them could sit down with her. He hoped Della would consider that. She was a good woman, and he had loved her. In the end, however, their marriage fell apart as their interests diverged. *Maybe I could never love her enough,* Tim thought. It was sad, but it happened every day. His big regret was it was tough on their children.

Della and he had worked very hard to keep things upbeat when they were all together, but still... when your Dad isn't living in the same home, it has an impact. Tim couldn't help them with their homework every night or just ask them about school or their friends at dinner. He missed that so much.

He thought the divorce would become broader knowledge soon, so he planned to tell his team and change the picture on his desk. Gerrie, his assistant, knew all about the split, as there had been lots of calls and meetings with the attorneys, which she helped arrange.

Thank God, Della was reasonable about the money and assets involved in the divorce. She would be well taken care of, and the kids would never have to worry about their future. How different that was from his upbringing, where money was scarce.

He knew his parents and siblings were proud of him for what he'd accomplished. He just wished he didn't live so far from them now.

Tim had gotten a fantastic, modern condo in downtown Boston when he moved out of the beautiful suburban home he'd shared with Della and the kids. He loved the city so much, but his new "home" didn't feel like a very warm place. Comfortable, yes. Warm, no.

At this point in life, Tim had no desire to become seriously involved with anyone. He couldn't accommodate any new people in his life. There just was no room. Maybe that's why he left the photo on his desk.

The buzz of the intercom brought him back to business. "Tim, everyone is assembled and ready for the acquisition meeting," Gerrie said.

"Send them in," Tim answered. He headed over to join them in his adjacent conference room, as lawyers, financial folk, and bankers filed in and seated themselves around the table.

"Welcome, everyone," Tim said. "Let's get down to business on the acquisition of a great American company, WHK Industries."

chapter four

Molly beat Cissy into the office the day following their dinner, and this didn't happen very often. They had enjoyed such a wonderful evening together. Women help other women get through difficult times in their lives, and Molly was grateful for Cissy's friendship and outstanding support at work.

Celebrating Jim's life and their marriage felt right to her, and while talking about Tam had been difficult, she actually felt okay with it.

She chided herself, though, saying out loud, "You only talked about the good times, Mol. How will you handle it when you get to the part where you felt like your heart was being torn out of your chest?"

Cissy appeared at her doorway. "Talking to yourself?" She laughed. "I guess that's what happens when we share a bottle of wine with dinner."

Molly smiled. "It was a lot of fun, and it helped me get through a difficult and taxing day. I can't thank you enough."

"No thanks required," Cissy said, coming in and flopping down in one of Molly's desk chairs. "Anyway… you didn't get to the end of the story." She paused expectantly.

Just then, Molly's phone rang, and she could see it was Ken. "Saved by the bell." She laughed as she picked up the receiver.

After a brief exchange, she said, "Sure, Ken, I'll be right over." With that, Molly grabbed her notepad and headed over to see her boss.

When she reached his doorway, he waved her in and asked her to shut the door. Molly was surprised, as she thought there would be a whole gang of folks to talk about the acquisition, but it was just her and Ken.

She was startled to see he was white as a ghost. She'd never seen him like this, and she hated to admit it, but she was worried, really worried.

"Read this," Ken said.

Confidential
Dear Mr. Squareton:
It is the sincere hope of the board of directors of TBBM Technologies that we can explore a combination of our company with WHK Industries.

We hope to sit down with you and your chief legal counsel to discuss whether there may be common ground for pursuing a combination of our great companies.

It is strongly suggested that you meet with our team before this becomes public.

I would appreciate the courtesy of a prompt reply.

Sincerely,
Tim Bart
Chief Executive Officer and Chairman
TBBM Technologies

"Well, let's talk to our bankers and get our outside counsel in right away," Molly said, immediately in business mode and taking appropriate action.

Ken shook his head slowly. "I know you're my senior legal counsel, and I pay you for your expertise, but I want to meet with them. There's no way this can make sense. We're bigger than them," he said firmly.

"They may have smaller revenues, but their market cap could be much bigger than ours. Yes, I've heard of them, but I don't know their company, their strategy. I strongly urge you not to meet with them," Molly said, her eyes flashing with real concern. "And we have a fiduciary responsibility to tell the board."

"Molly, I know you well enough to see you feel strongly about this. I want the facts, and we will, of course, fulfill all our duties to inform the board and the public as required.

"For now, cancel all your meetings and examine all their SEC and legal filings to see what you can find out. I will do some research as well about the CEO and the company," Ken declared. "I'll make sure all the meetings we had planned on our acquisition target are delayed."

"Ken—" Molly was going to protest again, but he interrupted her.

"This is my decision. My call. You work for me, so please get on with it. And do *not* speak to anyone about this. I mean *anyone*."

She nodded and headed out obediently.

When she returned to her office, she told Cissy to cancel all her meetings, most of which were about the acquisition WHK wanted to make, which, most likely, would never happen now that her company was under attack.

Molly shut her office door and didn't come out all day. Cissy brought in a salad for her lunch.

She read through TBBM's 10K legal filings, other public Securities and Exchange Commission (SEC) records, and company press releases. She saw a few press articles on earnings and the like, but she wasn't interested in any of the "fluff" pieces on the CEO and the company. Ken would be looking at all of that, and he counted on her for her assessment of all the legal filings and the financial footing of the company.

Unfortunately, what she saw was a company that was more valuable than hers, had much higher growth rates, and a clear strategy laid out for the future. This was a solid corporation. *What a shame*, she thought to herself. Ken was so responsible for the success of their company, but he was foolish to think he could fend off this takeover attempt. Yes, some takeovers weren't completed, but it sure looked to Molly like TBBM had the ability to raise the capital for a very attractive offer.

Ken had never spoken to her in the tone he did earlier and that bothered her as much as the fact that she knew she was right to advocate calling in all the external advisors immediately.

They desperately needed expert external legal, financial, and public relations counsel, and that meant meeting with investment bankers, their own chief financial officer, strategy team, external public relations counsel specializing in takeovers, and more… Her head was spinning. Why wouldn't Ken listen to her?

It was Molly's job to make sure they were doing everything correctly along the way, and if these talks advanced, there would have to be public disclosure very soon.

Molly grabbed her head, overcome with a horrible headache. She'd sent Cissy home, as she couldn't tell her anything about this, so she couldn't be of any help.

It was after seven when Ken finally came to her office. "What do you think?" he asked. When she relayed to him all the information she found, his shoulders slumped. "Not good." He sighed and rubbed a hand across his forehead.

"No, it's not," Molly answered truthfully but gently. "We may have to tell the board very soon after meeting with TBBM, and then, of course, there will be public disclosure."

"I promise after the meeting with TBBM, we can pull in all

the external advisors. I'll have Nell set up some time for us with a few key people tomorrow, including the financial and strategy folks, as soon as we return from the meeting with TBBM. We'll meet all our fiduciary responsibilities, I assure you," he said, and Molly nodded her agreement.

"We're meeting with TBBM tomorrow at their corporate offices near Boston." Ken continued. "I'm picking you up first thing in the morning."

chapter five

Ken and Molly arrived with plenty of time to spare for their critical meeting at TBBM. After they checked in through security, they were greeted in the lobby by Gerrie, the very professional executive assistant to Tim Bart. She was incredibly gracious and welcoming, offering to pick up coffees for them and making them comfortable in the waiting area outside Mr. Bart's office.

Molly picked up a copy of the company's annual report and was studying the financial summary on the inside front cover when Gerrie brought their drinks.

Molly put down the report before she got the chance to see the CEO's letter and photo. She'd read the letter as part of the SEC filings, so Molly certainly knew what it said, but she hadn't seen all the graphics and photos, and those details could say a lot about a CEO and company.

Just then, a number of folks came over to introduce themselves, including TBBM's chief financial officer, head of accounting, their general counsel, their corporate secretary... Molly was quickly thinking they were *so* outnumbered. She knew the two of them taking this on alone was a very bad idea.

The TBBM team led them into a conference room next to the CEO's office, and they all took their seats. Ken was to sit next to Tim Bart, and the TBBM chief counsel would be on his left. Molly could see there was a door that led from the conference room to the CEO's office, so he would enter that way. Everyone had to be assembled and seated before he entered the room, per protocol.

Molly didn't want it to be "us versus them," so she sat across from Ken, a few folks down. She didn't need to be close to the CEO. Besides, he might be able sense her anger and frustration with him.

Just after she took her seat, she couldn't believe it. Molly could tell she was just getting her period. She knew if she didn't get to the ladies' room, it could be very embarrassing later. She discretely excused herself and rushed out, asking Gerrie to direct her to the restroom. Gerrie graciously got up from her desk and escorted her.

"Can you believe my body took this exact moment to figure out it was that time of the month?" Molly whispered. "I would never be late for the start of a meeting like this, but I guess I can't tell this room full of men why." Molly laughed nervously, breaking the tension. "I hope you'll keep my secret," she added.

"I am sworn to secrecy," Gerrie said, waiting outside the ladies' room. When Molly emerged, Gerrie said to her, "Now we can see if we can get back before Tim joins the others."

To Molly's chagrin, the CEO was already in the meeting. He had his back to her and was chatting with Ken. She hurried in, took her seat, and Ken jumped in to introduce her formally, "Marjorie Parr, I want to introduce you to Tim Bart, TBBM's CEO."

At that moment, Tim had sat down and picked up a crystal pitcher to fill his water glass and then turned to look at her.

She looked into his eyes and lost all composure. "Tam," she shrieked.

Tim jumped up, dropped the pitcher onto his glass, and it

shattered, sending shards flying everywhere. In trying to steady everything, his hand went right into the fragments, and he screamed out loud, bleeding profusely. The CFO shouted for Gerrie to call the company doctor.

Molly ran over to him with a few napkins from the table and her scarf and tried to stop the bleeding.

He said, "Washroom," and led her to a door that went directly into his office and then into a private restroom.

She grabbed towels and pulled a piece of glass from his hand, then wrapped the hand in a towel, holding it tightly.

"Molly, I can't believe it's you. It's great to see you, but not necessarily under the circumstances…"

They both tried to stop the bleeding while they talked, Molly wrapping extra towels around his more injured hand.

"I'm sure the doctor will be here in a minute," Molly tried to assure him.

Tim nodded and grimaced in pain.

"Who the heck is Tim Bart? That isn't your name. I had no idea it was you," Molly said with some agitation, but she also couldn't help but have sympathy for him, as he was clearly struggling with the pain.

"I changed my name to make it easier for business. I was always spelling Rozomolski for everyone. It drove me nuts." He chuckled, holding the towel tighter. "I didn't know it was you, either. I saw your name was Marjorie Parr. That didn't ring any bells because I knew you as Molly Greenly. So is Parr your married name?" He stared down at the bloody mess between them.

"Yes, that's my husband's name. I mean *was*…" Molly stammered. "He died just about a year ago, pancreatic cancer."

Tim turned apologetic eyes toward her. "Oh, Mol… I am so, so sorry…" he said with real emotion.

She started when he used the affectionate nickname he had

for her, but she continued to use a wet towel to clean his other hand, face, and neck of the spattered blood.

Just then, Gerrie and the doctor ran into the washroom. "I'll let you take over. He's really bleeding quite a lot," Molly said to the doctor, who quickly declared they needed to head to the hospital.

As they rushed out, Tam said, "Molly, we need to finish our conversation as soon as possible…"

All the people who'd been around the table were standing now, shocked and confused because they had no idea what just happened.

"I'm sorry, but we'll have to reschedule this meeting as soon as Tim is available," Ken said. He grabbed Molly's arm, and they headed out as fast as they could to exit the building.

They got into the car waiting at the curb and the driver sped off. "What the hell just happened?" Ken barked. "You obviously know Tim Bart *really* well. Why didn't you tell me?"

"Because I had *no idea* Tim Bart was Tam Rozomolski, the first love of my life," Molly cried back, working hard to keep hold of the whirlwind of emotions tumbling through her mind at the moment. "Just as he didn't know Marjorie Parr was me."

"Didn't you see his photo in the annual report or any other press articles?" Ken asked.

"No. I focused on all the legal filings online. I was just about to see his letter and photo in the annual report when we were sitting outside his office, but all the people in the meeting came by to introduce themselves," Molly answered. "When we were driving here, you kept talking about his MBA from Dartmouth, and Tam had a masters in engineering from the University of Wisconsin, not an MBA."

"According to one of the articles, he worked outside the United States after receiving his advanced engineering degree and then returned to the States and was accepted at Dartmouth,"

Ken said. "Very bright guy, it seems, except for smashing the glass and pitcher and cutting up his hand," he added smugly.

"That's not fair. He was as shocked to see me as I was to see him," Molly stated with a bit of anger.

"Oh, so now you're defending him, the black knight who wants to take over our company," he replied with contempt.

Molly stared at him but remained silent.

"This complicates things," Ken said on a defeated sigh.

"*Really?* No kidding!" Molly answered with less restrained emotion.

For the first time, she looked down at herself. There was blood everywhere. Unfortunately, she'd chosen a beige suit, and it was stained, along with her blouse, and her hands, which were shaking, still had some blood on them. It was then the flood of emotions broke free and she started crying.

"I am so sorry. I'm a total mess, and I don't just mean my clothes," she shouted through her tears.

"Okay, okay, let's just calm down," Ken said, patting her hand while the driver made the turn off the freeway. "You've had the worst year of your life, and today is adding to your stress, and unfortunately, I'm not helping.

"We're taking you home. You don't need to come back into the office if you really feel like you can't," Ken said gently, putting his arm around Molly. "You need to clean yourself up and take time to gather yourself. We both need to think about this situation as well. Can you call me later?" he asked.

Molly used a tissue to dry her tears and blow her nose and said calmly, "No need to call. I'll be in the office as soon as I can put myself back together.

"Don't tell Cissy what happened. I'll explain everything later. Just tell her the meeting will be rescheduled and I needed to stop home before coming into the office. I would appreciate it."

The driver turned the car into Molly's driveway, and Ken regarded her with concern. "Molly, I'm so sorry I got upset, but as you can attest, it was a pretty bizarre scene.

"We'll figure a way through this... on the business end. I know what a consummate professional you are and have been for the fifteen years we've worked together. On the personal side, Jen and I will do what we can to help..."

Molly smiled. "Thanks. I'm sorry I lost it. I just can't talk about this right now. I need some time to process what's just happened... See you later," she murmured as she exited the car.

She walked in her front door and dropped her purse and briefcase with her computer on the couch. She crumpled to the floor, crying again. Seeing Tam, the blood, her emotions, the takeover, Jim's death... it was all just too much.

She thought of Jim, their lives together, which started just after Tam's betrayal. Tam... How could Tim Bart be Tam? How could she face him over what would most likely be a hostile takeover of her beloved company?

It was too much to contemplate. She stopped crying but stayed on the floor for a long time, curling up into a ball. As she lay there, Molly listened to her breathing, trying to gather herself and figure out what to do next.

Just then, her cell phone rang. She didn't want to talk to anyone, but she needed to see who it was. "Hello," she said, sitting up, resting against the couch.

"Molly, I'm so sorry to bother you, but this is Gerrie from Tim's office. He asked that I call you to tell you he's just fine, but they had to take him to surgery to sew up his hand properly. There may have to be some plastic surgery.

"He's very anxious to talk to you. Could we set up a time for a meeting?" Gerrie asked.

Molly was silent for a moment. She wasn't sure what to

say. Did she want to talk to Tam? What would she say to him? Could she handle it? How could she talk to him about their relationship with the takeover looming between them? This was just too hard.

"Thanks, Gerrie. I'm home now and need to take a shower and get my suit to the cleaners," Molly said, hoping to sound like she was okay, but her quivering voice betrayed some of the emotion she felt.

"The doctor said you did a great job stopping the bleeding quickly and made a real difference," Gerrie added.

"Well, I'm glad of that," she answered softly.

"In addition to setting up a time to talk to you, Tim also wanted to be sure you were okay," Gerrie said gently.

"While I appreciate the call and your concern, please tell Tim I am far from okay." She hung up. She didn't want her emotions to betray her any further.

Molly stripped off all her clothes and jumped in the shower. She let the hot water stream over her face and hair, and she lathered all over to clean off any last vestiges of Tam's blood. *Tam's blood!* How could this have just happened?

She had so many questions to *even start* the process of figuring out what to do next in her personal and professional life.

When she thought about Tam and their relationship of so long ago, Molly's head started spinning, and she tried to focus instead on how to address the complex business issues of the takeover, but that was fraught with peril as well, and she couldn't maintain her concentration.

Molly closed her eyes and tried to see Tam, the Tam of today, not her love of seventeen years prior. She remembered looking into his eyes, the same steel blue. His hair was shorter now, of course, still thick and dark but flecked with gray and styled in a contemporary fashion that suited his face.

As she recalled, he wore a stylish, dark-blue suit with pin-stripes, and he had on a blue, patterned tie with a white shirt; at least it was white until it was spattered with his blood. He had a few more lines around his eyes and had no stubble like the old Tam. Perhaps he was also more serious and less mischievous.

Was he still kind or did he turn into a cold-hearted business-man ready to gobble up her company? What would it be like to know him now? Would she want to?

Was he reaching out to her because he wanted to manipulate her over the takeover, or did he still care about her? She shuddered at the possible answers to her questions.

Molly realized she'd totally lost track of time in the shower, trying to reconstruct what had happened at Tam's office.

She turned off the water and buried her face in the plush towel. Steam filled the bathroom and fogged all the mirrors. She needed to get ready to go back to work, so she would focus on that. She resolved to put one foot in front of the other to try and move forward. It was the only thing she could handle right now.

chapter six

Tam woke up in a fog in the recovery room after his surgery. His left hand was wrapped in an ample bandage. *Lucky,* he thought to himself, as he was right-handed. He could see sheets or curtains that hung loosely, providing him privacy, but he could hear things going on outside his closed-off area.

Someone walked by briskly, a nurse perhaps. He could hear moaning across the room.

Tam tried to sit up but was still pretty dizzy. He flopped back down and began to think about the day's events. How did he get here? He remembered blood, lots of blood. But what happened before that?

He went to work… had an important meeting… and then something happened. It was Molly. *Molly's the lawyer for the other side in the takeover. Oh my God,* Tam thought to himself as the details of the day came rushing back.

Now he really wanted to get out of here, but he fell back down as he tried to sit up again. He just wasn't strong enough yet. *Okay,* he told himself, *think this through.* He was desperate to talk to Molly right away. She needed to know the truth about what happened all those years ago.

Wait a minute… He remembered he told Gerrie he wanted to talk to Molly after the accident. *Good.* Tam knew his strong desire to speak with her didn't mean she wanted the same, but he must find a way.

Molly was so beautiful. It was hard to believe they hadn't seen each other for seventeen years.

Tam had never seen her in a business suit, and her hair was shorter and in a more business-conservative style. It was corporate Molly. How was she different than *his* Mol, the woman he fell in love with so long ago? Tam had so many questions in his foggy brain.

He chuckled to himself as he thought of how she would have sized him up after all these years. Tam had never worn anything but jeans with Mol... *his Mol*.

He jerked himself back to reality. She wasn't his Mol, and her anger with him was palpable; he felt it even as she was helping him stop the blood flow. *If you only knew the truth, Molly.*

She will know the truth, he assured himself as he tried to fully recover from the drugs. He started to sit up again just as a nurse came in.

"Hello, I'm Marie, your nurse. How are you feeling, Mr. Bart?" she asked in a cheery voice.

"Marie, I've had an incredibly busy day, and I can't wait to get out of here to get back to the office," he answered groggily.

She chuckled quietly. "Well, Mr. Bart, you can't go back to the office. You have to go home and rest until all the anesthetic has worn off. You've also lost a great deal of blood.

"You can't push yourself too hard. You're going to be in pain," Marie said with some authority. "You'll have a prescription for pain medication, and I strongly urge you to fill it as soon as you're discharged."

He saw an older man in a white coat enter, and he looked vaguely familiar.

"Do you remember Dr. Johnson, Mr. Bart? He did your surgery, and he's here to check on you," Marie explained.

Tam seemed to recall his company doctor knew this other doctor, and the two of them were speaking with him before the surgery.

He was impatient with being treated like a child, but he knew they were doing their jobs and he was still under the influence of the drugs. Tam went along with the doctor's examination and answered all his questions.

"Well, it looks like you came through the surgery well, so I'm giving you this prescription and will release you," Dr. Johnson said, examining Tam as he spoke. "You're not to drive for the rest of the day, and keep your hand elevated above your heart as much as you can for the next three to five days. You're also going to feel a bit weak with the loss of blood you experienced."

"I do feel like everything's a bit fuzzy," Tam admitted.

Marie left the enclosure and told them she was checking to see if someone had arrived to pick him up. She came back quickly and told him he was all set to go but had to be taken to the car in the wheelchair.

"Is that really necessary?" Tam asked with some annoyance.

Marie chirped back, "Hospital policy. Oh, there's your wife."

"My wife?" Tim said with some surprise. "I thought my assistant was coming to get me."

"Well, there must have been a change in plans," the nurse said, looking at him strangely.

Della approached and held his good arm as he got into the passenger seat.

Once they were belted in, Tam turned to her and said carefully, "Della, I really appreciate this, but you didn't have to come pick me up. We're divorced, and I'm not your responsibility."

Della looked at him with tears in her eyes. "I know that, but you are the father of my children and you were hurt. I was worried and wanted to see for myself that you were okay... so I could tell the kids. Remember, you were supposed to see them tonight," she said with an expression of hurt.

"Gosh, Della, I totally forgot with everything going on today. I am so sorry," Tam said, shaking his head.

"Tim." Della called him by the name he'd used since business school. "You don't have anything to apologize for. You just had surgery. I'll explain everything to them."

She made sure he was as comfortable as possible in the passenger seat. "It's better that you go to your condo now and get some rest. It might scare them a bit to see you like this."

Tam looked at his heavily bandaged hand, imagined he looked pretty terrible, and agreed with her reluctantly.

Della pulled into the underground parking for his condo and helped him out of the car, into the elevator, and through his condo door.

She got him settled on the couch and then checked the fridge. "Tim, you don't have much in here. I'm going to run to the store to get you a few things and pick up your prescription."

"You don't need to do that..."

"I know I don't have to. I want to. In fact, I insist, so hold your protests," she said, bringing him a glass of water. "They told me you need to have a lot of liquids, so please drink this while I'm away." With that, she grabbed her purse and rushed out, keys jangling.

She was a wonderful woman, and he'd tried to be a good husband, but he knew he wasn't. He worked and traveled all the time, and then there was his inability to remain faithful, which ultimately doomed the marriage.

He sighed and sipped his water, gazing out the window at the beautiful view of Boston Common. His thoughts returned to Molly. He must speak to her, see her, but he needed to have all his wits about him.

chapter seven

Seventeen Years Earlier...

It was graduation week, and Molly felt like she was on top of the world. First, all her hard work was paying off, as she would graduate near the top of her class, and second, she and Tam had been planning their first real date. Both had last-minute exams and he had a number of gigs, so they planned to get together in the next few days.

It was also a hive of activity at Molly's flat. All the roommates were preparing to move out and were packing their belongings and marking their boxes to avoid confusion. They were cleaning like mad to make sure they got their apartment deposit back.

Molly planned to spend the summer at her parents' house before taking off for law school. Tam's place was well over an hour away from her parents' small farm, but the two of them would make it work, especially if she ended up staying over with him. She smiled to herself, thinking about spending the night with him as she carried one of her boxes to the dining room where everything was being stored for the movers.

"I would ask you what you were thinking about, but I'm pretty sure I know the answer." Ruth laughed as Molly set her box on the floor next to her other things.

"There's so much to think about. Graduation, moving, the

summer, and seeing Tam of course," Molly replied with a smile. Ruth had been accepted to the business school at their university, and Bobby was headed to get his MBA at the University of Chicago. Thankfully, they, too, would be close enough to see each other often.

"Lots of changes," Ruth said. "I hope we can remain friends, no matter where we end up, no matter what happens. I can't tell you how much I value our friendship."

Molly felt the same way about Ruth, despite their early differences over Tam. "Ditto," Molly said, giving her friend a hug.

The phone rang, and Ruth ran over to answer. "It's for you," she said, smiling, handing the phone over. "Tam."

Ruth headed back to her room to finish packing and give Molly some privacy.

She couldn't wait to hear his voice.

"Hi, Mol. How's everything going?" Tam asked.

"Better now, for sure," she said, feeling a bit embarrassed for telling the truth. "But hearing your voice makes me wish we could see each other right now, but I know you have a gig tonight…"

"If I didn't, I'd be on my way to see you right now." He chuckled. "Listen, the reason I called is I wanted to ask you about our date night. I thought we might have dinner at a place near my apartment. It's nothing fancy, but I think you'll like it. I could pick you up about six, since it'll be a bit of a drive."

Molly's heart was beating so fast. She was trying to take deep breaths without him noticing so she could calm down.

"That sounds perfect, Tam. I can't wait."

They hung up, but Molly held the phone to her chest, smiling dreamily, for a minute before replacing it in the cradle.

chapter eight

Present Day...

Tam had fallen asleep on the couch, his injured hand stacked on pillows, and he woke up to the morning light filtering into his condo. His hand really hurt as he moved it off the pillows.

He couldn't believe he'd slept until morning. It seemed like he'd moved around a bit, as the blanket Della had covered him with was hanging off the end of the couch. Thank God he had a really comfortable sofa.

He got up gingerly and made his way into the kitchen. Della had left him a note:

Dear Tim: I got some groceries, including juice, soups, and bread, and put them away for you. Your prescription is right here on the counter. Let me know if you need anything.
Best, Della.

Her note made him feel like a real jerk. She was a wonderful woman, and she'd been very kind to do this for him. It was too bad they couldn't make it work, but he just couldn't give her what she needed.

If he were honest with himself, he'd never gotten over Molly. After his international assignments and travels, he dated a bit at Dartmouth, but most of the students were a bit younger than him and he just wasn't ready for anything serious.

Tam always called the international period of his life his "exploration" phase, but he knew damn well he was running away after he lost Molly. He winced thinking of it.

Tam made some cappuccino in his new, fancy coffee maker and then drank a cup as he elevated his hand with the pillows and thought about his next move.

Unfortunately, he felt horrible, sick to his stomach, in a lot of pain, and with a throbbing headache, so he took the pain medication and waited for it to kick in.

He couldn't see anyone in the state he was in, so he resolved to work from home, recover his health, and then try and see Molly. He had to talk to her before pursuing any next steps on the takeover of WHK.

There was a knock on the door and then he heard a key turn in the lock. A tall man with long hair and a mustache, wearing scruffy jeans and a cowboy hat, pushed through the door with his duffle bag.

"What the hell'd you do, little brother?" Tunney said, shocked at the bandaged hand.

"Hello to you, too," Tam said, smiling. "It was a helluva day. I'm really glad you're here. You're probably the only person who can help me."

"Well, Tam, over the years, it's always been you helping out your poor excuse for a brother, so I'm happy there's something I can finally do for you, Mr. Successful and Rich CEO Bastard." He laughed affectionately. "Do you need me to stay here and help while you recover?" Tunney asked in his deep, resonant voice. "Don't tell me what you need. Let me guess… You wanna rejoin the band." Tunney chortled.

"I'd be grateful if you stayed to help for a few days, but the recovery shouldn't be that bad. Things are just kinda awkward with only one hand," Tam said. "You know you're always welcome here. Although, I do wish you'd settle down. A man your age on the road with a band... I don't know." He shook his head.

"Look at the Rolling Stones. They're still going strong," Tunney said. "And they're lots older than me."

"Yes, but they make millions, travel by private plane, and stay in the best hotels." Tam contradicted. "You drive a van, stay in dives, and probably make what their roadies earn in a year."

"That's for sure, bro." He laughed. "But what you see is what you get with me. I could never work in an office like you. You've known that your whole life... Anyway, I don't go on the road as much now." He shrugged, changing subjects. "So what do you need me to do?"

"It's about Molly," Tam said, and Tunney looked genuinely stunned.

chapter nine

Seventeen Years Earlier...

Molly couldn't calm down all day in anticipation of her first date with Tam that evening. The two had talked on the phone frequently to finalize the plans, and hearing his voice was the highlight of her day.

She kept thinking about every detail of their date... including the big question: would she lose her virginity to him tonight? Molly wondered if most women knew when they would lose their virginity or if it was a surprise. Had they planned it? Did they just know this was the right person? She was glad she'd gone on the pill to regulate her periods, so that was one really important thing she didn't have to worry about.

Molly thought back to what Tunney had said to her at the party. She didn't have a lot of experience with men, and Tam had plenty of experience with women.

Could she have misjudged Tam? Was he a "womanizing musician" as Ruth suggested? Should she be apprehensive about tonight? Molly concluded she was certainly overanalyzing what could happen.

He'd insisted on driving over to her parents' to pick her up. She offered multiple times to meet at his place, but Tam said no. In the end, Molly was glad he was driving, because she was so nervous. She could see herself getting distracted and running into the back end of another car.

Tam would meet her parents when he picked her up, which was a blessing and a curse. She'd warned them she might stay on his side of town, as they would have wine with dinner. She certainly couldn't say they were planning on having sex, could she? Even though she was twenty-two years old and she could talk to her parents about almost anything, there were some subjects that were off-limits, and this was certainly one of them!

Thinking of Tam arriving at her house that evening, she created a scenario in her head.

"Mom, Dad, this is Tam. Isn't he gorgeous? I'm planning to lose my virginity to him tonight…"

Molly laughed out loud. There was definitely something wrong with her!

She tried to pick out the clothes that were exactly right and make sure her hair and makeup were perfect. She had to admit she was obsessing over all the details, even her jewelry.

Molly felt this incredible passion for Tam, and she knew this was the exact right time for her to make love to him. She hadn't known him very long, but their connection was strong and deep. She wanted to be with Tam so much more than any other man she'd ever known. She needed this, and she needed him so much. She also trusted him, despite all the warnings from Ruth and even his own brother. Molly hoped she wouldn't regret that trust.

As Tam drove over to Molly's parents' house, he scanned the flat farmlands. He shook his head in disbelief, talking to himself. "I'm meeting this girl's parents, and we haven't even slept together… This is our first real date. Am I out of my mind?"

He had no answers for himself and just chuckled. He knew

Molly was special, and he was hopeful about the future. But meeting the parents?

Tunney had certainly given him a piece of his mind when Tam asked him to clear out of their apartment that night so he could be alone with Molly.

"She's a virgin?" Tunney shouted when they spoke that afternoon. "Oh, great," he said, still agitated.

"I need to ask you a question," Tam said, a bit angry himself. "Why is it you seem to be against me, your brother, and take sides with a woman you've known less than a month? Can you tell me that?"

Tunney looked his brother over and took a deep breath. "You know what you mean to me. We're blood. We shared a bedroom growing up, and now we share an apartment and play together in the band. Frankly, I don't know what I'd do without you, but…" Tunney paused.

"But what?" Tam asked.

"You know I think Molly's fantastic, one of the best women I've ever met. There's just something about her. You have this amazing connection. It's hard to miss, really."

"That all sounds good. I didn't hear the 'but' yet," Tam pressed.

"The reality is I'd feel horribly guilty if you hurt her, because I introduced her to you. I met her first when we got together before the gig. If I didn't take that little graduation gig—for much less than we usually get—you'd have never met her. So that's it," Tunney said with a tinge of sadness.

"Wow," Tam said, sitting on the couch in his living room. "I didn't even tell you I'm meeting her parents when I pick her up."

Tunney rolled his eyes. "Well, isn't that just super?" he uttered ironically. "Fantastic. Talk about expectation setting on a first date." He shook his head. "Meet the parents, have dinner, and then screw their daughter."

"Tunney, that's not fair. I have real feelings for Molly," Tam protested.

"I don't question that, bro, but will they last beyond the summer?"

Tam stared at his brother but didn't answer because he didn't know what to say.

As he drove to Molly's, that conversation haunted him. He rode along deep in thought and then realized he was getting close to a turnoff. He fumbled with the map on his lap and found the right road without losing his focus on driving. *They sure do live out in the country,* he thought to himself.

Molly had told Tam quite a bit about her parents. Her father worked for the phone company, installing lines, and her mother had a business selling homemade soaps she made, and they also raised vegetables on their small plot of land to sell at the town farmers' market. Molly said her mother was an amazing cook, using all her fresh vegetables in so many wonderful dishes and canning what was left over. They sounded like good folks to Tam.

He turned his attention back to the road, as it appeared he was just coming to the turnoff to Molly's parents' home. Sure enough, there was their pretty yellow farmhouse, just as Molly had described it.

Tam jumped out of his car and made his way to the door. Molly must have been close by, because she was right there to greet him before he could even ring the bell.

"Hi," she said and gave him a quick hug.

No passionate embraces right now, Tam thought to himself. He smiled and whispered in her ear, "You look gorgeous."

Molly smiled back and took his hand to bring him through the foyer into the living room. It was painted dark beige and decorated in a French country style. Tam was surprised the room seemed so sophisticated; he expected something more rustic.

There were photos of Molly on the mantelpiece above the fireplace and very interesting paintings on the walls. It was a warm and inviting room.

Molly's parents got up from the couch when he entered the room, and she introduced them. Her dad, Fred, was of average height with thinning light-brown hair and wire-rimmed glasses. He was quite trim, as Tam was sure his job really kept him on the go and physically active.

Molly looked so much like her mom, Margaret. They both were five foot five and had similar hair and eyes. Tam thought Margaret looked very good for a woman of her age.

"So nice to meet you, Tam," Margaret said. "We'd love to have you stay awhile, but I think Molly would prefer to get going. I know you have another long drive in front of you."

"It is very nice to meet you both." Tam nodded. "I'd love to stay for a few minutes and would really appreciate a glass of water."

Molly gave him a sharp look and said she'd get the water for him.

"Please, Tam, take a seat," Fred said.

He situated himself in a large wingback chair facing Molly's parents, who were sitting on the couch. "Molly is a very special woman. You must be proud of her."

Fred and Margaret literally puffed up at his comment. "We couldn't be prouder," Fred said. "We're glad you think she's special. I believe she feels the same way about you," he added, looking at Tam intently.

He could tell he was being judged, and it naturally made him uncomfortable.

Margaret jumped in. "Why don't you tell us a little about yourself?"

Tam told Molly's parents about his parents, his siblings, the band, and his interest in engineering. "In fact, I have some things to tell Molly tonight about my career plans, so I can't really spill the beans right now."

Molly came back with his drink and asked, "What are you going to tell me tonight?"

Tam said with a smile, "You're just going to have to wait until we have dinner."

Almost the second he finished his water, Molly popped up, more than ready to go. "Well, we really should get going, Tam."

As they walked out, Tam shook hands first with Margaret and then Fred, thanking them for their hospitality.

As the pair drove away, Fred and Margaret stood on the large, beautiful porch of the farmhouse, waving, as their only daughter took off for a special evening, one she would never forget.

As they headed to the restaurant near Tam's apartment, a light drizzle started, and they rode along to the steady hum of the windshield wipers.

"Thank you for being so charming to my parents," Molly said. "I know it's a bit unusual for someone to meet the parents on a first date."

Tam smiled at her, taking her hand, keeping his left hand on the wheel. "You're welcome. I have to say it's never happened to me before."

Molly cocked her head at him. "Is that because I'm special?"

Tam laughed out loud. "You are. My brother sure thinks you are, too. He's told me that more than once, most recently right before I left tonight." He paused for a minute before adding, "I asked him to give us some privacy later."

Molly took in the meaning of his words and blushed red. She looked the other way out the window in hopes he wouldn't notice.

"Mol, you don't need to be embarrassed with me," he said gently.

"I know," Molly said, "but I couldn't help thinking about being alone with you later. It'll be a first for us in more ways than one."

Just then, Tam pulled into the parking lot of the restaurant. She took his arm as they walked to the door, and Molly felt like she'd known him for a long time. Before they entered the restaurant, she pulled his face to hers and kissed him affectionately.

"What was that for?" he asked, a bit surprised but pleased.

"I've missed you and your touch," Molly said, looking into those steel-blue eyes that had such a profound effect on her.

Just as Tam was about to say something, they were forced to move into the restaurant and away from the door as some other patrons arrived.

Molly looked around at the cozy restaurant as the hostess led them to their table, which was right next to the window. Tam immediately asked for a glass of wine for each of them before they ordered their appetizers and entrées.

When their wine arrived, Molly suggested a toast.

Tam smiled and said, "Shouldn't it be my job to make the toast?"

Molly looked at him and said pointedly, "Tam Rozomolski, you should know something about me. I don't follow convention or care to, particularly when it comes to traditional roles for men and women. I hope that doesn't bother you."

"Not at all," he said. "I'm glad you challenge social norms. I'm also happy I figured out early that when you use my last name, I better be listening to what you have to say." He laughed.

Throughout the dinner, they had a lively conversation and learned a lot about each other. The time did really melt away as they enjoyed their salads, entrées, and dessert. Tam and Molly were having such a good time they didn't want to leave.

Molly was happy they had so much time to talk and get to

know each other. She felt this was a good sign. If he would have rushed through dinner to get to his place, she might have felt uncomfortable.

"You haven't told me your news yet, the career news you mentioned to my parents," she said.

"Well, I had a few interviews this week and have decided to start an engineering training program at a great company in Milwaukee," Tam told her. "It's a two-year program where I'll have the chance to work in different engineering disciplines and locations to decide what's the best fit for me."

"Tam, that's fantastic! I'm really pleased for you. Milwaukee isn't that far from Northwestern in Chicago, so I hope we'll have the chance to see each other."

Tam reached for her hand and said, "I was hoping for that too."

Molly just gazed at him, holding his hand, thinking about the future. *Could* she have a future with him?

"Why don't we get the check?" she asked.

"Don't argue with me about gender roles, 'cause I *am* getting the check," Tam said with a smile as he raised his hand to the waitress. "It's pure economics as well. You have two more years of school, and I start a real job soon."

"Okay, okay, you win." Molly relented, smiling.

While the wine had helped her relax during dinner, she became a bit nervous again on the ride over to Tam's apartment. All of her earlier concerns resurfaced.

It only took a few minutes to get to his place. It was in an old building on the third floor. While Tam put his key into the lock, Molly tried to calm herself.

Walking into the apartment, she was quite surprised to see it was spacious, with wonderful woodwork and built-in cabinets in the dining and living rooms. While it was clearly decorated in a masculine style, it was well appointed and welcoming. She wondered if he cleaned up for her visit, which made her smile.

"So what do you think?" Tam asked.

"It's wonderful. I like it a lot and I'm trying to envision you and Tunney living here together. I guess I have this image of an apartment shared by guys as being kind of messy, but this is very nice." Molly laughed.

"We're actually pretty neat. Our mom ran a tight ship, and we were taught to keep a clean and tidy house. See, Tunney and I don't fit the gender stereotypes, either." Tam laughed, giving her a jab.

"Please have a seat," he said, pointing to the couch. "I'll get us some drinks."

Molly sat down and thought about taking a tour around to see the rest of the apartment, but she was afraid that might seem too forward. She wasn't quite ready to see his bedroom.

Tam handed her a glass of wine and put his beer on the side table.

Molly took a sip while they both sat there a bit awkwardly, until Tam broke the silence.

"Molly, I want you to know we can do anything you want tonight… We can talk, watch television… We can…" Tam's voice trailed off as Molly set her glass down and grabbed his hands in hers.

"Tam, there's only one thing I want tonight, and that's you. I'd be lying if I told you I wasn't nervous. I am. I'm counting on you to help me," she said, touching his hair and face and looking straight into those steel-blue eyes.

He pulled her to him and kissed her softly at first, testing her. She responded eagerly, and their kisses grew more passionate as they began to touch each other all over.

Molly pulled back and whispered in his ear, "Please, let me…"

She started to unbutton his checked cotton shirt. As she got to the last few buttons, she slid her hand inside, touching his bare skin. He relaxed back against the couch as she opened the shirt and kissed him on his neck, moving down his chest, circling his nipples with kisses.

She could feel his arousal through his jeans and kissed him there, then loosened his belt and the top button on his jeans. Tam moaned with pleasure and couldn't stand it anymore, taking her into his arms and kissing her with increasing passion.

"Should we go into the bedroom?" he whispered, kissing her tenderly.

"We'll have plenty of time for that later. I just want to be with you right here, now," she said, overcome with passion.

Tam gently eased her down on the couch and pulled her top over her head before reaching around, unhooking her bra. He caressed her breasts and then covered them with his mouth. Molly wanted to scream with pleasure. She pushed his face into her breasts, and then he moved to unbutton her jeans and slide them off.

He skimmed his hand lower and lower on her stomach, and his fingers tingled on her skin in a way she'd never felt before. Then he moved his hand inside her panties and stroked her, moving his fingers inside her in a slow, rhythmic way. She felt intense pleasure to the point she thought she couldn't stand it. Then he slid her panties off and moved to kiss her there. It was beyond anything she'd felt before. She was sure she would explode.

Tam was as excited as her and whispered, "Molly, tell me what you want."

"I want you. Please, I need you," she said and felt him against her and how ready he was for her.

At that, Tam shed his jeans and underwear and murmured, "I know it's going to be a bit uncomfortable, so just let me know if it's okay. I don't want to hurt you."

She nodded and pulled him to her to kiss him, tasting herself on his lips.

He entered her slowly, and she rose to him as she took him fully inside.

It did hurt a bit, but it also felt so wonderful. They moved together, and soon she could feel herself coming and screaming with pleasure. Tam was soon to join her in climaxing, and they collapsed together, Tam still inside her. She held him tight and didn't want to let go.

Molly and Tam fell asleep together on the couch, holding each other closely.

During the night, they moved to Tam's bedroom, and she took great pleasure in facing him and watching him sleep for a few minutes. She couldn't believe she was with him, in his bed.

In the morning light, she was content to just lie there looking at him: his hair curling against the pillow, the shape of his chin, the hair on his chest and arms... There was so much to get to know about him.

It wasn't long until he was awake. Molly looked into his eyes, and Tam smiled, reaching for her.

"Hey," he said, taking her in his embrace. She wrapped her arms around his neck, and they had a long, warm, and sloppy good-morning kiss.

"Well, that's a lovely way to wake up," Molly said, stroking his hair.

"I kind of like it myself." Tam agreed. "Last night was wonderful," he said, nuzzling her neck and kissing her ear and cheek. They kissed playfully and then more passionately, and his hands moved over her breasts and then down over her stomach. When he felt her panties, he pulled back. "I didn't know you started to get dressed," he said disappointedly.

The last thing she wanted to do was disappoint Tam, but she needed to tell him the truth. "Last night was wonderful, magical, but 'cause it was my first time, there was a little bleeding…"

Tam pulled back, startled. "Mol, I didn't want to hurt you. Do you think you need to go to the doctor?"

Molly smiled and shook her head. "I wouldn't think so. It's natural. Don't worry about it at all. You were perfect, and we were perfect together. It's a night I'll never forget," she said, reaching for him and taking him in her arms.

He broke free, getting out of bed and going into his closet to pull on a T-shirt and shorts. Tam grabbed another old T-shirt of his that was extra baggy, and he threw it to her, smiling. "Here, you put this on and be a lady of leisure while I make us coffee and breakfast in bed."

Molly caught the T-shirt and pulled it over her head. She laughed because it was so big. She could almost wear it as a dress.

When Tam was in the kitchen, Molly took a good look around the room. It was a small bedroom with an old, beat-up dresser and a mirror on top. There was a wooden chair with some of Tam's clothes on it, and the door to the closet was a beautiful dark wood. These old houses had such character and quality.

The sun was shining in through the bedroom window, and she fully opened the curtains to look outside. *What a lovely day,* she thought to herself, *in so many ways.*

When Tam came back with a tray holding two coffee mugs and croissants, Molly beamed with pleasure.

"Another toast," she said. "Tam Rozomolski, I'm a different person this morning because of you. Thank you for a lovely evening and for being such a concerned and fantastic lover.

"I loved getting so lost in you," she added with real emotion, clinking her coffee cup with his.

They stayed in bed long after their coffee and croissants were finished, talking and laughing, never straying far from each other's arms.

chapter ten

The summer went by so quickly for Molly, too quickly really, as her love for Tam grew with each day. She helped her Mom make the soaps, pitched in on the farm, worked the farmers' market each weekend, as well as helped out in the law office of a family friend.

Tam was busy, too, doing an engineering internship and playing a steady stream of gigs at all the summer festivals.

Tam and Molly got together whenever they could. It was difficult for her to go a week without seeing him, so they always tried to make time, even it was just a few hours.

She brought some of her friends to see him when he had gigs, but it wasn't as much fun to share him with all the girls in the audience. Molly could see women flirting with Tam when he was onstage, and she had to admit she was a bit jealous, even though they had this way of communicating when he was up there.

She certainly understood the attraction, as he was gorgeous. What made Molly smile was she knew he was wonderful inside as well, and those women would never see that.

Both Molly and Tam were making arrangements to move at the end of the summer. She was relocating to the Chicago area and a furnished apartment to share with a couple other

Northwestern law students, and Tam was moving to Milwaukee to start his engineering training program.

He decided to get a very small apartment as a home base, as he would be doing assignments at different locations, perhaps even internationally.

Tam and Tunney had to give up their apartment at the end of August because Tunney didn't feel he could afford it on his own. He'd found a smaller place to rent, and he was moving in September as well.

All three of them were packing boxes whenever they could, and they laughed together about the joys of moving and trying to get rid of things they really didn't need.

Tam had actually volunteered to help Molly and her parents in August at their town's biggest farmers' market of the summer.

There was a music and arts festival going on all weekend, and Tunney made sure their band was booked for the festival on Saturday night.

Molly's parents had tons of fresh heirloom tomatoes, basil, strawberries, zucchini, green beans, green peppers, several kinds of lettuce, and wonderful fresh herbs. It was quite a harvest this year, and Fred and Margaret appreciated the extra help. As it was a long drive back to Tam and Tunney's place, Tam stayed over at Molly's for the weekend.

The problem for Molly was she couldn't sneak over to the guest bedroom to see him after her parents went to sleep, and it was killing her. Him, too. Tunney loved to rib them about it, but he never did so in front of her folks.

The couple had hatched a plan for the week after the festival to get together at his place just before she left to drive to Northwestern and her new apartment. Molly also had a secret plan to see him the night before, but she wanted to surprise him.

Molly's dad was so pleased on the first day of the farmers'

market, as they sold more than they ever had before. Tunney even helped out since he arrived early for the gig that evening. They all worked together to close up the stand for the day.

"Boys," Fred said to Tunney and Tam, "I can't thank you enough for your help. To start, Margaret and I would like to host you for dinner before you have to play tonight. I believe you may have heard from Molly that her mother is a fantastic cook."

"Well, sir, that sounds great to me, and we'll have plenty of time to get back here and get set up before we have to play. I think Brett and Murph are going to be really jealous we're going to have such a nice meal," Tunney said.

"I don't think they'll be jealous at all," Molly said with a smile, "because I called and asked them to stop by my parents' house before the gig. They're joining us for dinner."

Tunney poked his finger in Tam's chest. "That woman is always two steps in front of you, bro. You need to hang on to her!"

Tam laughed. "Don't I know it?" He put his arm around Molly. She threw her arms around his neck and gave him a quick kiss and hug.

Back at the farmhouse, Fred offered all the boys a beer, as Brett and Murph arrived in plenty of time for dinner. It was a beautiful summer evening, and they all sat on the porch while Molly and her mom put the final touches on dinner.

The feast Margaret had prepared was wonderful. She made a salad with all the ingredients from their own garden and a homemade salad dressing, marinated grilled chicken breasts topped with fresh herbs, green beans with toasted almonds, and new potatoes with rosemary and olive oil. For dessert, Margaret made a cherry tart with vanilla ice cream on the side.

"Ma'am," Tunney said, "that was the most outstanding dinner. We can't thank you enough for including us tonight. It's fair to say we usually don't eat like this," he said with a laugh. "Fred, if Molly can cook like her mother, I'd like to marry her right now. Forget my brother," he said with a twinkle in his eye, and everyone laughed.

Everyone helped bring the dishes into the kitchen, but Margaret shooed them out, even Molly. "I'm so glad you enjoyed everything," she said, "but you guys have to play tonight, so please feel free to get going. Fred and I will clean up here and meet you over there."

Tunney, Brett, and Murph thanked Molly's parents for the dinner and headed to the door. Tam lagged behind.

"Molly, I'm sure you'd like to ride over with Tam," her mother said.

Molly smiled because her mother had read her mind. Time alone with Tam this weekend was hard to come by, so she'd relish a few minutes alone with him on the ride over. They would take his car, as he had his guitar and some other gear in the trunk.

"Now, kids," Tunney said in one of his silly voices, "we don't expect you to take the long way to the festival."

Tam smiled and saluted his brother. "Yes, sir. We'll be there as soon as we can." With that, he grabbed Molly's hand, and they ran to his car.

But Molly and Tam didn't head over to the festival right away.

"Okay," Molly said. "It was a little fib. We are going to make a stop on the way. I think we can take ten minutes. I want to show you a special spot."

Molly directed Tam to the side of a creek not too far from her parents' house. They parked by the side of the road, and Molly grabbed a blanket from the trunk before they wandered down next to the water. Molly showed him an old tree with a trunk that stretched right over the water.

"That's my tree," Molly said. "I used to come over here by myself or with my friends as a kid, climb this tree, and then sit on that trunk over the water. It was my sanctuary. The sounds of the water flowing, the birds, the sunshine…" Her voice trailed off.

Tam reached for her and took her in his arms. "It's a beautiful place for a beautiful girl who has grown into an even more beautiful woman," he said and then kissed her gently.

Molly dropped the blanket and put her arms around his neck and pulled him to her. After they kissed, she looked into his beautiful steel-blue eyes and held him for a minute before breaking free to spread the blanket on the ground.

Tam walked over to the tree and took a small knife out of his pocket, carving a small heart in the base with their names in the middle.

"Now every time you come here, you can think of us," he said, coming back over to sit next to her on the blanket.

"Thanks. It will always be a reminder of our times together. I can't believe this summer is almost over," she said, stroking his cheek. "It's been the best summer of my life."

Tam kissed her gently, and she pulled him closer. As the passion rose between them, they rolled around off the blanket onto the grass. As they held each other and continued to embrace more passionately, Molly pulled back and looked Tam straight in the eyes.

"Tam Rozomolski, I can't imagine loving anyone the way I love you," she said. Tam took her in his arms and kissed her neck and then lifted her T-shirt over her head and unhooked her bra, covering her breast with his mouth.

She moaned in pleasure as he undid her jeans and then his. It wasn't long until they were back on the blanket, making love to the sound of the birds, the locusts singing, and the rush of the creek. When they finished, they held each other.

Molly wished they didn't have to leave but knew Tam had to get to the festival as soon as possible to play with the band. They dressed quickly and left reluctantly to make the short drive to the festival grounds.

When they arrived, Molly and Tam tried to make sure they were both presentable before seeing the guys and family and friends. Tam laughed as he pulled some grass out of Molly's hair.

"I think I'll take a spin around the festival while you set up," she said with a smile. "I know your brother will figure out what we've been up to and embarrass me for sure. You know how easily I blush," she said, giving him a kiss and wandering off to explore.

Molly walked around to see all the booths at the festival while the band set up. There were stands with artwork, jewelry, leather goods, clothes, and all kinds of food.

Her mother was so busy with the vegetable stand that she was unable to set up a separate booth for her soaps and had asked her friend who exhibited some pottery to give her a little space for them. Molly stopped by to see the display and chat with her mother's friend. The soaps smelled wonderful and looked great next to her friend's original pottery.

As Molly walked back to the stage where the band would soon be playing, she saw Tunney, Tam, Murph, and Brett run through their sound check, and she watched Tam intently as he tuned his guitar. She was so proud of him, and she looked forward to showing him off to all her childhood friends that would come to hear the band tonight.

She could see Tunney and Tam talking onstage.

"Bro, it sure looks like you enjoyed your detour tonight," Tunney said with a knowing smile. "The two of you have a pretty serious thing going on."

"Hmm," Tam responded.

"That doesn't sound like much of an answer."

"Technically, you didn't ask me a question. You made a statement," Tam responded.

"Quit getting technical on me and tell me what's going on with Molly," Tunney demanded.

Tam paused a second before answering. "To be honest, it's scaring me to death."

At that moment, Murph came over and signaled it was time to start.

Molly had run into a few of her friends and walked with them to the first several rows in front of the stage and sat on the bench seats. She described Tam and pointed him out to her friends, glowing with pride.

When the band started to play, Molly stopped talking to her friends and just listened to his voice. As usual, Tam found her in the crowd, and they exchanged glances.

She hummed along with the song and envisioned herself dancing with him. It would be wonderful to dance with him someday. It was sort of hard to do when he was playing. Molly laughed to herself.

She knew she was deeply in love with him, but did he love her? Molly just wasn't sure, but she had a feeling she would know soon.

At the end of the evening, there were still plenty of folks at the festival, cheering the band on as they reached the end of their set. Tunney stepped to the mic.

"Hope everyone is doing great out there," he said, answering the crowd's cheers with a great bass line. "We are Rockster Tunney and would like to thank all of you for coming out tonight." He garnered more applause. "I'd like to thank a special lady and her family for everything they did for the band this weekend. You know who you are, Miss Molly, and we can't thank you enough for a fantastic weekend," Tunney said as the band blistered through the end of the song, with Tam taking the lead on guitar.

He looked into the audience and saw Molly, then smiled and bowed to salute her. She blushed, and she was glad it was dark so her friends couldn't see the color in her cheeks. What a fabulous evening.

When the band did their last song after an encore, Molly waited on the bench seats with her friends as the band packed up their equipment and got ready to drive back home.

Tunney came over to Molly and her friends first. "Brett, Murph, and I are gonna hit the road. Your parents have already left, so please thank them again for everything," he said, giving Molly a big hug.

After saying good night to her friends, Molly and Tunney walked over to the band's van together.

"Tunney, that was fantastic," she said. "Thank you so much for doing the gig tonight. I know you could have done something closer to home, but it meant a lot to me that you'd come and play in my little town."

Tunney gave her a big hug and kiss. "Well, *boss*, you know I've got a real soft spot for you."

At that moment, Tam came over carrying his guitar case. "How come you always get more time with my girlfriend than me, brother?" Tam said, laughing, as he put his arm around Molly.

"Hey, you're going home with her tonight so you're all set," Tunney said with a laugh. "See you tomorrow, bro, and Molly, see you next weekend," he shouted as he headed out.

The weekend with Tam at her parents' went by so quickly. Molly had a hard time wishing him good-bye on Sunday, but she knew he had to get back to his apartment to finish packing and then travel to Milwaukee on Monday for a few preliminaries before officially starting his job in a week.

Tam had to do some interviews and training but would be back at his place to pack up next weekend. Tunney had booked two gigs for next weekend as well, which made the schedule impossible.

Tam and Molly had worked out that she would pack up her car and spend Saturday night with him before she drove to Northwestern on Sunday. Saturday would be bittersweet for Tam, as it would be his last night with the band. He would leave for Milwaukee on Sunday as well, and Tunney would close down the apartment. It was a whirlwind for all of them with the changes ahead.

Molly wanted more time with Tam, so she decided she would drive to his gig on Friday night to surprise him and then they'd have two nights together.

She didn't say anything to Tam. She had plenty to do in getting ready for the move and had promised to help her parents prepare for the next farmer's' market. Molly was fairly sure she could wrap everything up by Friday evening.

When she walked Tam to his car Sunday morning after breakfast at her parents', she felt so sad to let him go. This weekend was the most time they'd ever spent together, and she loved every minute of it.

Tam stashed his guitar and bags in the trunk and came over to stand next to Molly. "You'll thank your parents again for me?" he asked, and she nodded. She seemed upset. "What's wrong?"

"This weekend was just so wonderful. I don't want it to end," she said, putting her arms around Tam's neck and her head on his chest.

"It was pretty great," he said quietly, stroking her hair. "We'll be together again next weekend, and the week will go by in a flash. You'll see."

Molly looked up at him and touched his cheek. "I know. I just hate saying good-bye to you. It just gets more difficult each time."

Tam hugged Molly again and kissed her good-bye before he got in the car. She watched him drive away before slowly walking back into the house.

She felt this unbearable sadness that dogged her all day. It was strange because she knew she would see Tam again next weekend. She tried to shake it off and enjoy the day, as it was the final Sunday she would have at home in quite a while.

Molly's final week before leaving for law school was hectic, as she also was finishing up a project at the law office in town.

She was sure the practical experience she'd gotten at the law office would be very helpful in her law studies and hoped she might return in the summers if possible. It was busy but fun, and she learned a lot.

Tam was right that the time would fly this week, because it certainly had.

Driving home from town, Molly pulled her car off to the side of the road near the creek and decided to make her way over to her tree. She felt she needed a minute of solitude in this busy week.

Grabbing a bottle of water, she went over and sat in the thick grass at the base of the tree and ran her hand up and down the bark.

Molly could see the place where she carved her name when she was ten years old and traced the letters with her fingers. Now, in addition to the experiences of her childhood, she added the new memory of making love with Tam at the base of the tree. She felt herself flush just thinking about it and then touched the heart Tam carved for them.

"Well, tree, what's going to happen next in my life? I know I'm headed for the next phase with law school and, of course, Tam…" Her voice trailed off.

Molly laughed to herself, glad the chances were remote of anyone being around and seeing her talking to a tree. The tree was a constant for her, and she came to this quiet spot as often as she could when she needed time alone to think, to contemplate. It was calming for her, so she stayed for about forty-five minutes, drinking her water and listening to the sounds of nature around her.

Molly wished she could stay longer, but there was so much to do, and her parents would be waiting for her to help finish up the preparations for the farmers' market. She felt a bit sad as she left, because she didn't know when she would be able to return.

When Molly got back to her parents' house, they were outside picking the tomatoes for the market the next day. She helped them until dinnertime, and they all felt good about the progress they had made, with not much more to do the next morning.

Her mother prepared an excellent light pasta primavera with a wonderful salad, and Molly figured it was the right time to approach the subject of her early departure.

"Mom, Dad, I was wondering if you wouldn't mind if I left tonight. I wanted to surprise Tam at his gig, and then we can spend time together tomorrow before his last performance with the band on Saturday night. As you know, we both have to take off Sunday morning."

"While we'd love to have you for another night," Molly's mother told her, "we understand you'd like to see Tam. You've been a big help to us in preparing for the market, and you don't need our permission to live your life. Fred, don't you agree?'

Fred nodded. "You know we always want to see you and spend time with you, but you're a grown woman now, even if that's hard for us to admit at times. It appears you have something special with that young man," he added.

"Thanks so much. I really hate to rush off, but if you don't mind, I should finish loading my car and get going," Molly said.

"You two put everything in the car, and I'll clean this up," Margaret said.

It didn't take long for Fred and Molly to load the car, and Margaret had everything back in order in the kitchen very quickly.

When Molly got her final things together, she could see her mother was crying. "Mom, please don't be upset…" she said, giving her mother a hug.

"Honey, it's just this may be the last time this is your home. After law school, you'll probably get a job and could live anywhere in the country. I can't help but be emotional. Your dad and I just love you so much," she said, hugging Molly tightly.

When Molly pulled away, she could see the tears in her dad's eyes, and she gave him a big hug as well. "You're making me cry, too!" she said, the tears running down her face.

After a few final hugs, her parents walked her out to her car and watched as she drove away. Molly felt terrible. She missed them already and kicked herself for not thinking about how hard it would be for her parents to see her leave for law school.

Molly scolded herself for being so self-absorbed, as she had spent all her time thinking about herself and Tam. As she sped away, she wiped her eyes with the embroidered handkerchief her Mom had made for her. She made a mental note to herself. *Always think about others' feelings and never take for granted the people you love the most.*

Molly was glad the light lasted so long in the summer, as she would get to the dance hall where Tam's band was playing just as it was getting dark.

She put the emotion of saying good-bye to her parents behind her and began to get excited about seeing Tam. He would be so surprised and pleased to see her.

Molly pulled into the lot for the dance hall and parked her car right under a light. All her important worldly goods were in her car, ready for her to take to law school.

As she walked in the club, she paid the cover fee, hearing the band playing already. Making her way through the crowded club, she heard Tunney thanking the crowd and telling them the band would be taking a break. Molly thought her timing was perfect.

The crowd was clogging all the aisles, and it took her a few minutes to make her way to the dressing room. She could see Tam going through the dressing room door, and right behind him was a gorgeous blonde.

As Molly walked up to the door, which was open a crack, she saw the woman put her arms around Tam and kiss him passionately. She reached down and pulled off her top, and Molly gasped. She couldn't believe what she was seeing.

Molly bolted and crashed into a guy, spilling the three beers he was trying to balance. She called out, "I'm so sorry..." as she ran out of the club, beer dripping down her top and jeans.

Molly was crying as she got to her car and quickly buckled up, speeding out of the parking lot and onto the highway. She wasn't sure where she was going, but she couldn't get away from that club fast enough.

chapter eleven

Present Day...

About Molly?" Tunney said. "You haven't seen her for years. What are you talking about?"

Tam looked down at the floor and took a deep breath, still feeling woozy. "I saw her yesterday. That's how I got this." He held up his injured hand.

"Well, obviously, this is a story I wanna hear." Tunney turned to his brother with great interest.

"Before I tell you the whole story, you need to understand I'm making you an insider and you can't tell anyone—I mean anyone—what I'm going to tell you," Tam warned seriously.

"What kind of insider will I be? An insider to your life...? I thought I already was." Tunney laughed.

"No," Tam said. "You'll have inside information about two companies, and you're not to tell anyone or buy stock in either company. I'm deadly serious about this. My job and integrity are at stake."

"One." Tunney began. "I would never do anything to hurt your integrity. Two, I don't have any money to buy any stock, so this is a really ridiculous conversation."

"I understand, but I had to say this to you. You need to understand what happened with Molly, and you will hear some extremely confidential information."

"Bro, I'm all ears, and I understand it's between you and me."

Tam told him the whole story of the ill-fated meeting, Molly screaming his name, the shattering of the glass pitcher, and the blood.

"Tun, I can't tell you what it was like to see her again. She looked so beautiful. I've been trying to reach her since, but she won't take my calls.

"It's more complicated 'cause she's the attorney for the company we want to acquire, so if we do talk, we'll have to disclose it. There can't be any perception of collusion—"

Tunney interrupted. "Disclose what?"

Tam frowned. "Do I really have to go through all the Securities and Exchange Commission rules with you? Can you just take my word that any communication between Molly and me is very complicated?"

"Sure, Tam, sure. You're the CEO, and you have to *disclose* all your conversations with Molly. This is so weird…"

Tam shook his head. "Tell me about it. Molly needs to know the real story of what happened all those years ago, and I may need your help."

"You know I'd do anything for you," Tunney stated, "but you have to tell her yourself. She needs to hear it from you—the whole, unvarnished truth."

"I understand." Tam agreed. "But she won't talk to me, and I think I'll need your help to convince her to even see me. But once she agrees, we'll both have to tell our companies. Molly and I need to go above and beyond the disclosure rules because of our personal relationship."

Tunney sighed. "There's that disclosure junk again. You corporate types are so strange. Why does just talking to each other have to be so complicated?" He walked to the kitchen to make coffee for them. "It's easier for me to do this since I have two hands," he joked, "but you may have to help me figure out this convoluted machine." He chuckled. "Do you know if Molly was married, had kids…?"

Tam turned very serious. "She lost her husband a year ago… pancreatic cancer."

"Oh man. Poor Molly. And now you turn up *and* threaten to take over her company. She must be a wreck," Tunney replied.

Tam accepted his espresso from his brother. "She did seem very upset. Remember, she thinks I'm this horrible man who betrayed her. Then she sees me for the first time in years at a meeting that's one of the most important of her career.

"You're the only other person who knows the whole story…"

chapter twelve

Molly walked into her closet to find an outfit to wear back to work. *Back to work?* How could she be thinking about that right now with her mind stuck on Tam, the same Tam that destroyed her world years ago? She pulled her fluffy robe tighter around her and grabbed the step stool.

At the back of the closet, there was a box of old photo albums. She had what she called the "censored" album, the one she didn't share with Jim when he was alive. It wasn't that she was trying to hide it from him; he knew about Tam and how he'd hurt her.

No, that album was about her and Tam, and she didn't share it with anyone. She couldn't, really, as it laid bare this incredible pain for her. The album had pictures of their summer together, at gigs, at the farmers' market, at her parents', with the band, and lots of photos with Tunney... Oh, Tunney. She'd loved him like the brother she never had.

That summer would always have meaning for her despite its disastrous end. The photos captured a place in time that was almost perfect, but then...

Molly placed the censored album next to her purse. She couldn't look at it now. It was just too much. She knew she would be dragged back to those days through the circumstances around the takeover attempt, and she was going to have to figure out how to deal with it. No matter what, she would be strong.

Just then, the phone rang, and it was Cissy. "Just checking on you," she said cheerily. "When do you think you'll be back?"

"I should be there in about an hour," Molly said. "I don't know what you've heard about the meeting, but I'll tell you everything later. It's been quite a taxing day."

"I heard there was an accident at the meeting and you actually know the CEO, but that's about all."

"That's all true, but I'll tell you the whole story. I need to talk to someone—"

"You know I'm here for you. I've heard from Ken's office that there's an important meeting in about an hour, and I wanted to let you know."

"Okay. Thanks for the call. I'll be there as soon as I can." Molly hit the button to end the call and slid her phone back into her purse.

Molly dressed and finished her hair and makeup in record time. As she ran out the door, she grabbed her purse and glanced at the censored album before grabbing her briefcase and her soiled suit.

When she arrived at her office, Molly fired up her computer to try and catch up on all the emails she missed while she was at home. Cissy had left some notes on her desk to call her attention to the most important messages.

Molly had about five minutes before Ken walked in her office and closed the door. "I wanted to talk to you before the meeting in a few minutes. I did reach out to our lead director to let him know there had been a takeover communication.

"I told him we've scheduled a meeting this afternoon with a small team of leaders and I would update him afterward, as well as work with him on informing the rest of the board.

"We'll have finance, members of your legal team, and our mergers and acquisition folks in the meeting. We'll work on our strategy today and then call in the bankers and external legal and PR counsel tomorrow," he concluded.

"As you know, I totally agree this is the right approach," Molly said. "Why do I sense you're uneasy?"

"Molly, we're going to have to disclose your relationship with the CEO, Tim Bart, and any conversation you may have with him in the future. I feel it makes sense to go above and beyond the guidelines here because of the roles you both hold in your respective companies and your personal relationship with him. You understand, don't you?" Ken asked pointedly.

She sighed, nodding. "I've tried to put it out of my mind, but yes, I do know any substantial communication going forward should be fully disclosed to you, our external counsel, and, most likely, the board. It is very uncomfortable for me, but we need to be squeaky clean on this. I'll tell you about all conversations, even the personal ones."

Ken nodded, as he understood more than anyone at this moment the difficult road ahead for her.

"I've thought about this disclosure as well," she told Ken, "and I would like Bill Stewart, the external mergers and acquisitions attorney we've used in the past, to be fully briefed on my relationship with Tam. I'll consult with him going forward to understand what should be disclosed to whom and when," Molly added quite formally.

"I will get together with him privately in advance of our meetings to give him the background. You're also free to talk to him anytime, with or without me. Does that meet with your approval?" she asked in her most professional voice.

Both Ken and Molly felt awkward about this, as they'd always had such a close working relationship and were friends outside the office. "Yes, that's fine and should work perfectly.

"I want you to know that personally, Jen and I are here for you if you want to talk about anything else."

Molly smiled sheepishly, grateful for the reminder of friendship. "Thanks, Ken. I may take you up on that. I'd like you to know everything, but it may be better for me to talk to you and Jen about all the personal details outside the office."

Ken looked a bit startled. "That man didn't do anything to hurt you physically, did he?"

Molly shook her head slowly. "No, nothing like that. He would never do that. I suppose you'll learn this eventually, so I'll tell you now, off the record… I loved him, and I thought he loved me, but he betrayed me.

"I was warned not to trust a womanizing musician, but I did. I also learned too late that one should never surprise a musician.

"As my mentor and friend—and to lay everything on the table as we discussed earlier—you should know I lost my virginity to Tam. I was madly in love with him… Then I found him with another woman."

"I am so sorry, Molly. What a complicated situation." Ken's eyes shone with genuine sympathy.

"Yes, I'm all too aware of the complications, both personally and professionally. I'll do my best to navigate both in the best way I can. I'll keep you up to date on all fronts. You have my word on that."

Ken nodded and left her office, and Cissy immediately came in with some urgent business she needed to go over with Molly before the meeting.

Molly threw her hands up in the air, surrendering to the schedule. There was just too much to do right now, and she had to push aside her emotions. Perhaps the hectic schedule was a blessing in disguise.

The meeting was in just a few minutes, so she would have no more time to worry about it or think about Tam Rozomolski and/or Tim Bart, the man he was today.

Molly walked into Ken's conference room and nodded to the small group of people around the table, Ken and the top leaders of the company. The assemblage included the chief financial officer, corporate secretary, chief accounting officer, head of strategic planning and mergers and acquisitions, and surprisingly, the head of human resources, Dennis Menas.

It dawned on Molly that Dennis was there because of the relationship she had with Tam, which would have to be divulged to everyone. She actually sort of laughed to herself because whenever there was any discussion about sex, HR was involved.

She sat next to Dennis and thought to herself, *Is there anything worse that can happen at work than to have a conversation with a group of high-powered corporate executives about your sex life?*

She glanced around the table again: all men. *Why aren't there more women executives in corporate America? This is like hell on earth.*

Ken opened the meeting in a very professional tone. "Gentlemen and Molly, this is a confidential and serious meeting. You are not to reveal the nature of this meeting or what we discuss to anyone," he emphasized, looking at those around the table.

"We have received an invitation to enter discussions on the combination of our company with TBBM Industries," Ken revealed, and there were gasps in the room. In that one sentence, each executive knew their professional futures were at stake, as well as those of their teams.

"Molly and I went to their headquarters for an informal meeting with their CEO, Tim Bart, and his key executives. The meeting was aborted for reasons I will allow Molly to explain shortly.

"Our goal today is to plan our strategy, decide which external advisors to call in, and develop our communications to the board. I'm handing out the letter I received from Tim Bart, TBBM's CEO, but I will ask to collect this at the conclusion of this meeting.

"Needless to say, this is our number one priority right now, so please be sure to clear your calendars." Ken continued. "If this situation progresses, we will have to make a series of public disclosures, but for now, it is totally confidential. You know the SEC rules on insider trading, so I'm, as of this minute, closing the window for trading in our company stock by all executives.

"Jerry," Ken said, turning to the company's corporate secretary, "please make sure the window is closed immediately following this meeting.

"Now, I would like to turn the floor over to Molly to tell you what happened at the meeting. Let me give you all a warning. This is not an easy story for her to tell, and there are personal details that are now part of this takeover attempt. I expect you to treat this information sensitively and appropriately, as it is very personal in nature," Ken said pointedly, gazing over at Molly.

All the faces in the room turned to her; she had their undivided attention. She took a deep breath and forced herself to think through every word. Molly wanted to tell this story as professionally as possible. All she could do was her best.

"Gentlemen." Molly started, looking at all the men focused on her around the table. "Ken asked that we attend the meeting at TBBM to get the facts, as he wasn't sure this was a serious attempt at a takeover," she said, taking another deep breath.

"Prior to the meeting, I had reviewed all the legal filings as well as their financial reports and could see this was a company with outstanding results and a solid future—one that could obtain the financial backing to make this takeover happen.

"I stepped out of the room just before the meeting started and returned to rush to take my seat as the CEO had entered the room and was chatting with Ken.

"When Ken turned to introduce us, I saw the CEO, Tim Bart, was someone I knew—in fact, knew well. He was my first love, Tam Rozomolski." Molly paused for a moment, taking a breath and surveying the stunned expressions.

"He had changed his name for business purposes, and I'd never seen a photograph of him, so I didn't know he was the CEO. Prior to yesterday, I hadn't seen him in seventeen years." Molly paused once more. There was stunned silence in the room.

"At the moment he saw me, he was picking up a glass pitcher to pour himself some water and dropped it on the glass, shattering the pitcher and glass, and injuring his hand seriously. I tried to help stop the bleeding as best I could.

"Then the company doctor arrived, and Ken and I left, as Tam—I mean Tim—was taken to the hospital and had to have surgery on his hand." Molly continued.

"To finish out the personal part of this drama, Tim wants to talk to me about our past. We had a terrible breakup that was never resolved.

"I realize any conversations I have with him have to be disclosed and will be; you can be assured," Molly said. "I will be working with Bill Stewart, our expert M&A counsel, who many of you know, to ensure we have accurate and full disclosure at every level.

"I would like to turn it back over to Ken to discuss our options going forward," Molly said as she got up. "Excuse me just for a moment. I will be back shortly."

She walked out and went directly to the ladies' room. Once in the stall, she closed the door behind her and backed up against the closed door, hugging herself, gulping deep breaths to help calm herself. Her eyes burned, but she refused to shed any tears. After a few minutes, sure she could present a properly composed façade, she washed her hands and went back into the meeting.

Many hours later, the executives came out with a plan of action. By the time Molly got back to her office, it was six, and Cissy was waiting for her.

"I thought you might need some help on some things, and I wanted to go over a few urgent requests," Cissy said, seeing her boss was beyond drained.

"Tim Bart's assistant, Gerrie, has called several times to set up a time for you to talk with him. He's out of surgery and doing well but on pain pills at home for a period of time, and he wanted to meet you there, perhaps tomorrow," Cissy said, looking intently at her boss. She maintained her professionalism, but she was also Molly's friend and knew this must be a big deal for her.

"I know about the surgery and that he's okay," Molly answered, "as Gerrie—who seems like a terrific person—called me at home to tell me. I honestly don't know what I'll do, but I won't make that decision until after the meeting tomorrow.

"I must talk to external counsel about the ramifications of having any private conversations with him, so please let Gerrie know there will be no call tonight or meeting tomorrow with Tam," she replied wearily.

Cissy quickly ran through the important items and took notes on all the actions she would need to take the next day to set up meetings and calls and prioritize Molly's schedule. Only urgent business could be accommodated right now.

Cissy could see Molly was disappointed that all the meetings around strategic planning for their global philanthropy efforts had to be postponed. She enjoyed that work, and there always seemed to be something that pushed it off the schedule.

"Well, it looks like our work is cut out for us tomorrow,"

Cissy stated. "Do you need anything now? Do you want to talk about what happened today?"

Molly glanced up at her with weary eyes and shook her head. "No, I'm a bit too tired to talk right now. I need to finish up some emails, and then I'm going to go home and collapse. Let's have a fresh start in the morning."

When Molly finally arrived home, she took a sleep aid and went directly to bed. She woke up early in the morning and looked down at the Stevie Wonder concert T-shirt she put on the previous night before she went to bed. Jim had gotten it for her, so she touched it affectionately.

Years ago, Jim and Molly went to see Stevie Wonder at the college's performing arts center, and Jim surprised her with a really large concert T-shirt that she could use as a sleep shirt.

Molly loved the shirt because Jim got it for her, but it always made her think of Tam, too, as Tam and Tunney's band covered a lot of Stevie Wonder songs. Tam and the band played "Superstition" and a few of his other hits at the graduation party. She thought it was ironic the shirt made her think about the only two men she loved in her life.

Molly honestly wasn't thinking of any of that last night when she pulled it on and collapsed into a deep sleep, as she felt numb when she prepared for bed. She must have slept for ten hours, which helped her feel ready to face the day.

Molly decided to bring the censored photo album along to work. She thought she would like to talk to Cissy about Tam and what had happened at the meeting yesterday.

Driving to work, she actually laughed out loud thinking about the scene at the meeting at TBBM yesterday, as all those executives at Tam's company must have been so shocked. They probably still didn't have any clue about what was going on, and Molly laughed again because she wasn't entirely sure she knew either.

She made a mental note that she was going to have to keep her sense of humor through all of this personal and professional turmoil. Perhaps laughing at this absurd situation could help her stay sane.

She was still chuckling when she stopped at a traffic light. It was a beautiful spring day, and the trees boasted lots of buds. New England in the spring, summer, and fall was always so beautiful. It did actually lift her mood. The winter could be another story, though.

Molly was glad she got into the office early for a head start on the day. It was only about 6:30 a.m., so she could catch up on emails before the important takeover meeting.

When she opened her office door and flipped on the light, she was startled and dropped her purse when she found a tall man with long hair, wearing jeans and cowboy boots, sleeping on her couch. When he sat up, the cowboy hat that was covering his face dropped to the floor.

"Tunney," Molly screeched. "You scared the life out of me. I was going to ask you what you're doing here, but I think I know."

"Molly, listen, I didn't mean to scare you, and I didn't think you'd be in so darn early. I was afraid you wouldn't see me since you're refusing to see Tam." Tunney immediately started in, picking up his hat as Molly gathered her purse and briefcase and dropped them on her desk.

Tunney walked over to her and said gently, "Molly," and gathered her in an affectionate hug.

She collapsed into his arms and said, "Oh, Tunney," and started to cry. "You know I never stopped caring about you, the brother I never had."

Tunney smoothed her hair. "Molly, I never stopped thinking about you, caring about you. Tam, either."

Molly stiffened a little and pulled away. "Well, he had an

odd way of showing how much he cared," she said bitterly. "I was such a fool, Tunney," she cried. "Why didn't I listen to you and Ruth? In the end, he was a womanizing musician, and I was totally taken in. How could I be so stupid?"

"You need to hear the whole story from Tam, not me," Tunney said. "Things aren't always as they appear."

"Right!" Molly tossed up her hands. "I really wish that were true," she almost whispered. "How did you get in here anyway?" she asked, changing the subject for a minute.

"You have to promise me you won't get anybody in trouble and I'll tell you." Tunney flashed her that wily grin Molly loved so much.

"I won't. I promise," Molly vowed.

"One of your night security guys plays in the band from time to time. He let me in and told me where your office was. I know he can be fired for helping me, so I'm trusting you on this. Your door was unlocked, you know," Tunney half teased.

"Well, as you've heard, yesterday was quite a day. I had a lot of things on my mind." Molly still spoke softly, though the corners of her mouth tipped up a bit. "I must have forgotten to lock the door."

"Listen, I know how upset you gotta be about what happened yesterday with Tam," Tunney said more seriously. "And I know about your husband and am so, so sorry…"

"He was a wonderful man," Molly said sadly. "You really would have liked him. We were very happy. At least we had sixteen years together."

Tunney walked over and gave her another big hug and just held on for a minute before breaking free. "There are so many things I want to say to you, but it's not my place. You don't know the whole story of what happened so many years ago, and I do. But you have to hear it from my brother, from the horse's mouth.

You gotta see him," Tunney said beseechingly. "I know you loved him and he loved you. Geez, I love you, too." He laughed.

Molly smiled at that. "Tunney," she said with great affection, "I love you, too, but I know what I saw."

"But you don't know what you *didn't* see," Tunney answered, "including a few important things that happened that night and later. Please see him.

"I've decided to stay with him and help for a few days while his hand heals. I don't think he had a chance to tell you, but he's divorced so he's on his own. He's got two great kids, though, and they visit and stay with him, but we need to get him healed up a bit first."

"Well, I'm sure his divorce is due to his inability to remain faithful, isn't it?" Suddenly, Molly was steaming, remembering that night and imagining what Tam must have done to his wife, too.

"Molly, I'm not going to talk about his marriage, his life, and what happened in the past, because you have to hear it from him."

"You think it's that simple, that I talk to him and everything will be okay?" she asked, starting to cry again.

"This must be a terrible time for you with your husband's death and then everything with Tam…" Tunney said, gazing sorrowfully at Molly.

"Yes." Anger, sadness, and confusion warred in her heart. "You realize he's trying to take over my company and take the leadership from my boss, who's like a second father to me.

"Oh, great," Molly explained, clapping her hands once. "Now you're an insider, but I'm sure Tam told you about what he's trying to do.

"Now I need to tell you this is inside information and you cannot tell anyone or buy or trade on any stock in our company or Tam's. I take my legal responsibilities very seriously. Is that clear?" Molly said forcefully, grabbing a tissue.

"Geez, I got the same speech from him, too. You corporate types have a way with language. Why don't you just say, 'Do the right thing?' because I think that's what you're trying to say with all this 'insider' and 'fiduciary' junk," Tunney said.

Molly laughed, wiping at her eyes. "Okay, I can see you fully understand."

"Hey, it's not like I have any money to buy stocks or know anybody who spends money on stocks, except you and Tam," he said sarcastically. "That's exactly what I told him when he gave me the FEC speech."

Molly corrected him gently. "It's the Securities and Exchange Commission, SEC, not the Federal Elections Commission, which is the FEC."

"Any way you slice it, you corporate suits have too many abbreviations and too many rules. It's really a tough way to make a living, but I suppose that's why you and Tam make the big bucks," he said, smiling.

Molly walked closer. "Do you remember the last time we saw each other?" she asked quietly.

"Of course I do, Molly," Tunney answered. "It was at the festival near your house. It was such a great time, and your family and friends couldn't have been nicer to us. When I walked away to the van, I thought we'd see each other the next weekend…"

"Yes, me, too." Molly snaked her arm around his waist and rested her head on his shoulder. "And we didn't see each other again until now, seventeen years later."

"That shouldn't have happened, and that's why you gotta talk to Tam." Tunney rubbed a comforting hand between her shoulders.

"Listen, Mol, I know you're busy and have lots to do, so I

should get outta your hair before anyone else comes in. Please think about what I said about seeing Tam. You owe it to yourself to know the whole story."

Molly watched as he put his cowboy hat on and came over to her to give one more hug.

Just then, Cissy came in.

"Well," she said, startled. "I'm sorry to interrupt." She was clearly confused about what was going on.

"Cissy, I'd like you to meet Tunney, Tam's brother," Molly said. "It's a long story as to why he's here, but I'll tell you everything tonight."

"Cissy, it's a pleasure to meet you," Tunney said, taking off his cowboy hat in a grand gesture. "Molly, if all the women who work at this company look like you beautiful ladies, I may have to apply for a job," he said with a wink.

"Can I get you some coffee?" Cissy asked, obviously flattered by Tunney's comments.

Molly narrowed her eyes at both of them and guided them toward the door. "Listen, I've got tons of work to do, so why don't you two get coffee?"

"I'll grab you a latte," Cissy said.

As he walked out, Tunney grabbed Molly in another long hug. "I'll see you again soon. It won't be seventeen years; that I know for sure."

Molly looked at him with great affection as he walked out. Then she shut her door to focus on the important work at hand. *What an incredible two days,* she thought to herself.

Cissy and Tunney walked down the hall to the cafeteria, and they got a few odd looks, as Tunney certainly wasn't dressed in corporate attire.

"How in the world did you get in?" Cissy asked him.

"Well, I can't really tell you that, but I did promise I wouldn't do it again." He laughed. "But from now on, I can call you," he said with a twinkle in his eye.

"I'm actually glad you're here. Maybe you can help me help Molly. I'm looking forward to talking to her tonight about everything, but right now, she needs this time by herself to catch up and prepare before she goes to the meeting this morning," Cissy said.

Tunney looked around and took in the industrial cafeteria and all the people rushing around to get their coffees. Cissy and Tunney got their cappuccinos and sat at a table that afforded them some privacy.

"You know, Cissy." Tunney began, scanning the crowd. "I really hate this 'business casual' look for the guys. It's terrible. Bad khakis with some stupid polo shirt. It's really the worst.

"However," he said in his distinct deep growl, "the women always look great. I notice the same thing at Tam's company," he added.

"Oh my gosh," Cissy said, putting her well-manicured fingers lightly over her lips. "We're going to have to disclose your visit today. You reminded me when you mentioned Tam's office. But I'm sure Molly's thought of that already.

"You have to understand she's the chief legal counsel responsible for our ethics and integrity programs and, of course, all appropriate disclosure as defined by the Securities and Exchange Commission," she added, quite officially.

Tunney groaned. "You're the third person to lecture me on this. First my brother, then Molly, and now you. This is *exactly* why I chose not to work in corporate America. I love playing in the band, and I've never had to put up with the BS you guys have to deal with every day or wear stupid business casual outfits. Damn."

Cissy laughed out loud. "You're really funny. I think it's good from time to time to experience something or someone out of the ordinary. Maybe we can be that for each other."

Tunney and Cissy talked for twenty minutes. She told him about her kids, her short marriage, and how she loved working for Molly. She also gave him some background on Jim, what a wonderful man he was, and how hard the last year had been for Molly.

Tunney told Cissy a bit about his brother and Molly and Tam's relationship but was careful not to say anything he felt Molly should hear directly from Tam.

"I hope Molly decides to talk to him," Tunney emphasized. "It's really important. There's some things that happened that she needs to know. I think if she does, she'll see him in a different light. I sure hope you encourage her to consider it," he urged earnestly.

"Hmm… I feel like I'm in a tough position. We're planning to have dinner tonight because she hasn't had one minute to tell me what happened yesterday. I can't promise anything," she said honestly.

"I understand. I'll see Tam tonight and tell him about my impromptu visit," Tunney said.

"You mean he didn't know you were coming?" Cissy asked, surprised.

"No. He told me what happened yesterday, and he said he needed my help to think this through. I was shocked to hear he'd seen Molly after all these years and under pretty darn strange circumstances." Tunney shook his head and rubbed the back of his neck.

"Cissy, there's something you need to understand," he said, looking her straight in the eyes. "Molly's one of the best women I've ever met and that was clear from the first minute I laid eyes on her. She's very special to me and Tam.

"Listen, my brother is far from perfect, but he's a good and decent man who's made mistakes. But haven't we all?

"I love him, and I know Molly loved him, too. She deserves to know the truth about what happened, and she needs to hear it from him."

Cissy nodded, and after a little more conversation, they got up from the table. She grabbed a latte for Molly and walked Tunney out past the security guard without letting on that he'd never signed in properly. She would be sure to take care of that next time he visited, and she hoped that was soon.

chapter thirteen

Tam was sitting on the couch in his condo, hand elevated on pillows, looking out the window and talking on the phone with his assistant, Gerrie. She'd set up a series of meetings for him that he was able to take by phone, and they were going over the schedule.

Tam had a doctor's appointment the next day and expected to get the okay to return to work.

"You haven't seen or heard from my brother, have you?" Tam asked.

"No, he hasn't called or come around. I will certainly let you know if I hear from him. Do you need anything else?"

"I did have another question." Tam cleared his throat. "Have you heard anything new from Molly?"

"Sorry, Tim, I haven't. I've tried multiple times, but the only conversation we had was the one I told you about earlier when she answered her cell right after the meeting. It was clear she was really upset, sorry to say. I feel like she needs a little time," Gerrie said gently.

"At some point, I can tell you more of the story, but I have to talk to her first. I owe it to her and myself… She's a wonderful woman, Gerrie."

"I only had a couple conversations with her, but I thought she was really terrific. Very engaging, funny, and alive with energy," Gerrie explained.

"Those are good words to describe her. She's also warm, kind, beautiful, thoughtful…" Tam's voice trailed off. "Remember, I'm on drugs now, and I will revert to your cold and calculating CEO at some point in the near future." Tam laughed.

"You're a great boss and very good at what you do, not at all cold and calculating. You also know I'm the only person in the company who calls you a jerk when you are one.

"I'm very hopeful Molly will talk with you soon. I do understand the business complications of your relationship, since she's the chief counsel for the company you want to acquire." Gerrie acknowledged.

"As do I." Tam agreed.

After Tam hung up with Gerrie, he wondered if he forgot something Tunney told him about his whereabouts. He wasn't one hundred percent lucid while they were talking. Maybe he was getting some of his things from his apartment to bring over for a few days.

When Tam moved to the Boston area for his job, Tunney was playing lots of gigs all over the Midwest and East Coast, so he decided to move out east. Tam was glad he did, because they'd always been close, and he was happy Tunney could see Tam's kids growing up.

Tunney was a huge help when Tam needed to talk to someone about his divorce. He was a straight shooter and didn't hold back on what he thought of Tam or what he should do when his marriage started falling apart.

It was interesting that during one of their discussions, Tunney said no woman would ever match up to Molly, that she was Tam's gold standard. He thought about that comment, and after seeing her again and reigniting all those long-buried feelings, he could finally admit to himself Tunney was right.

It had hurt Tam very badly when Molly wouldn't return his calls or see him years ago. He shook his head slowly. What would have happened if he could have explained everything back then? But it was water under the bridge now.

Tam hoped Molly would give him another chance. He would do everything in his power to make that happen, but the impending acquisition of her company could break them apart again.

Just then, Tunney came through the door with a few of his things. Tam had given him a key so he could come and go as he pleased.

"Hey, bro. How're you doing?" Tunney asked as he dropped his things in the foyer.

"I'm fine. Doing better. I have a doctor's appointment tomorrow, and then I should be able to go back to work. Where have you been?" Tam asked.

"I went to talk to Molly," Tunney answered simply.

"What?" Tam exclaimed, agitated. "Why didn't you tell me?"

"I thought it was better in case I didn't get to see her." Tunney shrugged.

"Did you see her at the office?" Tam asked, really curious now.

"Well, one of their security guards sits in with us in the band sometimes, and he let me in the building, so I slept on her couch. She got in really early and woke me."

"Oh my God, Tun, what have you done? Don't you think Molly's had enough shock and surprise in the last couple days? I can't believe you did this…

"Well, what did she say?" he asked, apprehensive.

"She was surprised at first. I did give her a shock, but we had a good chat. She said she loved me like the brother she never had, and I told her I loved her and you did, too. I asked her to give you a chance.

"She didn't exactly say yes, but she didn't say no either. She did tell me about all the disclosure stuff like you did, so it isn't easy for her to talk to you.

"I know she had a bunch of really important meetings today and she's going out to dinner with her assistant tonight. They're really close and she hasn't had a chance to tell Cissy what happened with you."

Tam hung on his brother's every word.

"I also had coffee with Cissy and asked her to encourage Molly to talk to you, so I think I've done what I can to help, bro," Tunney added.

"Well, when do you think I should try and see her?" Tam asked eagerly.

"I have an idea, but I'm not sure you'll like it," Tunney said with a sly smile.

chapter fourteen

Thank God this day is almost over," Molly said to herself as she got back to her office after back-to-back meetings. Her dinner with Cissy couldn't come quickly enough.

She started the day with Bill Stewart, the expert external mergers and acquisitions counsel, and told him all the details of the takeover attempt, the meeting, the accident, and her relationship with Tam. She knew and trusted Bill, and he needed to know everything to help protect the interests of her company.

It was kind of fun to see his face when she told him the whole story. Bill did say this was one of the most interesting hostile takeover attempts he'd ever been involved in, and he had thirty years of experience.

Bill sat in on all the rest of the meetings during the day to help them refine their defense strategy and craft communications to the board. He also assisted the head of corporate communications in drafting a holding statement and questions and answers in case TBBM went public with their bid.

As Tam was injured and not yet back to work, Bill and Molly didn't think anything would happen immediately, but they had to be prepared.

Molly felt pleased with the work they'd done so far and was

looking forward to reviewing some of the documents that were under development as soon as possible.

It was about five thirty, so if she could finish up some phone calls and emails, she'd be ready to go in about an hour. Molly felt exhausted from the day, and she was so busy she hadn't had any time to think about Tam and what she might do in the future about seeing him.

The external legal advice was as she suspected. She would have to report on any contact from Tam to Ken and the committee they set up to manage the takeover attempt. There would have to be written accounts of any communication between them, as it couldn't appear they were trying to collude on takeover terms in any way.

She planned on talking to Bill privately if any contact did occur. It would be better if Molly didn't talk to Tam, but she couldn't imagine sitting across from him and seeing him again without any closure on their personal lives. She had visions of fighting it out through the media when the hostile takeover went public, which would inevitably result in bad blood between the leadership of both companies.

All the choices in front of her were unappealing.

Cissy came in with some questions for the meetings of the next day, and they covered everything quickly, as both were ready for some wine and a great meal at Bellini's. The staff there always took good care of them, and Molly very dearly needed that tonight.

Just as Cissy walked out of her office, Ken walked in. "Hello, Molly," he said. "I just wanted to check in to see how you're doing. We haven't had the time to talk one-on-one with all the back-to-back meetings on the takeover."

He took a seat across from her. "I also wanted you to know my conversation with our lead director went well, and we'll have a board conference call tomorrow. You'll see that on your calendar. I'd like you to disclose your personal relationship with Tim Bart on the call," he said, locking eyes with her.

"Of course," she said, looking down at her desk, busying herself with organizing pens and paperclips.

"Molly, you've been doing a terrific job under the circumstances. You've been extremely professional in every way. Bill Stewart pulled me aside to say you were handling this superbly, given the difficult personal complications."

"I can't tell you how much I appreciate your comments," she said, now fiddling with the papers on her desk, "but it's early in this process, and I'm sure we need to be strapped in for a bumpy ride.

"Personally, I feel there will be a number of difficult moments for me. It's inevitable that I will talk to Tam about our personal lives. I just don't know how or what the right time will be," Molly said, overwhelmed by her mental exhaustion.

"I don't have any answers for you there," Ken said, "but I have spoken to Jen, and we're here if you need us."

"You and Jen are just so wonderful and your invitation is appreciated, but I wonder if we can work our way through the week, see what unfolds. I may be over sooner or later, depending on what happens," she said.

"Fair enough. You probably need to get out of here soon." He stood and turned for the door.

"I will. You have my commitment on that," Molly said, waving at Ken as he exited.

She packed up her bags to leave for the restaurant, remembering to bring the censored photo album.

Molly and Cissy settled into their favorite booth at Bellini's and ordered a bottle of Pinot Noir. This week felt twice as long as usual to both of them, and relaxing a little with a glass of wine and a great dinner was perfect.

Molly spent a good part of the meal talking about her relationship with Tam and how she'd never seen him again after spotting him at the nightclub with the blonde.

"That's the strange part. Why didn't he try and find you to explain?" Cissy asked. "Something just doesn't make sense."

"Well, he did call me multiple times at my parents', and I never returned those calls. He also wrote letters. Since I'd just moved to start law school, he didn't have my address or phone number, and I didn't have a cell phone back then.

"I didn't make it easy for him to find me. I was so hurt. Perhaps I should have heard his explanation, but I couldn't erase that image in my head… him kissing that woman and then her taking off her shirt.

"Ruth and Tunney warned me about his womanizing ways and how he might hurt me, and then he did. I just felt like a fool who should have listened to those around me who offered solid advice." Molly rubbed a hand over her aching forehead.

"When I spoke to Tunney today, he asked me to encourage you to see Tam because he knows the whole story and feels you need to hear it," Cissy told her.

"He said the same thing to me, and to be honest, that carries weight with me. I always trusted Tunney and feel like he was always looking out for me, so I'm a bit torn…" Molly trailed off, fighting with herself as she tried to make a decision on what to do.

"It's really a tough one. You also have the disclosure requirements around the takeover, which makes everything extra uncomfortable. But you can't change that. You just have to deal with it, as you're doing.

"I'm sure it isn't easy to talk about your love life with your boss and a lot of executives," Cissy acknowledged.

"No, it's not." Molly laughed. "And I've resolved that I have to keep my sense of humor about all this.

"So here's a toast. To keeping a sense of humor," Molly declared, clinking glasses with Cissy.

After ordering coffee, Molly reached over into her bag to pull out the photo album. Cissy stared at her quizzically when she slid it onto the table.

"This is what I call the 'censored' album, my time with Tam. I put it away when he hurt me, and I started my life with Jim. Jim knew everything about Tam, but I never showed him this," Molly said softly.

Cissy scooted over next to her in the booth so she could see the photos better. There were photos of Tam and Molly at the farmers' market, at gigs, with her parents, the whole band, and lots with Tunney.

There was one of Molly with the whole band, Tunney on one side and Tam on the other, looking at her with unabashed love. There was another of Tam sitting up in bed, smiling at the camera. Molly ran her finger over the photo and Tam's face.

"Molly, he loved you. Look at how he looks at you in that photo. That's not fake; it's real. God, he's so handsome, too," she said, staring at Tam's photo.

"Yes, and the sex was spectacular," Molly said, "which I can readily admit after two glasses of wine. Let's hope I don't have to disclose *that* to a bunch of corporate executives!"

"What are you going to do? Are you going to see him?" Cissy asked, wide-eyed.

"I will," Molly said as their desserts arrived. "It's just not clear how and when right now."

When she got home from dinner, she dropped her bag on the kitchen counter to get a drink of water. She took out the censored album and looked at it again, taking a sip of water. Seeing the photos of Tam and her filled her with so much emotion. When she thought of the love they had and lost—

Just then, the doorbell rang, and Molly thought it was her neighbor, who probably locked himself out *again.*

When she opened the door, she was startled to see Tam. He was dressed in jeans, and his hand was still wrapped from the surgery, held up awkwardly in the air.

"Molly, please don't shut the door. Tunney's waiting in the car, and I still have to elevate my hand, so I won't stay long. I promise. Please, can I come in?" he begged.

She opened the door and let him enter. "Please, sit on the couch. You can stack those pillows to elevate your hand." She paused, fidgeting nervously for a second. "I'm really glad you're okay."

"Thanks for seeing me and doing what you did to help me when I cut my hand."

"In a way, it was really partially my fault it happened, because you were as shocked to see me as I was to see you," Molly told him.

"Yes, but I'd never blame you for this. It was stupid on my part, but I do admit I was so surprised to see you. In my heart, I always hoped to see you again…"

Molly realized when he said this that she wasn't ready yet to fully delve into the past. "Tell me about your life in the last seventeen years, but *please* do not discuss the takeover. As I'm sure you know, I have to disclose any conversations or meetings with you," she said a bit formally.

"I'm aware," Tam said. "I'll have to disclose my visit this evening, too."

Molly laughed out loud. "Can you believe the situation we're in? It's incredible."

Tam smiled. "It's absurd and difficult, but I'll not let anything come between us again. You deserve to know the truth."

118

Molly looked at Tam apprehensively. "Tam, I want to know, but I'm sure you understand to relive that time…" Her voice trailed off. "Those months we had together were magical, and when I saw you with that woman… Well… I couldn't get out of that club fast enough.

"I know you tried to reach me, but I guess in my heart of hearts, I thought you'd come after me if you really loved me… but you didn't." Despite her efforts, she started to cry.

"But, Molly, I did," Tam said, coming over and taking her hand in his good one.

chapter fifteen

Seventeen Years Earlier...

Tam stood onstage as Tunney sang a song requested by the crowd. He found his guitar playing to be a bit uninspired tonight. He was thinking about how his life was changing with his new job and Molly going away to law school.

They were both so busy now, but Molly and Tam always squeezed in time together, even if it was only a few hours. She also came along to gigs, and Tam loved seeing her in the crowd, knowing he would have time with her later.

Life would be changing so much. He was set to start his new engineering job, which had rotational assignments that most likely would take him to a number of other locations, and Molly would be beginning a whole new chapter with law school.

It did concern him because he knew this could cause them to drift apart. They needed to work hard to stay together.

Wow, Tam thought to himself. He really was in deep with Molly. He loved her so much. It scared him; he knew they were young, and with all the changes coming—

Tam's train of thought was interrupted by the applause at the end of the song and Tunney telling the crowd they were taking a break.

Thank God, Tam thought.

He put his guitar in its stand and was the first off the stage, rushing into the dressing room, not paying attention to anything going on around him. Just as he went through the door, he felt someone come in after him and spin him around. It was Linda, a girl he'd gone out with a few times, but she went away to Europe for the summer. He liked her, but it was nothing serious in his book, and he'd very much moved on with Molly.

"Linda—" he said, surprised to see her.

"I've missed you." She grabbed him and kissed him and then quickly pulled her T-shirt over her head.

"Whoa…" Tam said, pushing her away. He grabbed her shirt and told her to put it back on.

"What's wrong?" Linda asked, seeming a bit drunk. "You certainly had no problems with our *special connection* before I left for Europe."

Tam recalled they had a pretty intense physical connection several times before she went away, but that was about it. Tam didn't have any emotional feelings for her, and then she was gone.

"I'm sorry, Linda. I've met someone else. I can't be involved with you like this. And you're drunk."

While he rushed to the dressing room, Tunney was talking to Brett and Murph about the set list for after the break and was cursing his brother for his inattentive playing during their first set.

As he left the stage to go to find Tam, he saw someone who looked like Molly making a beeline for the exit, but he thought he must be mistaken. Molly was coming to the gig tomorrow night, not tonight.

When he got to the door of the dressing room, the door was open a crack and then flung wide as a blonde burst out and brushed past him.

"What the hell was that?" Tunney asked his brother.

121

"Do you remember Linda, the girl I went out with before I met Molly?" Tam asked.

"I can't say I do, bro. You've gone out with so many. I can't keep track." He chuckled.

"Well, she kinda jumped me when I came in the dressing room and then stripped off her shirt. Totally drunk. I pushed her off and told her I was seeing someone else. Then she just stormed out." Tam rubbed his hands down his face.

"Well, I was gonna dress you down for your god-awful playing out there, but I guess you've had enough to deal with already. But can you pick it up a bit for the rest of the night?" Tunney asked.

"You're the boss," Tam said, giving his brother a sarcastic salute.

He did try and focus more on the music in the second set, and Tunney seemed more pleased.

It was a late night, and when they got back to their apartment, both went straight to bed. Tam's last thought before he went to sleep was of Molly.

The next morning, Tam got up, made coffee, and called Molly at her parents' house to discuss the day's plans.

Margaret answered, and when Tam asked for Molly, she said in a cold tone, "She's not here, and she doesn't want to talk to you."

"What... what do you mean? What happened?" Tam asked, panicking.

"It's not my place to discuss Molly's feelings with you. I'm sorry," she answered.

"Please, Margaret, can you have her call me? I need to talk to her," he pleaded.

"I'll give her the message, but I don't think you'll hear from her. I need to go. Good-bye, Tam," she said and hung up.

Tunney walked into the kitchen, yawning, as Tam hung up the phone, but he saw immediately his brother was upset.

"I don't know what happened. Molly isn't home and doesn't want to talk to me. It doesn't make any sense. What the hell...?"

Tunney looked intently at Tam and then remembered what he saw last night. "Oh God, Tam—"

"What? Do you know what happened?" he asked, stricken.

"I think... I thought I saw Molly rushing out last night, but then I told myself it wasn't her 'cause she was supposed to come to the gig tonight. She must've come early to surprise you, then saw you with that other chick."

"Oh my God... I have to find her." Tam pulled on his hair, completely out of his mind with frustration.

"Well, you got a gig tonight and start your job Monday. I'm not sure you can find her if she doesn't wanna be found. I'm so sorry about this, bro. I know how special she is to you," Tunney said sadly.

"She's beyond special, Tun. I love her."

chapter sixteen

Molly was asleep in her car very early in the morning outside her new, shared furnished apartment in Chicago. After the scene at the nightclub the evening before, she'd taken off driving without knowing exactly where she was going and finally stopped off the highway to calm her nerves. She was angry and upset and probably shouldn't have been driving at all, much less late at night into the early morning. Thankfully, she made it to the apartment, safe and sound.

Molly would call her parents as soon as she was able to get inside to tell them she arrived okay, since Tam would most likely be calling later in the morning.

Tam! How could you do this to us? Molly thought, pounding her fists on the wheel. *Calm down right now. Just get yourself moved in. Don't think about it right now.*

Molly had arranged to get the apartment key on Sunday, so because it was Saturday morning, she decided to sleep for a few hours in the car until it was late enough in the morning to ring the buzzer. She didn't feel comfortable waking her new roommates at 6:00 a.m.

As there was no way she would go back to sleep, Molly decided to get a coffee and something to eat. Once she returned to the apartment, she found Bernadette, one of her new roommates, carrying boxes into the apartment.

Molly helped her bring some things up the stairs, and then Bernadette gave Molly her own key so she could start carrying in her stuff. Luckily, Bernadette had some folks helping her early this morning, and they were kind enough to help Molly as well.

She was glad to have her own bedroom, and once everything was in, Molly collapsed on the bed. She called her parents and told them the bare minimum. It was just too raw for her right now.

When she hung up, Molly started to cry, but she had to try to hold it together. She'd just met all three of her roommates and didn't want to seem like she was an emotional wreck on their first day together.

After composing herself, Molly went out into the kitchen where a couple of her roommates were chatting, and she joined in. They set rules on food, cleaning, guests, and early and late-night comings and goings.

Once all that was settled, Molly thought she would head out to do some grocery shopping to keep herself busy; it certainly wasn't because she was hungry, because her stomach was still tied up in knots.

After going to the store and taking a walk around the neighborhood, Molly worked for the rest of the day to get herself settled in and ready for her first day of law school on Monday. It would be the start of her new life, in more ways than she'd imagined just yesterday. She had to push Tam out of her mind.

Her first day of school went smoothly as Molly navigated the campus and enjoyed her classes so far. When she got home after the full day at school, she grabbed a yogurt from the fridge and ran into Bernadette.

"How was your day?" she asked.

"It was fine. I found all my classes okay. Met a few great people in my hardest law class, and we decided to form a study group. I think it will be very helpful."

"Any good-lookin' guys?" Bernadette asked.

"I really wasn't paying attention to that," Molly said with a chuckle, "but now that you mention it, there was this one guy. Light-brown hair, hazel eyes…"

"Sounds promising." Bernadette smirked.

"Oh… I'm not looking for a relationship right now. I've just broken up with someone," Molly informed her, tears coming to her eyes.

"I'm so sorry, Molly. I didn't mean to upset you." Bernadette softened quickly, patting her on the arm. "Let me know if you want to talk about it."

"It's not your fault," Molly replied quietly. "I can't really talk about it yet. It just happened Friday night. When I can, I'll be sure to find you." With that, she tried to smile and made her way back to her room.

As the weeks went by, Molly slipped into a routine and kept herself busy. She talked to her parents frequently, and they both told her Tam continued to call and had written her some letters they were saving for her.

She declined to speak to him, as the hurt she felt was still so fresh. There was no way she could trust him again. She just needed to put their relationship behind her.

Molly worked very hard to do well in her classes, joined the law club, and did some volunteer work for the school paper. She hung out with her study group and other students she met in her classes.

Of all her new friends, she spent the most time with Jim,

the guy she'd found attractive that first day. He was so kind and smart and helped her think through a couple really difficult assignments.

Judy, another member of the study group, pulled her aside one afternoon and asked her to get a coffee. "Molly, your defenses are up because you were so hurt, and you haven't noticed Jim is crazy for you."

"We really click, but I guess I've held him at arm's length. It's only been a couple months," she told her.

"I understand the timing doesn't feel right, but it sure seems Jim is an unbelievable guy. He probably has a dozen girls banging on his door." Judy giggled.

Molly laughed softly. "You're right. He probably does."

Judy looked her straight in the eyes. "Well, are you going to do anything about it?"

"I don't know. I'm not sure I'm ready. But if I were, I'd definitely go for a guy like Jim. He seems so sincere… I don't think he'd ever hurt me," Molly answered.

It took Jim a few more weeks to finally ask Molly to go out with him. He never talked to her about Tam, but he knew she was still reeling. He didn't push anything too fast. He could see she was warming up to him a bit, and he asked her if they could have a picnic Saturday afternoon in the park near the law school.

Jim was thrilled when she said yes, and he took care of all the details. On the day of the picnic, he filled a basket with freshly baked bread, some meat and cheese, a salad, and some cookies and special chocolates for dessert.

Trying to impress Molly, he picked out a French wine he thought she'd like and found some plastic wine glasses. He brought a multi-colored blanket for them to sit on and real cloth napkins. He was hoping this would be a turning point from friendship to something more.

When he went to Molly's apartment to pick her up, he chatted with a couple of her roommates. Since her study group often met at the apartment, he was trying hard to make an even more positive impression now that he was hoping to date her.

Once at the park, Jim got everything ready and laid it out on the bright blanket.

Molly was impressed. "Gosh, this is quite a spread, Jim. Thanks so much for doing this." She smiled. His returning smile was ear to ear, and she noticed a sparkle in his beautiful hazel eyes.

The pair ate their lunch and talked for hours, drinking the whole bottle of wine. The alcohol gave him some courage and helped her open up more.

"Molly, I…" Jim began, looking right at her and taking her hand. "I think you know how I feel about you. You had a difficult breakup and you were hurt badly. I don't know the details, but if you ever want to talk about it, I'm here for you.

"I'm hoping you consider today a fresh start and a real beginning for us," he said, hoping for a clue to her feelings.

She squeezed his hand and said, "I do. I'm grateful you've been patient with me. I can't guarantee it will be smooth sailing, but I'm willing to try. To see where things go from here."

At that, Jim took her face in his palms and kissed her tenderly. She responded by putting her arms around his neck and kissing him back.

At that moment, a man walking on the path was startled as he recognized Molly and moved quickly to hide behind a tree. Tam had driven down from Milwaukee after trying to reach her for months. He'd parked his car near the park and was planning to walk around campus to find some contacts for the law school and see if there was any way he could track her down.

When Tam saw how Molly kissed this guy and how the man

sitting on the blanket looked at her, he knew it was over between Molly and him. This guy clearly was crazy about her, and Molly looked to have a connection with him.

Now he knew why she hadn't responded to any of his phone calls or letters. Molly had moved on. Perhaps her feelings for him weren't as strong as he thought.

With tears in his eyes, he turned and headed back to his car as quickly as he could.

chapter seventeen

"Tam, I had no idea you were there that day or that you ever came to find me," Molly said, staring at Tam, a bit in shock. "Or that you totally rejected that woman at the club."

"Tunney can verify everything if you don't believe me," Tam replied genuinely.

"Of course I believe you..." Molly bolted to her feet and then felt a bit dizzy, as she had just had a shock and got up too quickly. "I need a glass of water," she said uneasily.

She rushed into the kitchen and got water for Tam, as her glass was still on the counter. Molly took a big gulp of water to help calm herself. She felt at a breaking point after learning the truth about their breakup.

Tam had followed her into the kitchen. He could see she was struggling, so he took the glass from her, set it on the counter, and took her in his arms, carefully protecting his injured hand.

Overcome, Molly cried on his shoulder, wetting his shirt. Tam smoothed her hair and tried to calm her, but it was emotional for him, too, so he tried to keep it together.

She pulled away and grabbed a napkin to wipe her eyes. "Tam, if you would have found me that day, maybe I would have never married Jim… And he was the most wonderful man…" The emotions hit her again, full force.

He gathered her in his arms again and held on tightly. "And I wouldn't have had my kids, who I love more than anything…"

"Nothing is simple," Molly said, "particularly our relationship." She looked into his steel-blue eyes.

"I'll never give up on us again. Seeing you after all these years…"

Molly put her arms around him and just held him as she cried softly. He stroked her hair and shoulders, and they stayed like that for a time.

As they stood there, Tam spotted the censored photo album on the counter behind Molly, and he broke from their embrace gently to look at the old pictures.

"Wow, I know you sent me a few photos years ago, but I don't have all of these. Murph, Brett, your parents, Tunney… these are just wonderful. Mol, we were so happy," he said sadly, looking straight in her eyes.

Molly touched his hair and stroked his cheek. "Yes, we were." Hesitantly at first, she kissed his forehead, his eyes, his cheeks, and then his lips softly. He pulled her closer and kissed her gently and just held her again for a few minutes.

"As much as I'd love to stay here with my arms around you, it's late and you're tired. And I'm still on drugs after the surgery." He pulled back and looked down at her. "I don't want to pressure you right now, but I hope we can get together again very soon and talk about the future. I won't give up this time, no matter what," Tam said softly but firmly.

"I agree. It's late, and I have so many meetings tomorrow… Ironically, they're because of you, but let's not get into that right now," Molly said with a tinge of irritation, as the romantic mood of their reunion was abruptly changed. "We already have plenty of disclosures to make about tonight."

Tam groaned. "Unfortunately, yes. Listen, Tunney's been in the car for a long time. I certainly won't invite him in right now, but you have to promise me you'll make copies of the photos for me and show them to him. He'd love them. He already loves you." He smiled as he started to make his way back into the living room to take his leave.

"My big brother..." Molly said with great affection.

She walked Tam to the front door, and as she opened it, he took her in his arms and held her before gently kissing her good night.

"See you very soon, Mol," Tam said, walking out.

Molly leaned against the doorjamb and watched him walk to the car, astonished at what had just happened.

chapter eighteen

Tam went to his doctor's office first thing the next morning and got his okay to return to work, so he was at his desk by nine thirty.

He was still glowing from seeing Molly the night before, and he was happy the new bandage on his hand allowed him to maneuver so much more efficiently.

Tam's mind was racing, as he knew he had lots to catch up on at the office. One of his first meetings was with his CFO, his head of mergers and acquisitions, and his legal counsel. Tam knew he had to disclose his meeting with Molly last night and create a written record.

He worried about how to navigate this takeover. It was going to be very upsetting for her and messy. How did he spare Molly's feelings and not let business come between them? He was definitely conflicted.

Before his first meeting, Gerrie came in with a list of things to go over to get a few things moving that were stalled during his time out of the office. They got through the list rapidly, and Gerrie asked him how he was feeling.

"On top of the world," Tam said with unbridled enthusiasm.

"I know you're glad to be in the office again following the accident, but there's something else going on with you." She observed him quizzically. "You saw Molly!"

Tam whispered, "Yes, I went to her house last night, unannounced. I told her some things she didn't know from all those years ago, and I think it's made a difference in our relationship. At least I sure hope so. I want her to give us a chance."

"I'm really happy for you, Tim, and for Molly," Gerrie said. "And don't worry. I won't say anything to anyone."

"I appreciate that," Tam replied, "but as you know, I'll have to disclose that I saw her last night during my first meeting this morning. We didn't talk about the takeover, but she did seem agitated when she mentioned all the meetings she had today.

"This romance by disclosure is going to be very difficult for both of us and the companies, too."

Gerrie stepped out as the three gentlemen arrived to meet with Tam, and they all moved over to his meeting table.

Tam's CFO ran over all the numbers in the acquisition offer and the financing terms, and the head of mergers and acquisitions talked about the strategy to reach out to WHK following the aborted meeting.

They agreed the WHK executives would most likely not meet with them again and that TBBM would have to send another letter to the WHK CEO. A draft would be developed and reviewed as soon as the next day.

As their time together was winding down, Tam's chief lawyer, Bryne Tena, asked if Tam had anything else he wanted to cover.

"Yes, I need to disclose that I met with Marjorie Parr last night, but it was personal in nature. There was no discussion about the deal," Tam asserted. "I will create a written account of our conversation, with Gerrie's help."

Bryne asked point-blank, "Tim, you need to tell us what is going on. How will this affect any potential deal?"

"Let me explain my relationship with Molly... um, I mean Marjorie," Tam stumbled. "We met when she was finishing her undergraduate degree and I was completing my masters in engineering at the University of Wisconsin. We broke up over a misunderstanding.

"I was able to tell her some things last night that she didn't know to help clarify what really happened at that time.

"You may not know, but Tim Bart isn't my real name. I changed it to simplify it for business purposes, and that's why Marjorie didn't know I was the CEO of TBBM. And I didn't know she was the chief legal counsel of WHK because I didn't know her married name was Parr.

"That's why we were so shocked to see each other. We hadn't laid eyes on each other in seventeen years. And I'd love for all of that to be kept private," Tam explained. "When I had the accident and Marjorie helped me, she indicated her husband died of pancreatic cancer last year, so it has been a very difficult time for her.

"I went to her house to tell her the truth about the past and ask her for another chance. My eventual intent is to pursue a relationship with her, which I understand is difficult at the moment as we plan to take over her company, which is a sore point between us, as you would expect," Tam added.

"Well," Bryne said, "that is quite a story. I can't guarantee it will never be public, however. Reporters have a way of finding out everything when these deals go hostile, and it sure looks like we're headed that way."

"Understood." Tam nodded. "And I pledge to disclose any meetings I have with her that are personal in nature so it will all be detailed.

"I felt it important you know this, since you will be key in any negotiations, offers, disclosures, and public communications. It is my hope this not become hostile and we can come to an agreement with WHK," he added.

"Of course that is our hope, but I don't believe it's in the cards, frankly," Bryne admitted. "I'm sure the leaders at WHK are circling the wagons, have contacted outside counsel and the bankers, and are ready for the incoming. For us, the problem is, with your accident, they've had more time to prepare their defense. We need to move quickly."

Bryne asked to meet privately with Tam to discuss the timing of the next move and asked those leaving to shut the door behind them. "Tam, is there anything else I should know about your relationship? I know you're divorced now. Is this about sex with the Parr woman?"

"One, you can call her Marjorie. Two, if I have my wish, it will be a very serious relationship, just as it was seventeen years ago.

"I don't appreciate you implying anything about her reputation," Tam said. "For your information, as we've pledged to be totally transparent, Molly lost her virginity to me, and the next person she slept with was the man who was her husband." His anger built with each word. "She isn't someone who sleeps around. She's a wonderful woman, and I expect you to speak of her respectfully."

"I will. I meant no offense. I just wanted to understand the nature of your relationship," Bryne answered calmly. "I also want you to know this could get very bumpy and your judgment shouldn't be clouded by any personal considerations.

"I'm not sure anyone else on the team would say this to you, so I feel I have to, as I'm trying to look out for the best interests of the company. If this was a good deal before, it should still be now, regardless of your personal relationship with Marjorie Parr," Bryne said, sensing Tam's increasing anger.

"I can see this woman means a lot to you. There are red flags everywhere, and we have to proceed fully aware of unique challenges this deal presents."

Tam got up from the table and walked over to the window to calm himself. He learned in leadership development training to walk away from the person or the keyboard if he felt he might say something he would regret later. Once he took a breath, Tam knew Bryne was right to say this to him. He loved Molly and that *did* influence his judgment around the deal.

Bryne needed to be able to tell Tam things like this if developments really went sideways during this acquisition.

The complication of Molly's involvement made everything much more difficult, but he knew as the CEO, he couldn't walk away from this deal because it would upset Molly. That was difficult to admit to himself. He knew he had to move forward, and she could have no warning of it.

He turned back to Bryne. "I understand fully. How quickly should we make the next move?"

chapter nineteen

Molly got into work very early the morning after seeing Tam, as she could hardly sleep thinking about the evening before.

She was happy to learn he never encouraged the woman she saw him with at the club so many years ago. The knowledge was bittersweet. It made her envision so many "what ifs." Molly kept thinking about Tam seeing her kiss Jim for the first time and what it must have done to him. He most likely felt the same way she felt when she saw him with the blonde. But instead of pushing Jim away, she'd married him.

She picked up the photo of her and Jim from her desk and spoke out loud. "I would never regret one minute of our life together, Jim. I loved you so much, but I am so confused.

"I'd like to give Tam a chance, but can I trust him? Especially since he's about to launch a hostile takeover of our company."

Cissy dropped her things on her desk and could see Molly in her office, looking at the photo of Jim. "Rough night?" she asked as she walked in.

"It was a wonderful night in many ways," Molly said wistfully. "Tam came by after our dinner and cleared up what happened so many years ago."

"Wow! I'll run over and grab some lattes. You've got to tell me this story before we start our busy day."

When Cissy came back, Molly explained what happened the night before.

"Amazing," Cissy sang. "I'm really happy for you, Molly, but this does complicate matters." She sighed. "I guess the first thing is you'll need to disclose Tam's visit to Ken and then Bill Stewart."

"Exactly." Molly agreed. "I'd like to catch Ken before he starts his day and then have a brief call with Bill. He'll help us determine the best way to keep a written record of the evening and our discussions."

Cissy rushed to her desk to set up the appointments and then buzzed Molly to let her know she could see Ken at 7:45 a.m. It seemed everyone aware of the takeover attempt was in early and on high alert.

Molly came into Ken's office and sat in front of his impressive walnut desk. He nursed a coffee and looked like he'd been in the office for some time as well.

"I need to let you know Tam surprised me and came to my house last night. We didn't talk about anything related to the takeover attempt; it was all personal in nature.

"He cleared up some things for me that happened between us years ago," Molly said in a matter-of-fact fashion.

Ken got up to shut the door. "Are you sure he isn't trying to manipulate you to get you to support this takeover?"

"All I can say is I believed what he told me about our relationship. Can I trust him? I have no idea," Molly said, throwing up her hands.

"Did he make a pass at you?" Ken asked.

Molly groaned. "I wouldn't call it a pass. Did we touch? Yes. Did he hold me in his arms? Yes. Did he kiss me? Yes. Did it progress any further? No…

"Do you have any idea how uncomfortable it is to have this type of discussion with your boss?" she asked.

"Well, I imagine it isn't the easiest," he said, smiling.

"The bad part is I have to talk to Bill Stewart and go over the details with him as well," Molly said. "I told you I'd let you know of any contact I had with him, and I'm committed to keeping my word." She got up to leave, pausing near the door. "I'll see you at the meeting at eleven to review all the materials, unless you have any other questions for me."

Ken shook his head. "Thanks, Molly. I do appreciate your candor and how difficult this is for you. Unfortunately, I think the takeover battle is about to get much worse."

Molly got into her office early again the next day, and things seemed eerily calm.

Tam had texted her a brief message yesterday.

Thanks for seeing me last night, Mol. Hope you're okay.

As a result of the disclosure, they agreed to have very few, if any, texts or emails between them. Their relationship couldn't be private, and unfortunately, any communication between them would be seen by scores of people.

As usual, she had a packed schedule for the day. She was pleased she was able to make some headway on emails and had been able to return some European phone calls already this morning. Molly was diligent about meeting all of her commitments, regardless of the heavy workload caused by the takeover attempt.

Cissy would be in soon, and they could compare notes on the day. Molly felt the WHK team had done everything they could to prepare for what TBBM would do next. All the documents had been drafted and approved, and the board had been fully briefed and approved the course of action.

Molly saw Cissy arrive and plop her things on her desk and start up her computer. Her assistant was a gem and a great friend, for sure.

Molly was intrigued by the relationship between Tunney and Cissy, as they were so different but appeared to be attracted to each other and planned to get together. She loved them both, so she hoped everything worked out between them.

Cissy hadn't had a lot of luck in the romance department, and Tunney's band lifestyle just didn't help him establish and maintain relationships. Their potential friendship had some complications with the takeover as well, but nothing like Tam and Molly's relationship.

She wondered if she and Tam *would* have a relationship. What was going to happen? *Too many questions and circumstances to contemplate*, Molly thought.

Cissy came in with her notes, and they got to work. They weren't far into the schedule for the day when Vanessa Cachum, head of corporate communications for WHK, rushed in.

"They've gone public and put out a press release about their offer," Vanessa said with some urgency. "We need approval to put out our response. I'm already getting media calls."

"Let me see what they said," Molly said calmly as Vanessa handed her a copy of the TBBM press release. "We are in hostile territory now," she muttered as she finished reading it. "Let me call Ken so we can go to his office to get the okay to put out the press release. Do you have our response and Q&As? He'll want to take one last look, as do I," Molly added.

With that, Vanessa and Molly went to Ken's office with the press release and the final draft of the questions and answers for the media and the statement for employees. They also called the head of investor relations, as he would be inundated with calls from the investment community and it would be important that WHK was consistent on every statement they made internally and externally.

After the approval from Ken, his assistant, Nell, sent an

email to the board with the copy of the TBBM press release and the WHK response. Vanessa sent a similar email to leadership to alert them and advise them not to make any statements, as their press release and communication to employees would be going out in a few minutes.

The WHK press release would also be sent to the Securities and Exchange Commission before it went public.

As it was before the market opened, the stock was soaring in premarket trading. While a big gain in the stock price was usually a cause for celebration, this wasn't one of those times, as everyone knew they could be losing their company.

Unlike most of the other stakeholders, the investment community was only interested in making money, so the large shareholders would pressure WHK leadership to meet with TBBM and strike a deal. Other stakeholders had more complex concerns. Employees would want to know if they would still have jobs if the company were taken over, as most combinations would mean the shedding of hundreds, if not thousands, of jobs, particularly at the corporate level.

Government leaders would be concerned about job loss in their districts, and community leaders at all locations would be worried about losing charitable giving and other company support. Suppliers would be concerned about their ongoing relationships and contracts.

There were no answers right now, as the process had just started. It would be an uneasy and busy time. The company's position was that it could deliver more value as an independent entity, but Molly knew their position could change over time as events unfolded.

It was sad to think Ken might not be the leader of the firm in the future. He'd put his heart and soul into WHK, and it was a great organization. If TBBM won, Tam would take over as CEO.

She cursed him under her breath.

The eerie calm of the morning vanished and uncertainty hung in the hallways at WHK as its leadership contemplated the next move.

At the end of the day that the takeover was made public, Vanessa put together a review of all the media coverage, which was extensive with national, international, and local stories. While the WHK leadership didn't like it, the overwhelming conclusion expressed in the media was the deal would be done eventually and the only real question was the price.

It was after six when Molly wandered over to Ken's office to discuss the day's developments, actions, and plans going forward. It was a deflating day, and Ken appeared to have aged five years.

He had his hands full with all the stakeholders looking to him for answers. He was masterful in this role, informing the board, trying to reassure employees, helping the leadership team communicate as effectively as possible with their staff, and guiding all external communications, particularly with investors and the media.

When Molly walked in, he was just finishing a call. She plopped down in the chair opposite him, and they stared at each other as he hung up the phone, understanding the exhaustion both felt.

"Ken, you were spectacular under very trying circumstances today. You personify what leadership is about, and I am honored to work for you," Molly told him.

"Aren't I supposed to be bucking you up right now?" he said with an ironic smile.

"I think we both need encouragement at this moment," she replied, "as this is the first day of a trial that will go on for some time."

Ken nodded. "I'm afraid so."

Just then, Molly's phone beeped as she got a text. *Can I see you?* Tam's message read.

NO, Molly texted back.

She looked back to Ken. "Tam sent me a text and wants to see me. I declined. I can't see him right now. I'm too angry."

"If I'm honest, I'm not pleased with him myself," Ken admitted, "but I'm not surprised it played out this way."

Molly's phone beeped again.

Can we talk? Tam messaged.

NO! Molly replied.

"He's made our lives miserable, so I hope he feels a bit miserable right now, too."

"What will you do?" Ken asked. "You're going to have to talk to him eventually."

"That's a good question. When I saw him the other night, he was like the old Tam, and, yes, I did fall in love with him a little bit again. There's a problem, though. I don't really know if this Tam is the man I want him to be.

"This episode today doesn't give me a great feeling about his character or feelings for me. Clearly, this acquisition is much more important to him than me," she said quietly.

"I don't know what to say." Ken shook his head. "I have lots of misgivings about you being with him. I can't attest to his character, and today's events don't help.

"As a CEO, however, he has to separate his personal and professional considerations, and, unfortunately, that includes his feelings for you."

"I do understand that, but it's difficult to accept, as you can imagine." Molly sighed and rubbed a tired hand across her forehead.

"I'm also thinking about my own future. Perhaps closing this deal is the end of my career as a CEO. It's been a wonderful career, and I've been grateful for every minute, with perhaps today as an exception.

"I have an ego like any CEO, and I certainly would like to conclude my career on my own terms. This isn't the script I would have written," Ken said sadly.

Ken and Molly sat there for a few minutes, silently keeping each other company.

chapter twenty

Tam got back to his condo late. He ended the evening at work, doing a series of media interviews, which he thought went extremely well.

His senior leadership team and the external bankers couldn't have been more pleased with the way everything played out. Tam should have been overjoyed, but he couldn't stop thinking about Molly and what she was feeling.

There was no question in his mind that she was upset with him. Her one-word text answers made it clear. He wanted the takeover *and* he wanted her—he wanted it all. But could he have it all?

He went into the kitchen to get a stiff drink, whiskey. As he was pouring it out, Tunney walked in. Even though Tam's hand was much better, Tunney had still been crashing at the condo.

To be honest, Tam was glad to have him, as he really needed someone to talk to about everything going on: his divorce, the kids, Molly, the takeover... Tam chuckled to himself. Tunney wasn't the best guy to talk with about the takeover, but he was a great help on everything in his personal life.

"Hey, bro," Tunney said, slapping him on the back. "You bringing out the hard stuff, eh?"

"Wanna join me?" Tam asked, pouring Tunney a glass. "I've

had a rough but successful day, until the end. Molly won't see or talk to me now."

Tunney shook his head. "Well, I heard something about the takeover on the radio when I was driving over here, and those Wall Street guys commenting thought the combination of the two companies would work well. I'm no expert, but I'm sure Molly's none too pleased with you today."

"Molly knows full well there's no way I could have told her what we were planning," Tam said defensively.

Tunney took a swig of his whiskey. "No, but I'm sure she's thinking this is a fine way to show her you love her."

Tam stared at his brother. "You're supposed to help me feel better, not worse."

"Bro, I'm just telling you the truth. Can't sugarcoat it." He shrugged.

Tam looked into the amber liquid in his glass, dejected. "I know, Tun. I'm trying to figure out a way to fix this. I promised Molly I wouldn't give up on us again, and I won't. There has to be a way."

"As my legal counsel reminded me, I have to do the right thing for our company, regardless of Molly's feelings. Unfortunately, we had to do what we did today," he added.

"You've gotta find a way for Molly and that boss of hers to feel good about this in some way," Tunney said. "Molly thinks the world of him. He's like a second father to her. From what I hear, he's a good man and leader. If she feels he's damaged by this, she's going to hold it against *you*." He pointed at Tam.

"I get it," Tam said dejectedly.

"You know Molly. She always puts everybody else's feelings before her own. It's the hurt you're causing him that's really getting to her. You've got to get with Ken," Tunney said.

"It's a good idea, but it's as hard to talk to Ken right now as it is to talk to Molly, Tun."

"I'm actually going over there tomorrow to see Cissy, and I'd love to meet him," Tunney said. He watched Tam, and he could see the wheels in his head were spinning, coming up with ideas on what to do next.

The next morning, Molly had grabbed some breakfast from the company cafeteria when she got into the office. She arrived early, as she had so much work to do around the takeover, particularly now that it was public.

She thought she was losing weight. Eating hadn't been her top priority since the ill-fated meeting with Tam at his office. It seemed like most nights she went to bed without dinner. With everything going on, she didn't feel the least bit hungry, but Molly knew she had to eat something.

Back in her office, she picked around at her food and drank some orange juice. When Cissy came in, she plopped down across from Molly. It felt like they hadn't had any time to really catch up since the takeover started.

"Good morning," Cissy said in as cheery a voice as she could muster. "I'm glad you're having breakfast, but you're moving your food around more than eating it."

Molly gave her a crooked smile. "Well, I just haven't been hungry, and I'm sure you can guess the reasons—Tim, the CEO, and Tam, the man I love. Sometimes, I believe they *are* two separate people."

"Speaking of the devil..." Cissy leaned in conspiratorially. "Did I tell you Tunney's coming by at the end of the day to take me out on a date? I hope that won't be a problem, having Tam's brother in the building... Just to be clear, I was speaking of Tam as the devil, not Tunney." Cissy chuckled.

Molly frowned at the mention of Tam's name, particularly as the devil. He sure was causing her a lot of problems, but she still had strong feelings for him.

Cissy had gotten her one of those stress reliever balls that had a gooey filling, and she'd taken to squeezing it lately during meetings in her office. She grabbed it tight, thinking of Tam.

"I really don't think it's a problem." Molly shrugged. "I'm very sure he knows nothing about the business of the takeover. As a precaution, I'll send an email to Bill Stewart and mention it to Ken so they're both aware.

"You know how I feel about Tunney, but the deal really complicates everything. Despite that, I'm really happy the two of you have hit it off. We'll just have to worry about the rest of it later," she said a bit sadly.

"The rest of it being Tam and your feelings for him and the deal?" Cissy asked. "When will you talk to him? I'm sure he's been asking all the time."

"That's a really good question. I sure wish I knew the answer. As the discussions with the board progress, we may be ready to talk to the execs and advisors of TBBM soon."

Cissy frowned. "I wasn't talking about the deal. I know it'll take its course. I meant when you were going to talk to Tam about your feelings for *him*."

"That's just it." Molly rubbed her hand up her arm, shrugging again. "What *are* my feelings for him? Do we have a future together? Is he the man I think he is, or does he want the company more than me?

"Will I have a job? Do I have to work for him? It's all too much to contemplate," she said, putting her face in her hands. "Remember, in a takeover of this kind, the corporate office is just about wiped out, including your job, my job... Perhaps five hundred jobs will go away, just at WHK.

"You know how many acquisitions we've made, and the reality is the acquiring company keeps most of its staff as it combines with the acquired company. Of course, there can be lots of talent that can be absorbed, but unfortunately, many people will be gone.

"I keep thinking about all the great people here who will be out if the takeover happens, and Tam will be the reason for it. It just upsets me so much.

"Now you can see how my mind works. I try to think about the business ramifications, and then I switch to my feelings for Tam and then back again…"

Cissy observed her boss with concern. "It's clear all of this is eating you up."

"Listen." Molly waved aside her concern. "Forget about me. I'm so sorry to worry you, talking about all the job loss, including your job. It was really thoughtless of me—"

"You have lots on your mind, and I appreciate that you're always honest with me," Cissy said firmly. "I'll just repeat the words you've said to all the staff here: 'It's business as usual. Just keep doing your jobs, don't listen to speculation, and news will be communicated as soon as it can be.'

"Just thought I'd remind you." Cissy smiled.

Molly couldn't help but return her smile. "You are absolutely right. Thanks. I'm certainly hopeful we can continue to work together in the future."

"I'm worried about you, Molly, and I think you need to have some time to yourself to think all of this through. Is there somewhere you can go to get away?" Cissy asked with great concern.

"I've been thinking the same thing. It's Friday tomorrow. I was thinking about flying to Wisconsin to see my parents for the weekend. All the work has been done for the board meeting on Tuesday, so I think Ken would be supportive of my trip," Molly said.

"Say no more," Cissy declared. "I'll look at flights during your first meeting, and we can review it when we get a break. I think a trip home would do you a world of good, and I'm absolutely sure Ken would agree."

"I've tried to keep my parents up to date on everything, but I know they're concerned about me. I let them know about the misunderstanding that pulled Tam and me apart, and they were heartbroken. They really liked Tam... and Tunney, too."

"Your parents knew Tunney, too?" Cissy asked, wide-eyed.

"Absolutely." Molly nodded. "They thought the world of him. He made them laugh so much. Tunney actually helped us at the farm stand and had dinner at their house. He loves my mother's cooking." She laughed, her mood a little brighter.

At that moment, Tam was in his office, drinking a cup of coffee and gazing out the window. He was thinking about Molly, the deal, and their relationship. Did they *have* a relationship? Would the deal destroy any chance they had?

He knew he couldn't put the genie back in the bottle. He felt the deal would go through, as he knew TBBM would increase the offer after WHK formally responded next week following their board meeting.

The problem was the fur would probably fly, the media would get ugly, and Molly will be in the middle of it all. It had to be so stressful for her, and it was all his fault. He couldn't fool himself about that; he was at the root of her problems right now.

Tam wished he knew how she felt about him. Could she love him again after all this?

Just then, his train of thought was broken as Gerrie came into his office with a fresh latte and a scone. "I brought you something to eat and drink. You haven't given food much of a priority with all the meetings around the takeover and the business with

Molly. I have a feeling you were thinking about her when I came in," Gerrie said gently.

"You're a smart woman, Gerrie," Tam replied with a sad smile.

At that moment, Tunney popped up and swiped his cowboy hat off his face, as he was dozing on the couch in Tam's office. "Gerrie is the *most* wonderful woman," Tunney said overenthusiastically.

"Okay, okay," Gerrie said, laughing. "I'll get you the same thing, Tunney." She headed out of the office with a chuckle.

"Thank you, ma'am," Tunney said, getting up and tipping his hat to her.

Tam laughed. "You know, she didn't even seem surprised to see you there on the couch. I guess I should be concerned with all the media we've been getting lately that they might write a story about the CEO's cowboy musician brother bumming in his office. But I've got so many other things on my mind…"

"My guess is the main thing on your mind is Molly," Tunney said, matter-of-fact, as he walked over to sit down on the other side of his desk.

"Good guess," Tam said. "This takeover does occupy my schedule, but I have to admit my head and heart always return to Molly and how to win her back."

Tunney nodded. "I've been thinking about that, too, and I had an idea. You got in too late last night and up too early for a serious conversation, so I tagged along this morning to give us time to talk."

Tam looked at Tunney with interest.

chapter twenty-one

Molly had finished up her meetings for the day and was turning to answering emails and phone calls for a few hours. She would work late tonight because she was leaving in the morning to go to visit her parents in Wisconsin. Molly couldn't wait to see them, and she knew she needed the time away from all this business to clear her head.

It was a welcome break in her work when Cissy came in with Tunney, who had arrived to pick her up for their date. Molly got up to give him a big hug.

"Well, you just made my day," Tunney said with a laugh. "How lucky am I? Two beautiful women."

Molly was just about to tell him about her trip to Wisconsin when Ken walked in, seemingly deep in thought.

"Ken, I'd like to introduce you to Tunney Rozomolski, Tam's brother," Molly said, touching Tunney's arm with affection.

"What a surprise to meet you," Ken said. "Your brother has certainly made a lot of work for us." He reached out his hand to shake Tunney's.

"Yes, sir, I understand what he's done has caused quite a stir, but I don't talk to him about it, and I have no part in it." He tossed up his hands. "As you can see, I'm just an old, broken-down musician who happens to have a hotshot CEO brother."

"You're not broken down at all," Molly chided, linking her arm in his. "In fact, you and Ken are two of the best men I know in the whole world." She smiled at both of them with admiration.

"Tunney, that's high praise for us, coming from an impressive woman. It's very good to meet you. I just wish it were under different circumstances," Ken said warmly.

"I understand," Tunney answered. "It sure must have been some scene when Molly and Tam recognized each other in that meeting."

"That's an understatement. I'm sure I'll remember that meeting for the rest of my life," Ken declared.

"Me, too." Molly agreed.

"Sir, Molly's told me what a mentor you've been to her and the support you and your wife gave her when her husband died. I know you've helped her with this situation with my brother. I believe she feels like you're a second father to her, and I can tell you her father is a man to be admired, so that says a lot about you.

"I feel I should thank you. I've always been protective of her," Tunney said with a grateful smile.

Molly squeezed Tunney's arm again, eyes shining with emotion. "I've always felt Tunney was the big brother I never had, even though we've had quite a gap in our contact." She laughed.

"As you know now, that was all a mistake," Tunney said gently. "I sure wish we could've stayed in touch…" He trailed off.

"Well, I'm sure you and your boss have some work to do, so we should get out of your way."

"Cissy, unfortunately, I need one more thing, so if you and Tunney could grab a drink in the cafeteria, I'll just finish up with Ken," Molly said.

"I only need a few minutes," Ken said. "Wonderful to meet you, Tunney. I'd like to say it would be good to see you again, but with the takeover, I'm not really sure."

The tall cowboy tipped his hat at Ken, and he and Cissy set off for the cafeteria.

Tunney always liked to look around the offices, see what the people were doing, the photos on their desks, the posters and artwork on the walls. He never tired of taking it all in. He especially loved coming to the office to get Cissy so he could check on Molly.

"Ken's a good man," he said to Cissy as they strolled down the hallway. "I'm glad I had the chance to meet him."

"He is." Cissy agreed. "He's a great leader. We all certainly look to him at times like this.

"The stress is taking a toll on him. It looks like he's aged years since this thing started, but he never shows us how much pressure he's under. He's always confident and cool, which helps keep us all calm and things running smoothly. His leadership skills are a real gift."

Tunney nodded. "It's interesting. I think Ken shares many traits with my brother."

Cissy smiled and said, "On one hand, I can't wait to meet Tam. On the other, I'm a little scared."

"He's really not that scary, but I get where you're coming from," Tunney answered.

Cissy steered him to the cafeteria, and, as it was after six, they went over to the machine to get a couple soft drinks. The lights were down, so it was a little dark, and the music playing in the background was an instrumental version of a song Tunney sang with the band.

He put down the drinks, grabbed Cissy by the waist, and started dancing to the music with her and softly singing to her.

"This is a treat," Cissy whispered, linking her arms around his neck and looking up at him. "I don't usually get to dance with a handsome man in the cafeteria. It makes coming to work more fun." She smiled.

"Well, I knew I'd have to drag you out of this place to get you to go out with me because of all this takeover business," he said, "but I agree with you. This is fun."

Tunney smoothed Cissy's hair, then softly stroked her face as they continued to dance. She reached for him and brought his head down to hers, and they kissed very softly at first, then more urgently.

Cissy reluctantly pulled away, telling Tunney, "I wonder if I can get fired for kissing the brother of the CEO who wants to take over our company... *and* kissing him in the cafeteria at that!" She giggled.

"This is why I could never work for a corporation. Kissing is the most wonderful thing, and I'm sure there's something in your darn rulebook that says it's banned on company premises. That's just no fun at all." He joined in her laughter.

"Well, as much as I enjoy kissing you, I think we should get back now so I can do what Molly needs me to do, and then we can be off." Cissy grabbed his hand, heading back to Molly's office.

Molly asked her to rearrange a few meetings for her and set up a call for Monday, so Tunney came into her office for a few minutes and sat across from her.

"I'm so glad you came by so I had a chance to see you," Molly told him with a warm smile.

"Me, too." Tunney agreed. "It was good to meet Ken. He seems like a great guy. Cissy just raves about him."

"I'm lucky to have him as my boss," Molly said. "Most CEOs don't measure up to Ken. He's provided terrific leadership to this company, particularly through this takeover attempt."

"How are *you* doing?" Tunney asked.

Molly sighed. "Okay, but I need a bit of a break, so I'm headed to see my parents for the weekend."

"Will you say hello for me?" Tunney asked. "You know how I feel about your parents."

"Of course. They feel the same about you."

"And what about Tam? Are they upset with him?" Tunney asked, sitting up straighter in his chair, a bit anxious to hear her answer. He knew it would reflect her personal feelings.

"They've spent a lot of time listening to me, and I think they've kept an open mind about everything. It's difficult to have these discussions on the phone, so I really can't wait to see them in person to talk things through... and have some of Mom's cooking."

"I don't think I'll leave the house much," Molly answered.

"Your mother's cooking is out of this world. You're making me hungry just talking about it." Tunney laughed. "Wouldn't it be fun someday to have a meal around the table again, all of us?"

Molly squinted at him with suspicion. "I know what you're getting at, but I just don't know. There's so much ahead of us with this takeover, and it could get really ugly.

"I find it very difficult to separate my feelings for Tam from the frustration I feel over what he's doing with this takeover."

"I understand, to a certain extent," Tunney said, looking down at his calloused fingers, "but on the other hand, I know what you two meant to each other and the kind of love you had, and you just can't give up on that. Don't you still care about him?"

"Of course, but it's mixed up with all these other feelings right now and complicated with the takeover, as well as my love and grief for Jim. Even though Tam explained what happened all those years ago, I can't just erase years of hurt and automatically trust him again.

"On the takeover front, we have a critical board meeting, and there's just no way I can talk to him or see him right now." Molly sighed, closing her eyes for a brief moment. "It's actually helpful that I'll be out of town, seeing my parents."

Tunney looked straight in her eyes and said, "Molly, you know he wants to see you in the worst way. He's in agony right now."

Molly seemed a bit sad. "I don't doubt it, as I have the same feelings." She perked up a bit and laughed. "Tunney, are you spying on me for your brother? Are you trying to get business secrets so he can get an edge in the takeover?"

"Ha!" Tunney laughed. "I don't know anything about the takeover, don't want to know, and wouldn't understand it anyway.

"*And* I wouldn't use the word 'spying,' but I sure wanted to see you with my own eyes to see if you were all right," he said, taking her hand and rubbing her knuckles gently with his thumb.

Just then, Cissy walked in to announce she'd finished her work and was ready to go. Tunney and Molly hugged and said good-bye, and Tunney and Cissy walked out of the building, linking arms.

chapter twenty-two

Molly looked out the airplane window at the flat plains of the Midwest, with the countless farms and square patches of grass and fields. It wouldn't be long until they landed in Wisconsin.

She'd told her parents she would rent a car, but they wouldn't hear of it and were making the drive to the Madison airport from their small rural town to pick her up.

Molly was actually relieved. She'd been working so hard and under so much stress that she just wanted to collapse. The thought of her mother's cooking and the opportunity to just unwind was intoxicating.

She also wanted to sit down with her parents and fully discuss the new developments between her and Tam. Molly's parents had listened carefully on the phone and weren't judgmental. They knew how much Tam had hurt her so many years ago, but they seemed open to the possibilities of the future once they heard the real story about what happened when they broke apart.

Maybe they were just humoring her on the phone, so a face-to-face conversation would help her figure things out.

When Molly talked to Ken about the possibility of taking off for Wisconsin to spend the weekend with her parents, he was all for it. He knew how much she needed to get away and rest and told her the time away would allow her to refresh and be ready for the next phase of battle. With the board meeting coming up, it would be a busy and difficult week.

When Molly got off the plane and went past the security area, she saw her parents standing there waiting for her. She ran over to them and hugged them both so tight. She wasn't prepared for the emotion of seeing them, and she started crying, softly at first, but soon she was sobbing.

"Oh, honey," her mom said, holding her tight and stroking her hair.

"Mom, Dad, I'm so sorry," she said, wiping away her tears. "I guess I've kept my emotions all bottled up, and they're all coming out now... There's a lot going on in my life, and I have so many questions. Maybe you can help me sort it out. And I'm just so happy to see you, too."

"You're home now," her dad said, putting his arm around her. "It's time for you to relax and take care of yourself. Let us pamper you a bit. You clearly need it. We're also here to talk about anything you want to talk about."

With that, they moved to the exit to get the car and begin the long ride home.

Molly spread out in the backseat and looked out the window, watching the farms whizz by with their worn barns and lazy cows. What a different life she had growing up and living here. It really was idyllic, as she had wonderful friends and was under the caring and watchful eyes of her parents.

Her life was so different now. Stress-filled days, running from meeting to meeting, not having enough time to breathe, endless emails... It was all utterly unfulfilling, if Molly were honest with herself. But she hadn't always felt this way about work.

What had changed? Was it Jim's death? He could always make her feel better, even if she had a bad day. After trying days, they had a nice glass of wine and light dinner and just laughed at silly things. Now she worked twelve to fourteen hours and went home to a silent, empty house.

Molly knew she was good at her job. Her boss and staff told her so, as well as outside counsel. She knew she was yearning for something, perhaps a major change in her life.

Could she trust these feelings?

And what about Tam? Would it be disloyal to Jim and their marriage to consider a relationship with Tam? She had to block that out for now, as there were just too many issues around her feelings about him and the complications of the potential takeover.

Just then her mom asked, "Everything okay? It's mighty quiet back there."

Molly laughed. "Fine, Mom. I'm just trying to think everything through. Frankly, I have so little time lately just to think, and my personal and professional lives are a bit complicated at the moment."

Her mom looked at her with the steady and true gaze Molly recognized from her childhood. "You will have all your answers. You just need a bit of time. Don't rush yourself. Your dad and I are here to help you, but any decisions you make are yours and yours alone."

Molly smiled at her mother. Fred and Margaret, could there be any finer people or better parents? She was so lucky to have them, and there was no other place she wanted to be this weekend.

When they arrived home, Molly went upstairs to her old bedroom and unpacked. She just brought a carry-on bag since all she needed was a few casual things to wear.

Molly didn't want to go out and see anyone; she just needed time to do as she pleased—no meetings, phone calls, or endless emails.

She smiled to herself. She knew she'd have to look at emails at some point over the weekend, with the board meeting coming up, but not for a while.

Molly peeled off her clothes, put on her plush robe, which was still on the hook on the back of the door, and went into the bathroom to have a bubble bath. This was what she always did when she came home.

The hot water and bubbles surrounded her and she luxuriated in them. She relaxed and felt happy to be home, leaving behind her worries, if just for a few minutes.

As she dried off, Molly could hear the sounds downstairs of her mother preparing dinner, which was such a welcome sound. Margaret hadn't said what she was making, but Molly knew it would be one of her favorites.

Her mother had a wonderful herb garden. She canned vegetables in the fall and made her own jams and jellies. Margaret also made sourdough bread from scratch, and Molly could smell the bread baking.

For the first time in quite a while, Molly felt ravenous. She pulled on her jeans and T-shirt and went downstairs to help her mom set the table and finish the dinner preparations.

Her mother revealed the menu: lemon chicken with asparagus sautéed with garlic and slivered almonds, new potatoes with rosemary from their garden, and mixed salad greens with Molly's favorite homemade balsamic dressing. For dessert, her mother had made a peach galette with her own preserves.

"I can't remember the last time I felt this hungry," Molly announced.

"Good. You are looking a little thin," her mother said, smiling.

At dinner, they talked about everything: Jim, Tam, the takeover, and the toll everything was taking on Molly. She felt like a burden had been lifted, having the chance to express her fears and concerns in a way she couldn't before.

As they had a cup of tea with the excellent galette, Molly said, "I can't thank you enough for everything. Seeing you, talking things through, and having this wonderful meal have helped me tremendously.

"I feel like I can begin to deal with the toughest dilemma, my feelings for Tam." She glanced at both her parents.

Her dad looked at her with concern. "Honey, you need to know something. Tam was here earlier today."

"What!" Molly screeched, jumping up.

"Slow down a minute. Sit down and let us explain what happened," her father said calmly. "He arrived, unannounced, this morning. He knew you were coming and wanted to speak to us prior to your arrival. He flew out very early and left right after he talked to us because he didn't want to interrupt your visit or add any more stress in your life.

"Tam is fully aware of the pain he's caused and the pressure you're under. He was happy you'd have this time to decompress and relax," Fred said, pausing for a minute.

"I can't believe he was here…" Molly said, stunned, falling back into her chair.

Margaret touched her arm. "Honey, I think he wanted us to know how sorry he was for the misunderstanding and that he cares about you so much—"

"Maybe he came here to manipulate both of you *and* me." She pounded her fist on the table.

"We certainly understand, as we were a bit angry as well and totally taken off guard when he showed up on our doorstep," her mother said. "But as we talked about everything, we could see he was sincere in his feelings for you and his regret of the pain he caused to you and our family."

Molly sat back and thought for a minute. She was so distraught when she and Tam broke up that she didn't think about her parents' feelings at the time. Thinking back, she was sure they were devastated to see her in such pain and experiencing a loss that was so deeply felt. Her parents thought so highly of Tam as well.

"How long was he here?" Molly asked quietly.

"About an hour and a half," her father responded.

"Well, you've spent a lot more time with him than I have recently." Molly threw her hands in the air in frustration. "Oh, and by the way, I'll have to disclose that he was here. Did he mention anything about the takeover?"

"Only that he regrets that it's been so upsetting to you and has prevented you two from having much of a conversation about your relationship… and he wants that so much," Margaret replied.

"He told us he would disclose it as well," Fred told her.

"I'm not surprised he would do that. It's the right thing to do. He's a very good CEO, I believe," Molly said earnestly.

"That's good to know, honey, but what do you feel about *him*? He made his feelings for you crystal clear. What are you going to do?" her mother asked.

"On one hand, I feel a bit terrified to talk to him and secretly relieved the board meeting is coming up, preventing any contact. On the other hand, I can't wait to see him, to be with him, because I can't deny the feelings I have for him…" Her voice trailed off as she put her face in her hands.

When she looked up, she could see the concern in her parents' eyes.

"From a business standpoint, the takeover is a disaster, and so many good people will lose their jobs in the process. My job is one of those, but I'm not concerned about that.

"It's killing me that Ken will be forced out, as he's one of the finest leaders I know, and you're aware of how he's mentored me over the years." Molly sighed.

"Honey, is it possible to think about Tam personally, putting the business issues aside?" Margaret asked.

"I've racked my brains on this. Should I resign? No, as I would let down everyone I work with and value at the company, including Ken.

"Should I walk away from Tam personally, as I know how devastating it will be to see our company dismantled? How will I feel if we're together and I see him after a long day of watching people I really value walking out the door?

"As legal counsel, I'll be one of the last left and have to play a huge role in combining the companies.

"Personally, I wonder if we could be together, get married, have a family... I would so much like to have children. But I worry so much. He couldn't stay faithful to his wife... Is that me in a few years, licking my wounds because he's hurt me so badly again?

"Believe me. This is *all* I can think about. Tam, the man I love, taking an atom bomb to the life I have now," Molly said, tears streaming down her face.

"So you love him?" her father asked.

"Yes, of course. That's why this is so hard," she said, blinking back her tears.

chapter twenty-three

Tam walked into his condo and put his computer case down on the counter. He had gone back to his office and worked late after his quick trip to Wisconsin to see Molly's parents. Under the circumstances, they couldn't have been more gracious. Fred and Margaret were certainly surprised to see him on their front porch in his business suit. The last time they saw him, he had much longer hair and was dressed in ripped jeans.

By using the company plane, he was able to get there hours earlier than Molly. He paid for the trip himself, but it would still be in the corporate jet log so it could be discovered by the media, but he had no other choice.

Tam felt strongly that he had to see Fred and Margaret so they understood the events from the past and how he was feeling right now. He made it clear to them that he wouldn't give up on his relationship with Molly. His love for her was as strong as ever.

Molly and Tam just needed to get through this week. Then everything on the takeover offer would be public. He sincerely hoped they could start working on their relationship. It was just such a difficult time.

Molly was suffering, and it was all his fault. He couldn't talk to her, comfort her in any way. It was driving him insane. Did she feel the same way about him? Could she overcome her anger and frustration over the takeover and the embarrassment she felt about her personal life being discussed in two boardrooms?

At least Tunney had the chance to see Molly, and he felt she was doing okay. Tam wanted to call her parents after he left, but Molly would be there all weekend, and he'd made it clear he wouldn't try to see her or talk to her until after the board meeting on Tuesday. That made the most sense, but it was agonizing.

He sent a fruit basket to Molly's parents to thank them for their hospitality and for spending so much time with him. Tam felt a bit guilty because he ended up running by his own parents' house for only about thirty minutes. He would find time later to try and make it up to them.

Tam had kept his mom and dad abreast of what was going on as soon as he'd seen Molly again. Of course, his parents were concerned with the injury to his hand and were happy to see he was just about good as new.

He had to chuckle, as his parents read the reports in the papers and had plenty of questions for him. It was like dealing with the media!

He tried to separate his personal life and feelings for Molly from his business sense to keep an objective focus on the deal. His leadership team and board of directors were excited about the takeover and saw it as a huge opportunity for growth and global expansion for their company.

Tam's career success was now tied to the successful completion of the takeover. If the deal didn't go through, it would be seen as a career failure for him, possibly costing him his job. Ironically, career success could mean failure in his personal life.

Tunney walked in and saw the look of concern on Tam's face. "Hey, bro. What's up? I guess I probably know."

"Yeah, right now, it's Molly and business. Just trying to sort through it.

"With all this going on, I don't want to lose focus on the kids, either. I'm really looking forward to seeing them this weekend. I hope some quality time with them will get my mind off other things. Maybe we can have 'Dad and Uncle Tunney' weekend?" Tam suggested.

"Sounds good to me," Tunney said. "We just need to work it around the gigs I have Friday and Saturday."

"The kids come Saturday morning, so don't plan to sleep late," Tam said with a grin.

"Got it, bro. I'll try to get to bed by two thirty to be ready for them." Tunney laughed. He got more serious when he asked his next question. "How was your trip to Wisconsin?"

"I can't tell you how wonderful it was to be in Wisconsin, our home, and see our parents and Fred and Margaret. To walk into their house after all these years… What a feeling." He was obviously emotional.

Tunney looked at his brother with concern.

"We had great times there, didn't we?" Tam asked.

Tunney nodded. "We sure did. Those are some mighty fine people, none better. They must have been surprised to see the 'new issue' Tam, Mr. CEO. They probably remembered the old Tam in jeans, long hair—poor musician." He laughed.

"They did comment on that." Tam smiled. "I surprised them, no question. At first, I think they were a bit put off, but as we talked, they seemed to relax.

"I'm sure I looked like a different man. In so many ways, I am different, but in so many other ways, I'm not. I'm still that kid from Wisconsin, trying to make his way, but totally in love with their daughter…" He stared down at the floor.

"I know it's not going to be easy with this takeover and so much about your and Molly's relationship becoming almost public knowledge," Tunney said. "But you have to stay strong, focused on you and Molly. Don't let anything or anyone get in your way. And if I know Fred and Margaret, I think they'll be in your corner in the end," he said with conviction.

Tam nodded. "I feel that, too, quite strongly. I just don't know the obstacles that'll be in our way. The next couple weeks are so important for Molly and me. I hope we can both hold it together."

"Me, too, bro," Tunney said. "You have to do it for yourself and for Molly. In my book, you're both worth it, and your love can make it through."

Tam threw a towel from the counter at him, laughing. "That sounds like a song!"

"Well, it sure could be. I think you and Molly have a few songs in your story," Tunney said, smiling. "Let's just hope it's a happy love song, not a sad one."

chapter twenty-four

It was a beautiful day on Saturday, and Molly relished the time at home with her parents. She decided to take a little bit of time to review emails and get her work out of the way early so she could spend the rest of the weekend away from business.

Molly felt herself lighten with the thought of no work and no pressure. Well, at least she could do her job today sitting on her bed in her pajamas.

When she finished and showered and dressed, Molly, Margaret, and Fred decided to drive out to a scenic old town to have lunch and enjoy the glorious spring day.

They would have plenty of time at home later to chat, as Margaret was planning another feast for dinner, and Molly was loving being spoiled with all of her favorite dishes and having their long, leisurely talks after dinner.

Molly looked out the car window at the spring day with the buds on the trees and the hint of the flowers to come. For a moment, she felt joyful, seeing this rebirth. There was so much in her life currently that was keeping her from enjoying everyday pleasures.

It was time for a change.

That's quite convenient, Molly thought to herself, as she was about to be forced to change with the takeover. But no, she wanted to drive the change, not be forced into it by others.

"You're certainly deep in thought back there," Margaret said.

"I'm thinking about big changes in my life, Mom. I'm not entirely sure what the changes will be, but I'll know soon." She grinned at her mother, peaceful determination overtaking her features. "I can't tell you how much this time away has helped me."

"Honey, we want you to be happy, and you know we would do anything for you and support you in whatever decisions you make," Margaret said as Fred parked outside the café in the small town where they'd planned to have lunch.

They walked in and took one of the few open tables near the picture window.

"We've been worried about you for some time, but particularly since Jim's death. It seems like you wanted to bury yourself in your work to run from your grief," Margaret said quietly. "Whenever we'd talk to you on the phone, it was always about work, never about what you were really feeling. I know it might have been easier to hide your emotions in work, but all work isn't a life."

Molly gazed at her parents across the table. "How did you two get to be so wise?" she asked, smiling.

"It is interesting that you seem so full of life now, ever since this business with Tam, even as difficult as it's been. It's like a light has suddenly been turned on," Fred commented. "I was very angry with him at first, and I thought I might punch him if he hurt my daughter again. But that's not a very thoughtful reaction, is it?" He chuckled.

"I guess that's what Mom's saying. I may be running through the full gamut of emotions—happy, sad, frustrated, angry, joyful… but I am alive again. I can feel again, and I'm not just going through the motions of life.

"It did mean a lot to me that Tam didn't betray me years ago, that he really loved me. I'm still trying to come to terms with that and how my life could have been different," Molly said. "I'm really glad you didn't punch him." She laughed, lightening the mood. "Although, there have been plenty of times lately where that's exactly what I wanted to do."

They enjoyed their lunch and headed to the old bookstore on Main Street and spent quite some time looking through the secondhand books. Molly bought an old Betty Crocker cookbook with so many wonderful, old-fashioned recipes.

Molly actually was a good cook, and like her mom, she always tinkered with recipes and never followed them to the letter. She had almost stopped cooking after Jim died, so it would be fun to try some of the dishes when she got home but spice them up a bit. Molly hugged the book to her chest as they ambled back to the car.

When they got back to her parents' house, she asked her dad if she could borrow the car. Molly needed a little time on her own, and she wasn't going far.

Pulling over on the soft shoulder, just minutes from the house, she parked and walked along the banks of the creek to sit down next to her tree. It was a bit brisk outside, so she zipped up her fleece jacket against the wind. As there had been plenty of spring rain, the water was flowing freely, and Molly listened to the sound of the current.

She closed her eyes and thought of all the times she'd come here over the years to relax and think. Her mind kept coming back to the day she brought Tam here and they made love in this exact spot. Molly felt herself flush warm thinking about it.

They had the most intense physical relationship; their lovemaking had always been electric. She'd only slept with one other man, Jim, so she didn't have a huge comparison base. While

Molly and Jim had an active and satisfying love life, her physical relationship with Tam was something else entirely. She blushed deeper just thinking about it. Tam just brought something out in her...

As the wind picked up in that moment, Molly decided to head home. Right before leaving, she gently touched the heart Tam carved into the tree. *Still here,* she thought.

Margaret cooked another fabulous dinner that evening, and the three of them talked for a very long time. It was about ten when Molly excused herself, needing some time alone with her thoughts.

The next morning, her mother would make her favorite blueberry pancakes for a late breakfast, and then they would head to church and to the airport. Molly hated to see the weekend end.

As she dozed off, she was thinking of Tam and the first time they made love, when his touch made her skin tingle and they had fallen asleep, arms around each other.

Molly tried to squeeze in every last second with her parents, even though it meant she would get home very late. After a tearful good-bye at the airport, she got on the plane to return to the East Coast.

Her late return didn't matter, as all she was going to do was go to bed and get up at the crack of dawn to head into the office. *Back to the grind,* she thought to herself.

Molly considered checking her email when she got home, but she was exhausted and ruled out any work before she collapsed in bed. She was up by 4:45 a.m. and was ready to go in record time. She left so early the newspapers weren't in the driveway yet.

When she got into the office, Molly was surprised to see the corporate communications leader, Vanessa, sitting outside her door, working on her computer. It was just six thirty.

"Molly, I tried to reach you last night and this morning and sent multiple emails. You need to know about a story published very early this morning," Vanessa said, obviously concerned.

"So sorry. I was traveling and didn't check email. I got in so late, and I must have left my cell phone on silent. What's it about? Some other takeover speculation?" Molly asked.

"It's about you and Tim," Vanessa explained, laying the copy of the story in front of her.

"*Hostile Takeover is Love Story,*" the headline at the top of the page screamed in large type. The smaller decks underneath the headline gave more detail.

"*TBBM CEO hopes to rekindle romance with first love, WHK Senior Counsel.*"

"*Shock of seeing each other at meeting causes accident that seriously injures CEO.*"

The story started, "*It's not every day blood and sex are discussed at a board meeting, but that is exactly what happened at the first WHK Industries meeting after an unwelcome takeover offer from TBBM Technologies.*

"*At a meeting prior to the WHK board meeting when Marjorie (Molly) Parr, WHK's Senior Counsel, and Tim Bart, TBBM's CEO, saw each other across the table, Bart dropped a water pitcher, shattering it and seriously injuring his hand, shocked to see Parr across the table from him more than seventeen years after a messy breakup.*

"*Parr's shock matched Bart's, as she rushed to help stop the bleeding and was face to face with the man who allegedly took her virginity many years ago.*

"*Parr was reportedly still recovering from the loss of her husband of fifteen years, James Parr, an attorney who died at just forty years of age of pancreatic cancer one year ago...*"

Molly didn't need to see the rest. There were photos of her and Tam and even one of Ken.

Molly slumped in her chair. "How could this happen?" She sighed.

"There was a leak, and I suspect the bankers. I suppose they think this will get the deal a lot more attention, and, unfortunately, I think they're right.

"Molly, I want you to know I've been in contact with Ken, and we put together an email to the board so they wouldn't be surprised. When I couldn't reach you, Ken and I developed a plan of action.

"From the questions the reporter was asking me, I could tell it would be a very personal kind of story. He waited until the last minute to contact us for comments, as I'm sure they had the story confirmed through other sources before reaching out to us. I'm so sorry, Molly," Vanessa said, touching her arm.

Molly jumped up. "You don't think Tam—I mean, Tim did this, do you?"

Vanessa frowned. "In my professional opinion, no. There is no advantage to TBBM whatsoever. In fact, I believe it would make Tim Bart and the company look very bad if he or the company did leak it.

"I'm fairly sure their board isn't happy about this story, either, because it implies TBBM will pay an inflated price for WHK, partly because of Tim's desire to reunite with you."

Molly's phone rang, and Vanessa grabbed her arm. "Do not answer your phone unless you know who it is, as it's probably a reporter.

"Have Cissy take messages, and I'll return any media calls. I have a copy of a statement that Ken and I agreed to in your absence. I hope you approve," Vanessa said, sliding a copy of the statement over to Molly.

"It's fine," Molly said, reading the statement quickly. "I trust your judgment on this, as I have no objectivity. I need to call my parents and wake them up before they see this, and then I'll talk to Ken.

"I'll plan to address this story at the board meeting tomorrow. Let's review all the media coverage at the end of the day and see if we need to alter our statements. Needless to say, I have no comment on the article and am not doing any media interviews," Molly said.

"Agreed." Vanessa nodded. "Unfortunately, I have a number of requests already this morning. I'm afraid this story has some legs.

"I better get back to my desk now. I will update you throughout the day," Vanessa said, hurrying off.

Molly turned on her computer, and the phone was ringing again.

Cissy ran in, dropped her stuff on her desk, and answered the phone.

"No, she is not available. If you are a reporter, I will transfer you to our corporate communications department. Thank you," Cissy said very professionally into her phone.

"Molly, I am so sorry." Cissy rushed into Molly's office. "I was out with Tunney last night and didn't check emails until this morning.

"I know the drill. You can't answer your phone—" Just then, the phone rang again, and Cissy ran to answer it.

Molly shut her door and leaned back against it. This was a nightmare she couldn't wake from. She walked over to her desk and sent a couple critical emails before calling her parents, waking them, as it was only about six at home. Molly explained that she wanted to tell them before they turned on the news or picked up the paper.

Cissy walked in and heard Molly telling her parents, "I guess this weekend was the calm before the storm. Don't worry. I'll be okay. I'll give you a call later if I can. It's sort of a zoo around here, as you can imagine. Cissy just came in, so I have to go. Love you both," Molly said and hung up the phone.

"Molly, it's Tam." Cissy was the only one in the company who called him Tam rather than Tim. "I don't know what you want me to tell him," she said with a look of concern on her face.

"I'll talk to him for a minute, but please stay here to verify we didn't discuss anything about the deal," Molly said matter-of-factly as she picked up the phone.

"Hello, Tam," she said. "I just want you to know I'm putting you on speaker and have Cissy here so she can verify we are having no discussions about the deal."

"Understood," Tam said. "I had to call you, Molly. I've been trying to call you ever since I learned of the story.

"I was mortified by the article. We had nothing to do with it. It's just terrible and an invasion of privacy." He was clearly upset.

"Our head of corporate communications thought it was the bankers," Molly said, "but who knows? It is pretty awful. Listen, I really appreciate your call, but you know we agreed not to speak, so I should get going."

"Don't hang up," Tam said with urgency. "Molly, are you okay? I was so worried about you when I saw the article. I know we can't talk or see each other right now, but please, *please*, can we get together as soon as possible?"

"I don't know. Please try and be patient. We'll have to see what develops this week. I feel the same way about this article and the other stories it will generate. I'm so embarrassed, but I'll be fine. I've had to face worse things in my life, as you know.

"Again, thanks for the call. I'm so sorry we can't talk further. Good-bye, Tam," she said, putting the phone back in the receiver gently.

"Cissy, I'm going over to see Ken. Please set up a call with Bill Stewart for as soon as I return. I'll need to disclose the call from Tam, and you'll need to be part of that discussion to verify what was said. I suggest you type your notes on it right now," Molly said, hurrying out of her office.

Cissy said, "Got it," but Molly was already out of the office and down the hall.

As Molly suspected, Ken was in early and so was his assistant, Nell, who said, "I was just going to call you. Please go right in."

Molly came into Ken's office and shut the door. "Ken, I am so sorry I didn't see the emails or calls last night. I was traveling and turned off my phone." She sat in the chair across from him.

She was trying to stay calm, but she was clearly shaken by the article, the reaction to it, and Tam's call.

"Don't worry," Ken said. "Vanessa and I handled everything."

Molly nodded. "I really appreciate that. I also need to tell you Tam just called me this morning about the article." She continued. "He said they had nothing to do with it, and he was quite upset. I kept the call short, for obvious reasons, and had Cissy listen in to verify there were no discussions about the deal."

Ken picked up the intercom. "Nell, can you get two coffees for us? Thanks.

"I can't imagine how you're feeling right now," he said. "I just want you to sit for a minute. You don't need to worry about not being available last night. I told you to take off because you needed it.

"Vanessa and I took care of the communication to the board and senior management. We—I should say you—just have to handle the barrage of media stories and the reaction.

"I saw something on the business channel this morning…"

Molly put her face in her hands. "I can just imagine the fun people are having with this article. The problem for me is this is *my life.*

"I scanned the article; I didn't read all the way through it, but everything I saw was correct. Me, Tam, Jim, you. Oh, God, I am so angry right now!" Molly said, smashing her fists on the table.

"Anger is certainly one of the emotions I would be feeling at this point if I were you," Ken said, observing at Molly with concern.

"Totally embarrassed as well. I could go on," she said, agitated. "This is totally your call, Ken, but I would like to make a statement to the board tomorrow, after the official business."

"Of course." Ken agreed.

"I don't want to have to walk on eggshells," Molly said, "particularly as we're going to have a social hour and dinner with the board after the meeting. I'll draft something for you to take a look at."

Ken shook his head. "It isn't necessary for me to review anything. I agree you should say something, and I trust you'll be honest and straightforward, as you always are with the board.

"Perhaps you want to talk to HR today to get their guidance on things you might say more broadly to staff, as the article is so personal in nature," Ken suggested.

"I will, Ken, thanks."

Nell came in with their coffees. "Welcome to Monday morning," she said.

"It certainly has started out with a bang," Molly answered.

She spent the rest of the day in meetings and finalizing the board presentations for the critical meeting the next day.

Cissy had one of the other assistants helping her assemble the dozen binders. They also prepared electronic versions for the board members' tablets.

Many of Molly's colleagues wanted to come by her office

179

and commiserate with her, but she wanted none of it. She had too much to do and no interest in chatting about the article for others' amusement. She politely excused herself from any of those conversations.

She spoke frequently to Vanessa about the number of media requests that were coming in and her analysis of the coverage so far. They changed their response statement slightly as the coverage rolled in and decided to hire their outside public relations agency to do an analysis of all the takeover coverage, including this recent, very personal article.

Vanessa and Molly met with Ken to review everything at the end of the day, and Molly took the opportunity to deliver Ken's board book and tablet.

As they finished their review, Molly complimented Vanessa's work.

"Vanessa, I can't thank you enough for your professionalism through all of this. You have been a tremendous help to the company and me on what has been one of the most difficult days of my career," Molly said sincerely.

Ken chimed in. "Totally agree. Your quick action last night helped us respond as best we could and inform the board and the leadership about the article."

"You are both very kind," Vanessa said, "and I appreciate your support very much. However, our challenges are far from over. In fact, I do have another suggestion. It may make sense for Molly to have someone from security accompany her home tonight and to the office tomorrow morning. There's always the chance of a media ambush on a story like this, or some crazy person who may try and meet you," Vanessa said seriously.

Ken picked up the phone. "I'm calling security right now."

Molly nodded at Vanessa. "Unfortunately, you're probably right," she said softly. "It isn't what I want, but it does make sense."

She excused herself and walked back to her office slowly, stopping in the ladies' room. Molly looked in the mirror and didn't like what she saw, so she splashed some water on her face.

Just then, June, her favorite clerk from the cafeteria, came in, and Molly jumped. "Oh, Molly, I didn't mean to startle you. We were working late tonight to get ready for all the meetings tomorrow. I don't mean to be rude, but you don't look good," June said, concerned.

"It's been a rough patch, June," Molly said, drying her hands and face.

"I know about the article and your relationship with that CEO. I mean, everybody does. I can't lie to you," June continued. "We're all concerned about our jobs with this takeover. There's talk of closing this building if the companies are combined."

"It's natural that a potential takeover causes anxiety for everyone," Molly said.

"You're so highly thought of around here because you treat people right, Molly. Sure, a lot of people are gossiping, and that's natural, but what most people say is what I believe. We just want you to be happy," June said.

"Thanks for that, June," Molly replied.

"You've been through so much," June said, reaching out to give Molly a hug.

"You know what?" Molly asked. "I needed that hug. It's the best thing that has happened to me today," she said, laughing.

"I think you need a stiff drink tonight," June suggested, smiling. "You'll be fine, Molly. You're a strong woman."

"That means a lot coming from such a strong woman as yourself," Molly said, touching her arm warmly as she left the ladies' room.

When she got back to her office, Cissy was there and looked up as she walked over.

"Molly, Tunney and I would like to take you out to dinner tonight. Security's already called, and they're going to follow us to the restaurant and make sure you get home safely, as well as pick you up in the morning. I made the reservation in my name," Cissy added.

"Sounds great." Molly smiled. "If anyone's going to mess with me, I'll have you and Tunney *and* security to protect me." She laughed. "I've seen Tunney deal with rowdy drunks when the band was performing, so I know he can be a force to be reckoned with, for sure. Let me just check my emails and shut down my computer, and I'm more than ready to go."

Security informed them there was a local camera crew filming outside the gates, so Molly threw her coat over her head in the passenger seat and crouched down while Cissy drove through the gates. She didn't get up for several blocks.

"Whew," Molly said, finally sitting upright. "To say I would appreciate a nice glass of wine is an understatement.

"I can't thank you enough for arranging this. I was thinking of asking you to go to dinner tonight, as I couldn't face a night alone where I would be seeing red over that article and all the follow-ups as well.

"I certainly don't want to turn on the television!" Molly said, exasperated.

"Almost there," Cissy said. "I'm glad you're smiling again. I don't think you did all day."

"No, there sure wasn't much to smile about today.

"I ran into June in the ladies' room, and she was so kind to me. I think so many of my colleagues just wanted to come by and chat so they could tell others they spoke to 'the woman from the article.' I'm not sure all of them were very concerned about me personally," Molly said. "I certainly didn't have time for any idle chatting today."

"That's for sure," Cissy said, pulling into the restaurant parking lot. They were going to Bellini's and were hoping they could have some privacy.

When they walked in, Tunney was already there. He stood, cowboy hat in hand. He enveloped Molly in a hug, and she held on tight.

"Molly, so sorry about this mess. If that reporter was here right now, I'd give him what for," Tunney said, smoothing down her hair and kissing her on the cheek.

When he let Molly go, he gave Cissy a hug and a more intimate kiss to say hello.

"Thanks, Tunney. I'm so glad to see you and Cissy tonight. I didn't want to go home alone. Well, I won't be entirely alone, since security is taking me home so there aren't any pesky reporters or weirdoes lurking about." Molly giggled.

"Well, I think I'll swing by with you to make sure it's all clear, if you don't mind," Tunney added. "I'd feel better seeing things are okay for myself, and I know Tam would, too."

At the mention of Tam's name, Molly sat and stared at the table in front of her.

"Tam told me he called you today," Tunney said. "I was staying over at his place so I was there when he got the call from his people about the story. He was fit to be tied, throwing stuff around. He was so concerned about you, not so much about himself," he said.

"I believe that," Molly said softly. "I thought for a second he might have leaked it, but I dismissed that. I know he didn't."

"Molly, I know he's my brother and my blood, but I can tell you in no uncertain terms that he would never do anything to intentionally hurt you like that. You must know that," he said with emotion.

"I do. I do," Molly said emphatically. "I just want all of this to be over. What else could happen?" she asked rhetorically.

She was interrupted by the waiter with the menus and wine list. Molly grabbed the list to pick out one of her favorites. She deserved it tonight.

Molly, Tunney, and Cissy enjoyed a wonderful dinner, and they were able to relax a bit. They chatted about everything and anything *not* to do with Tam or the takeover.

Tunney explained he'd cut back on playing, as he was establishing a piano-tuning business in the area so he could eliminate most of the late hours. As the members of his band were getting older, they had day jobs as well.

What he didn't say was his brother needed him more than ever right now, and he wanted to be there for him. Maybe he'd talk to Molly later about all that.

Molly seemed to be enjoying the evening, and Tunney didn't want to change the vibe with serious talk. It seemed she had the weight of the world on her lately. It was good to see her smile and joke around. She mentioned the wonderful visit with her parents and how relaxing it was for her. Too bad her good mood was ruined with the story today.

Molly rarely had dessert, but she ordered the mini cannolis Jim loved so much. She remembered she always shared them with him, and it brought a tear to her eye.

"Molly, everything okay?" Tunney asked, obviously concerned.

"I was just enjoying the evening and this wonderful dessert. It's the same dessert I used to share with Jim," she said quietly, wiping away a tear and finishing her treat. "How my life has changed in the last year. How could that reporter mention Jim like that in that stupid article today?" Molly asked sadly.

Both Tunney and Cissy looked at her with concern and affection.

"It was a low blow, if you know what I mean," Tunney said,

covering Molly's hand with his. "Let's get you home so you can get some rest."

Cissy grabbed her cell phone and called security to bring the car around and follow Tunney and Molly to her home.

When Tunney pulled up, security asked if they could have a few minutes to patrol the grounds before Molly and Tunney entered the house. When they got the all-clear signal from security, they went in, and Molly punched in the code to disarm the system. She was glad she remembered to the arm the system before going to work. She would do it every day now.

Molly got a glass of water for Tunney, and they sat in the living room, Molly kicking off her shoes.

Before settling in, she jumped up and said, "Hold on a minute. I promised Tam I'd show you something."

Molly came back with the censored photo album and sat next to Tunney, opening it to the first page. She'd taken photos at the graduation party so many years ago, and those were the first photos in the album.

"Well, well." Tunney laughed. "Look at those handsome guys in the band and the beautiful young lady."

"They certainly are handsome," Molly said, brightening. "God, I fell in love with both of you that night."

"Wait just a minute," Tunney said, faking outrage. "You fell in love with me the first time we met in the student union."

"You're right." Molly laughed. "I stand corrected."

"You've always felt like family to me, and you do now. You know that, don't you?" Tunney asked.

"Yes, I do. I've always felt that way about you, too. Maybe we will be family in a way if you end up with Cissy," she said.

"She's a real gem, for sure. I could do a lot worse," Tunney said, chuckling. "Seriously, I really like her, Molly. Maybe it could be serious. I've done a lot of thinking lately, and you can see I'm changing my life. I think Cissy and I could be good together.

"I'm not letting you out of my life again, and my brother, God help him, really needs me right now. Your life has been in turmoil for some time, but his has, too. I know how much he loves you, and he will fight for you, for sure."

"Yes, and now the whole world knows how he feels for me," Molly said, flipping the page in the photo album, "and that I lost my virginity to him and that he wants to buy my company for a very high price. This is so embarrassing," she said, running her hand over the photo of Tam.

"But you love him, too?" Tunney said, posing it as a question.

"You and my parents…" Molly chuckled. "You're exactly the same, trying to get me to admit my feelings. You've been around us. You knew the love we had was special, rare…" Molly's voice trailed off. "The question I have is could we have it again? Could it be destroyed again? He fooled around on his wife. Why wouldn't he fool around on me? And to tell the truth, I couldn't take that, Tunney. I just couldn't."

"I understand why you'd be concerned. Tam's ex-wife is a wonderful woman, but he didn't have with her what he had with you. I can say that 'cause I saw him with you and then later with his wife. It just wasn't the same," Tunney said, shaking his head.

"I've never said that to anyone before now, not even Tam. He did love his wife and was busted up when they broke apart. But to be honest, I could see them drifting apart for years.

"With all that going on, he was always a good father. His kids are very important to him. In fact, he's taken special care to focus on his kids lately, even with all the distractions," Tunney said.

"I don't question that," Molly answered. "I can tell he's a wonderful father by the way he spoke about his children when we were able to get together."

"With the divorce, I get to see the kids quite a bit. I'm over at Tam's a lot when they come for visits. Last weekend, when you were in Wisconsin, we had 'Dad and Uncle Tunney' weekend. It was lots of fun," he told Molly.

"We're both lucky to have wonderful parents, Molly, and I'm so glad you had time with Fred and Margaret this past weekend."

They leafed through the album, seeing their families and friends of so long ago. How young and happy they looked. Tunney asked if he could take two photos: one of Molly and Tam and another of the three of them together.

"I promised Tam I would get copies made, and I will," Molly said, handing Tunney the photos, as she had some similar ones in the album.

"It's fun to see us so young, happy and at home," Molly said. "The visit to Wisconsin this past weekend was much needed. With everything that happened today, I'm glad I got a little rest and relaxation. It doesn't look like I'll get much in the near future."

"Well, I should get outta your way so you can try and get some sleep. I assume you'll be in the office before sunrise tomorrow," Tunney said, getting up to leave.

"Yes," Molly said, taking his arm and guiding him toward the door. "Thank you for everything tonight. I appreciate that you really care about me."

"Always have, always will," Tunney said, giving her a hug.

"Love you," she whispered in his ear before he left.

As he walked down the front steps, out of earshot, she said, "And I love your brother, too, even though he infuriates me so much."

Tam was pacing the condo as he waited for Tunney to return after his dinner with Molly and Cissy. If Molly's day was anything like his, her nerves would be frazzled.

As soon as he knew about the article to be published on Monday, Tam called his ex-wife and his parents in Wisconsin. He was able to work with his head of corporate communications to get notifications to his board and his leadership team and commissioned an agency to track the leak. He was livid about this intrusion into his personal life and what it could do to Molly.

Tam was the CEO, so most people at work kept their distance and didn't bring the article up with him. He talked to his senior legal and HR leaders in depth about it and covered any issues that could arise as a result with those involved most closely with the deal.

Tam's head of corporate communications and his team handled the massive amount of media inquiries they received, using an agreed-to statement. At work, the only person he could talk to about Molly was Gerrie, as she understood how important Molly was to Tam.

He wondered how Molly would feel about the next steps in the takeover. Perhaps she knew what was coming, or would she be caught off guard? Hell, he had no idea how she would react or what would blow up next, as today's article clearly demonstrated.

Tunney came through the door. "Hey, bro. I thought you'd be up waiting for me."

"How is she?" Tam asked.

"Well, as good as can be expected when you have to have security escort you home at night," Tunney replied with a laugh. "I drove her home. I wanted to check it out as well. Told her you would've done the same."

"Thanks, Tun. You're exactly right on that. I'm glad you took her home to make sure she was okay," Tam said, sitting on the sofa.

"All of us relaxed a bit over dinner and tried not to talk about the takeover or you. We did talk about you back at her place, though." He fished in his pocket, handing over the old photo of Molly and Tam. "I have something for you."

Tam ran his thumb over Molly's face in the photo, wishing he could see her now. "Thanks for this. When I went to her house, she had the photo album out in the kitchen. I don't think she really wanted me to see it, but it was too late.

"There's so much love in the photos. Really brings me back, you know what I mean?" Tam said, still staring at the photo.

"I sure do, bro. Sure do," Tunney said thoughtfully. "You know, the way you looked at each other was always a gauge for me with others' relationships."

"Not sure I understand what you mean," Tam said.

"Well, when people look at each other the way you and Molly do in those photos, I know they're in love.

"As you know, I've played lots of weddings, and the bride and groom didn't always look at each other that way, and that's not a good sign. So you and Molly are my examples for true love," Tunney admitted.

"You never told me that before... maybe because our 'true love' didn't sustain," Tam said dejectedly.

"That's why you're fighting for it today. Once you find it, you can't give it up. You know that now," Tunney said.

"I do," Tam said, gazing at the photo. "But it's hard to wage a battle for Molly's heart when I can't see her or speak to her and have no idea when I can."

Tunney just nodded at his brother. He had nothing to say to help him on that.

chapter twenty-five

There was a camera crew at Molly's house in the morning, so she slipped out the back with the security guys, and they drove her into work. She hadn't watched any television or looked at the papers, but she could tell from her emails and the reports from the corporate communications team that the coverage was continuing in a big way.

When she got into the office, she tried to get through her emails, but there were just so many that she gave up.

When Cissy came in, she'd actually printed out some emails she thought were important, one of which was from her friend from college, Ruth.

Molly: I saw the article yesterday and stories about you on TV, and I wanted to let you know I'm here if you want to talk. You must feel violated with all this media coverage. I'm sure it's difficult for Tam as well. Whatever you need, I'm here for you. Love, Ruth

She took the time to answer Ruth's email thoughtfully and replied that she would like to talk at some point when she could clear both her calendar and her head.

Molly had seen lots of supportive emails and just couldn't answer them all. Ruth was someone who could help her, since she knew Tam and Molly and lots of details about their early relationship. Molly would be sure to take her up on her request later.

Right now, she needed to prepare herself for the board meeting and rehearse what she would say to them about the article and Tam. The business part of the meeting would go smoothly; Molly had no worries about that. It was the personal stuff that concerned her, and she had to keep her emotions in check.

Molly started squeezing her stress ball; it had gotten a lot of use lately.

As soon as the board meeting was over, Ken and Molly would approve the press release, which presented the company's position on the takeover offer by TBBM. The release would say they rejected the offer, as it did not provide proper value for the company.

Ken and Molly fully expected that TBBM would be ready to counter with their press release, increasing their offer.

Molly thought about all the members of the board; there were twelve, ten men and two women. They were very smart and accomplished people, respected in their fields of expertise.

Molly hoped the board would have empathy for her situation, as it was not of her making. She actually laughed to herself for a minute because the board could find her particular takeover drama more interesting than some of the more boring things they had to look at all the time—spreadsheets, technical lawsuits, engineering reports. At least the takeover drama did have some sex in it!

Molly finished the preparation she could, put her stress ball back on her desk, and grabbed her board book and tablet as she headed over.

The early part of the meeting went well, and when they broke for lunch, Ken seemed pleased with the progress so far, and the board was supportive of the direction Ken laid out and the plans for public announcement.

Molly made sure to make herself scarce during breaks, as she wanted to make her statement to the board members before discussing it with them individually. There would be plenty of time for one-on-one discussions during cocktails and dinner.

She respected and admired the men and women on the board so much and wanted the difficult discussion on her personal life to go well.

When the meeting resumed, things went exactly according to Ken's plan. He had one last thing to share with the board, and Molly knew she was up next.

Ken stood and spoke quite formally. "All, I would like to thank you for your engaged discussions around the potential takeover of our company. Your insights and input, and frankly, concern for this company are deeply appreciated.

"Now, before we head into executive session and the members of my leadership team leave the room, I know Molly would very much like to address the group. Molly?" Ken motioned for her to take the floor as he sat down.

"Ladies and gentlemen, thank you for your continued support and guidance during this attempted takeover," Molly told the group, standing and looking directly at the board members as she spoke. "This has taken more of your time, energy, and attention than your usual board activities, and we are very grateful.

"Ken is a tremendous leader, and I must thank him for all the personal support he has provided from the minute this ordeal started. His leadership has been superb.

"As you know, it has not been a 'normal' takeover attempt for me, as my personal life has been front and center from the start. I certainly appreciated all of your support when I explained my personal relationship with the CEO of TBBM.

"Yesterday, when I saw the article about Tim Bart and me, I was mortified, as you can imagine. Tim actually called me yesterday morning to assure me he had nothing to do with the leak.

"I had my assistant listen in on the conversation so there could be no assertions that there was any discussion about the takeover. It was a brief, personal conversation about the story.

"It is important to me that you know I have asked him not to contact me during the takeover process, and any contact there has been has been disclosed to Ken and external counsel. There has not been and will never be any side conversations about the takeover." Molly continued, taking a deep breath. "I am sorry for the attention this has brought the company, as I understand the coverage of the story has been global in nature and covered on entertainment as well as news channels.

"You have my full commitment to professionalism throughout the process, and please feel free to ask me any question at any time. I look forward to talking with you tonight during cocktails and dinner. Thank you for the opportunity to address you this evening," Molly said, stepping toward the door.

Before she could make it out of the room with other members of Ken's staff, the lead director stood. "Molly, on behalf of the board, we want to thank you for your comments. As chief legal officer, you are our main liaison with the company and leadership, and we know how hard your team works to support us.

"Your professionalism has never been in question, and the attention the company is receiving now connected to your personal relationship is not your fault. You did nothing wrong, and no apologies are necessary. Tim Bart is an important part of your past and you can't change that. I guess I am telling you something you already know," he said with a smile.

"Thank you, sir," Molly said. "I really appreciate your sentiments and look forward to seeing you a bit later."

Molly walked out with her colleagues and headed to her office. After the executive session, the press release would be issued and more fireworks would start.

Later that evening, WHK issued their release, and as predicted, TBBM followed quickly with their response, announcing they were substantially raising their offer for the company.

Would the board consider taking it? The financial community was certainly for it, but they were all about the money.

Prior to the cocktail hour and dinner with the board, Ken called an executive session to discuss the new development. The company would not comment further until the board and senior leadership had enough time to review the offer and consider their response.

Molly sat in her office and read all the stories coming across the wire, and most seemed to welcome the combination of the two companies. She felt sad, as the inevitable looked to be happening: her beloved company would be bought by Tam's.

Stopping in the ladies' room, Molly tried to make herself look more presentable before leaving for the posh hotel where the cocktail hour and dinner with the board would be held.

The board members and her colleagues attending the cocktail reception and dinner could not have been more gracious. She felt lucky to work with a great team and an engaged and concerned board.

Ken seemed to be in a very good mood, which felt a bit odd to her, as it sure looked like their company would be taken over.

What Molly didn't know at that moment was Tam had called Ken and requested a confidential meeting for the next morning. The takeover was only one of the topics he wanted to cover.

chapter twenty-six

Tam arrived at Ken's house at 7:00 a.m. sharp on a bright and beautiful morning. The two CEOs couldn't meet in public, so Ken suggested his home, which was a wonderful old New England Tudor with cherry wood floors throughout and beautiful architectural details.

Ken welcomed Tam and invited him into his study.

"Ken, thank you very much for agreeing to meet with me," Tam said cordially. "I'm anxious to talk with you."

Just then, Ken's wife Jen came in with a tray of coffee and pastries. "Thought you gentlemen might enjoy a cup of coffee at this early hour," she said, sliding the tray onto the table.

Tam popped up from his chair as Ken introduced him to Jen.

"Good to meet you," Jen said. "You've certainly made my husband a busy man lately," she added, smiling.

"It's very nice to meet you as well, and I appreciate your hospitality. Thank you for letting us meet in your home." Tam shook Jen's hand. "I also understand you've been a good friend to Molly and have helped her through very tough times. I'm grateful for that," he added.

Jen nodded. "She's a wonderful woman, but you know that.

"I'll take my leave so you can talk business," she said as she left the study and shut the door.

"Before we talk about the offer, I wanted to share my thinking on how the combined company could work." Tam got straight to business. "And I'd like to discuss a proposal with you.

"I know what an incredible leader you are. I hear it in the industry and particularly from Molly, who thinks you walk on water." He continued.

Ken nodded gratefully. "Thank you for the compliments."

"I know I could learn a lot from you," Tam said sincerely. "As you know, it's important for leaders to understand their strengths, weaknesses, and development needs, and I know you're a much more experienced global leader than me; you've led a board many more years than I have, and your external relations experience is much richer and deeper than mine." He maintained direct eye contact with Ken, who took a drink of his coffee but was listening intently.

"I believe we could create an incredible company together. If we're able to finalize this deal—and I realize that's a big 'if' at this point—I would love for you to be an executive chairman of the company, running the board as well as our external relations.

"I'd also like you to lead the task force that will combine the two companies to ensure we retain the best talent from each organization. You would also lead the formation of a single foundation for philanthropy and a new corporate social responsibility function that would consolidate our operations into a single organization."

Ken nodded, though he didn't necessarily agree. "Go on," he prompted, not betraying his thinking.

"I'd like to nominate a candidate to lead our new foundation and corporate social responsibility efforts. As the leader, it would be totally your choice, but I suggest Molly head up this new organization," Tam said, studying Ken for any reaction.

"I'm surprised you would suggest that," Ken admitted. "Does Molly know you're meeting with me today?"

"No, you're her boss and the CEO of WHK. I respect your authority and position. If our companies do combine, I would expect you would tell her about her new role, not me. You would continue to be her boss."

"Hmm." Ken now appeared more interested.

"I believe Molly's looking for a change in her life, and I'm aware she loves philanthropy and corporate citizenship, but she never has time for those activities with the demanding nature of her current responsibilities.

"In addition, she has outstanding experience in her work with the board and corporate governance and environmental issues." Tam continued, hardly taking a breath. "As we combine our companies, we'll have a truly global organization, and I believe you and Molly have advanced your global philanthropy and citizenship efforts well beyond what we've been able to do at TBBM." He finally paused to gauge Ken's reaction.

"I don't know much about TBBM's efforts in this area, but there's no question we've advanced this important function in our company, in large part due to Molly's leadership," Ken said.

Tam nodded. "Ken, your experience leading industry trade groups is invaluable because you understand the best practices in corporate citizenship, governance, and external relations across multiple industries. I would welcome your leadership in these areas, and Molly's as well," Tam said, again pausing to hear Ken's reaction.

"As you know, I need to talk with my board following our meeting this morning, so I can't give you an answer right now," Ken asserted.

"I totally understand you'll have to consult with the board on this as well as our enhanced offer, and I would want you to do so.

"If you agree to take on this new role, you would lead the combination of the two boards, as we're both lucky to have very capable and distinguished boards of directors," Tam said, observing Ken intently. "Are there any questions you have on our offer for your company or the role I've outlined for you?"

"No. Your offer has been spelled out to us in great detail, and you've given me a lot to think about and discuss with my board. I will do so and get back to you as soon as possible."

Tam took a drink of his coffee and put the cup down, rattling the spoon and saucer a bit loudly.

"Unless you have any other questions, I'd like to conclude the business portion of this meeting to talk to you on a personal level," Tam said a bit uncomfortably. "As this is a confidential meeting between us, I want to talk about Molly. I know how hard this has been for her."

"It has." Ken agreed, pressing his lips together tightly and running a finger along the rim of his coffee cup. "She's held up very well, but I can see the pain of losing her husband, the shock of seeing you again and learning your breakup so many years ago could have been avoided, and the takeover battle have taken a toll on her.

"She essentially works all the time, trying to avoid the tough professional and personal questions," he added.

"I know how you've mentored Molly and helped her when her husband died," Tam said quietly. "She told me how kind you and Jen have been to her and how she doesn't think she could have gotten through everything without you. I'm very grateful to you for that friendship and support."

"Molly is a special woman, as you well know," Ken said a bit more warmly, his eyes speaking of the tenderness and admiration he obviously held for her.

"Ken, I love her and hope she'll agree to marry me," Tam said suddenly. "I've already asked her father for her hand in marriage when I went to see her parents in Wisconsin last Friday.

I'm telling you this in confidence. I know you'll not tell Molly, and I have total trust in you."

"Well... thanks for that trust. I'm certainly aware you didn't need to tell me about your intentions. She'll make her own decisions about her future, both personal and professional," Ken said, a bit taken aback at the sudden confession.

"Understood." Tam nodded. "I've vowed never to let anything come between us again, and I mean it. It's been agony knowing I caused her pain years ago and again now, with this takeover.

"To have our personal relationship featured in the media around the world has been an embarrassment to both of us, but the personal details about Molly, her husband's death... It's more than most people could bear.

"The fact that we've been virtually unable to communicate has been extremely difficult. Thank God my brother has seen her so I know she's okay," Tam said with great emotion, and Ken watched him with intense interest.

"I had the pleasure of meeting Tunney the other day in Molly's office," he said. "He's quite the personality and does care about her a great deal. That's very clear."

"Yes, they were close years ago and that hasn't changed," Tam said. "I hope to find my way back into her life as well. We need to make up for so much lost time.

"Circumstances have kept us apart with the takeover, but, like Molly, I haven't let my personal feelings influence the deal in any way. What has occurred so far would have happened if she worked at WHK or not."

"I believe you, Tim," Ken acknowledged as he stood. "I'll get back to you later today on what you've laid out after a full discussion with the board." He shook Tam's hand, bringing their meeting to a close. "Well, this has turned out to be quite a get-together," Ken declared as he ushered him to the door.

chapter twenty-seven

Molly got into the office early as usual, as she knew the response to the enhanced takeover offer needed to be finalized as soon as possible. She was anxious to talk to Ken this morning but could see through the online calendar tool he wouldn't be available until about nine. She emailed Nell and asked to see him as soon as he was available.

Pushing her chair back from the desk, Molly went over to look out the window at the spring morning unfolding. She couldn't get the dream she had last night about Jim out of her head. Molly was in the car with him in the backseat, and the car was moving quickly. Jim took her in his arms and kissed her and held her. He pulled back and touched her hair gently and said, "I love you."

Molly held his face in her hands and told him, "Jim, I love you, too, and miss you."

Jim smiled at her. "Molly, I'm very well and happy, and I want you to be happy, too, but I have to go now," he said, as the car slowed down.

"I'll go with you," Molly said urgently.

"No," Jim replied firmly. "You have to stay. Don't worry about me. I'm really okay, and I need you to be happy."

Before she climbed out of the car, Jim turned to her to say

one more thing. "I love you, Molly." And then he was gone, and Molly woke up.

Instead of feeling sad, she felt incredibly calm and happy to have seen him and know he was fine and wanted her to be happy. She actually felt the glow of his love and the warmth of his kiss, and it enveloped her in happiness as she looked out on the crisp spring morning.

Was Jim trying to tell her it was okay to move on with her life, that she would always have his love, but she could find love again? With Tam?

Most of the time lately Molly had tried to push Tam out of her mind, but she knew she wanted to think about him now, to try and figure things out. Jim and Tam were the only men she ever loved, and she felt they were both with her now, part of her. *There are so many twists and turns in life*, she thought. Who would have believed she'd be standing here at this point, with these choices before her? It was frightening and thrilling at the same time. Her life was about to change drastically, but how exactly?

Molly knew she needed to get her mind back on business, because if WHK were to announce they would accept the offer from Tam's company, there would be tons of work to do in a very short period of time. They would have to come to an agreement in principle and then make the public announcements, and so many questions would have to be answered. After that, the two companies would work to complete the final agreement and close the deal.

If that were the case, she would be free to see Tam. Molly put her hand to her chest as she realized she could see him very soon, perhaps even as soon as tonight. She sucked in her breath. That scared her a bit. They had so much to talk about, but where would they start?

Molly thought about how wonderful it was when she and

Tam first made love. It was magical. She hadn't made love for more than a year, with Jim's sickness and death. She'd almost forgotten what it felt like to be intimate.

Would she make love with Tam soon? Tonight? She blushed at the thought of it. *Snap out of it*, she told herself. *You're not some silly schoolgirl. You are the senior counsel of a company that is in a takeover battle.*

But even the worry of the hostile takeover couldn't keep her from thinking of Tam, and she hugged herself as she continued to stand at the window.

Just as she turned around, Cissy came into her office. "Hey, boss, another early morning?" she asked cheerily.

"For you as well," Molly observed.

"Yes, but I didn't have to wine and dine the board last night. I assume you didn't get home until late?" Cissy asked.

"Not too late. They were fantastic to me, and I did address my relationship with Tam and the media coverage," Molly said, walking over to sit at her desk. "It is possible we're getting closer to a decision on the TBBM offer."

"The hallway chatter is we're going to be taken over." Cissy frowned.

"I think there's a real chance of that now with their sweetened offer," Molly answered truthfully. "I'm going to see Ken as soon as possible to begin work on the next steps and the public announcement of the decision."

"What does that mean for you? And what about you and Tam?" Cissy sat across from Molly, propping her chin in her hand, elbow resting casually on the edge of the desk.

"I sure wish I knew." Molly sighed. "For starters, we'll be able to meet and talk more freely if there is an agreement in principle for the deal today. I guess we would start over to see if we can have a relationship that sustains. It's scary."

"What do *you* want?" Cissy asked.

"On the business side, I can tell you right now I will *not* work for Tam. He cannot be my boss." Molly laughed. "On the personal side, I want to try," she answered honestly, quietly.

"What if we continue to fight the takeover?"

"We'll fight an increasingly bitter war of words in the media, and TBBM will be forced to increase their offer. WHK will be pressured from the financial community to accept. Other, less reputable companies may jump in to make a play for us.

"On the personal side, I would still have difficulty seeing or talking to Tam. This limbo would continue." Molly's brow furrowed.

Her phone buzzed, and she could see it was Nell. Ken was ready to see her, so she took her notepad and bottle of water and rushed over to his office.

She greeted Nell, and Ken motioned her to shut the door and sit down.

Molly desperately wanted to know what was going to happen.

"I'm going to recommend to the board that we accept TBBM's offer." He jumped right to it.

"Wow," Molly breathed out, intently observing Ken.

"As you know, our external financial advisors indicated it was a generous offer that was more than fair." Ken continued. "I've called a meeting of our senior team at ten to announce this and discuss the next steps.

"As soon as you're out of the ten o'clock meeting, you can work with the deal and communications teams to finalize the internal and external announcement documents. I know they've developed drafts for the various possibilities, and I'll need the drafts to share with the board this afternoon," he added as Molly nodded.

"Once we have board approval, we'll need to coordinate our external statements with the TBBM team, and I leave that in your capable hands. You'll be working with the corporate communication teams from both companies," Ken said. "Vanessa will be at the meeting at ten, so she'll have the details to update the statements quickly, and I'd appreciate your review before they're circulated."

Molly nodded and took another sip of her water. She felt a bit hot and sweaty with nerves, her throat dry and constricting.

"If everything goes as planned, we'll put the announcement out today after the market closes," Ken said. "Now, I want to talk about you." He turned to look her straight in the eyes.

"I'm all ears," Molly said seriously.

"I met with Tim this morning," he stated. Molly gasped a bit as Ken continued. "He came to the house very early to talk about how he'd like to run the company with me as his partner and mentor. Tim has asked me to be the executive chairman of the new board, oversee the merger, and handle all external relations, including governance and the combination of our corporate contributions and citizenship efforts into a new, global corporate social responsibility function.

"I'd like you to lead that function, reporting to me," Ken announced.

It was a lot to take in so quickly, and Molly sat in stunned silence for a minute. "It sounds like you covered a lot of ground in the meeting," she finally uttered.

"We did. I have to say I was impressed with him. Not many CEOs admit they have a lot to learn, but Tim did, very humbly. I believe he was sincere in asking for my help in mentoring him, especially in the areas he doesn't have the depth of experience I have.

"Of course, Tim's technical skills with his deep engineering background are stronger than mine, but I know there are many areas in which I can help him." Ken paused for a moment to gauge Molly's reaction. "If I lead the combination of companies, we can get the best talent in the right jobs. You know how I feel about this company and the people in it, so I don't believe there's anyone who could do that job better than me," he said, matter-of-fact.

Molly still was a bit taken aback with all these developments and took a deep, steadying breath before replying. "Well, I'm thrilled you had a good meeting with Tim and you got an opportunity to know him a bit.

"I can tell you he means every single word he said to you. He's not the type of man to say one thing and change it later. You're an incredible leader and mentor, and you could help Tam—I mean Tim—be a better CEO and make the combined company successful."

"Tim did say you sang my praises to him," Ken answered, "and I'm sure that helped in his decision to ask me to take on an important role in the company.

"But I want to get back to talking about you. I'm aware your life has been extremely difficult over the last year, after losing Jim. I know, recently, you've been thinking about making a major change in your life.

"I've always noticed your eyes light up when we talk about our corporate social responsibility efforts, but with your other broad responsibilities, you've had little time for it. So when Tim suggested this new role for you—"

"Tim suggested it?" Molly said, shocked.

"He did. And you can call him Tam." Ken chuckled. "I know how hard it is for you to call him Tim, although you'll still have to do that in business settings.

"Tim made it clear I should discuss your potential new role

with you, as I am your boss. He also said it was entirely your choice."

Molly thought about the opportunity to do something she was passionate about and answered Ken very quickly. "If I report to you, I will absolutely take that role. You know I really wanted a change, and I believe I can make a real difference for the company and organizations around the world doing so much good work. I would be honored to continue to work with you."

"Excellent," Ken said. "I'm very pleased. If you would, let's keep this between the two of us—and Tim—until later, as we haven't discussed any roles for your colleagues yet.

"Clearly, you are special, to both Tim and me." Ken smiled genuinely.

"If we're able to get the announcement out today about the agreement in principle on the deal, I'd like to talk to Tam this evening. Would that be appropriate in your view?" Molly asked, leaning forward for Ken's answer.

"It would be very appropriate." Ken's smile reached his eyes. "Tim and I talked about you, of course, and he made his feelings for you very clear. He wants to talk to you desperately."

"I share his feelings. It has been agony, not to mention frustrating and embarrassing. I never thought my life would be front-page news," Molly said, shaking her head.

"You just reminded me that you probably should add a question and answer on your relationship with Tim to our holding statement, as I'm sure the media will ask about your relationship and role. I don't think we can comment on your personal relationship, and I believe the only roles that will be mentioned will be Tim's and mine," Ken said, thinking through the possibilities.

"I totally agree. Only the CEOs' roles should be detailed in the press release. I haven't been formally offered or accepted any role yet, and I would not do so in advance of my colleagues,"

Molly said firmly. "Don't worry. I'll make sure the communications folks know the answer to any personal questions about me."

"The public scrutiny of your relationship will most likely continue throughout the merger review process. You and Tim will have to decide what you want to say and when," Ken told her.

"I've thought the same thing," Molly answered. "There are so many questions I have for him. I need to know if he's the man I thought he was so many years ago," she said quietly. "It's important personally and professionally now, as our company will be in his hands and perhaps my personal future as well."

Ken nodded. "It is difficult to imagine what the headlines will be. Something about merger romance consummated? Who knows? Unfortunately, you have to be prepared for the next wave."

"I will," Molly responded. "Right now, I'm more worried about seeing Tam for the first time in a while and what will happen between us. Will it be fireworks or a knockout fight?" she mused nervously.

"That's a question only the two of you can answer. Now, let's get ready for our senior leadership meeting," Ken said, clapping his hands together once.

chapter twenty-eight

Cissy sat at her desk, literally exhausted after a long day of important meetings, approvals of multiple statements, press releases, phone calls, and board meetings. She played an important role in supporting Molly in all of this activity and had to communicate with members of leadership, the board, and Molly's staff, who had questions throughout the day.

The news was out there now; it was official and there was full disclosure. TBBM would acquire WHK.

Cissy was glad Ken would have an important role in the combined company, which might even have a new name. *So much to do*, she thought.

Molly had told her not to worry about her position, so she wouldn't. Lord knew she needed her job. She was hopeful she could continue to support Molly and help Ken in the board combination, as she served as the executive assistant to the board as well.

Cissy was too tired to worry at this point and beyond glad she and Tunney were getting together that evening. She smiled thinking of him. What a delight and surprise he was. She had fallen pretty hard for Tunney, and she hoped he felt the same. She'd never met anyone like him. Tunney was kind, sweet, smart, funny, and wise.

Cissy's thoughts were interrupted by the buzz of Molly's phone, which had been ringing off the hook all day. She answered Molly's line at her desk for about the hundredth time that day.

"Hello, Cissy, this is Tam. Is Molly available?" he asked hopefully.

"Tam, Molly isn't here at the moment, but I'm sure I can find her for you," she said.

"Thank you. Cissy, while we have a minute, I'd like to thank you for all the work you've done today and throughout this process. I know how Molly depends on you professionally and is so thankful for your friendship and support personally as well.

"My brother can't stop talking about you, too. It seems you've made inroads in taming that bucking bronco." He laughed.

"Thank you so much, Tam... Or should I call you Tim?" Cissy asked.

"Well, I believe you and Molly are the only people in the company who are allowed to call me Tam." He chuckled again. "I'm sorry we haven't been able to meet yet, but I look forward to that very soon."

"I do, too, Tam. Tunney cannot say enough good things about his little brother," Cissy said enthusiastically, just as Molly returned to her office. "You probably heard I'm seeing your brother tonight," she added.

"Just be sure to keep him out *very* late," Tam teased, chuckling.

"Molly's just come back, Tam," Cissy said with a smile at her boss. "Thanks again for your kind words. She'll pick up in a minute."

Molly heard that Tam was on the phone and rushed into her office and closed the door.

"Hello," she greeted. "How was your day?" She couldn't help but smile.

"Well, my day was very similar to yours, I would guess. Lots of statements, press releases, employee communications, media interviews… Thanks for all your work in getting the agreement publicly announced so quickly," Tam said.

"Just doing my job," she replied.

"Well, that's the end of the business talk. The reason for my call is entirely personal," he declared with a decided change in tone.

"Oh, now it's getting interesting." Molly laughed.

"I've made plans for us to have dinner tonight, if you agree. We can't be seen publicly with all the scrutiny of our relationship, so I've arranged for us to get together at my condo," Tam explained. "A chef who's a friend of mine will cook dinner for us. I've kicked Tunney out and told him to stay at his own apartment for once." He laughed.

Molly laughed, too. "While I adore Tunney, that was the right thing to do."

"If that plan meets with your approval, I'll have a car pick you up at your house at seven thirty tonight," he said.

"You've thought of everything." Molly was truly touched by his invitation and thoughtful plans.

"I just can't wait to see you, Mol," Tam said softly.

"Me too, Tam. Me too," she answered.

When they said their good-byes, Molly hung up the phone and opened the door to ask Cissy to come in so she could finalize the last action items of the day and go home to change for the special evening with Tam.

She was surprised to see Tunney standing right outside.

He came up to her and gave her a big hug that lasted a long time. "Now that this thing is moving forward, I hope to see a lot more of you, boss." He released her. "I had to come by here to pick up Cissy, which is really an excuse to see two of my favorite women," he said, smiling cheekily at Molly and then Cissy.

"You always come to pick her up at the office. I believe you're checking on us both," Molly said with a laugh.

"I'm sworn to secrecy," Tunney said, crossing his heart. "But let me be clear that I'll continue to shine around here."

"I think I can speak for both Molly and myself when I say we'd welcome that," Cissy said, beaming at Tunney.

"Absolutely," Molly said. "As Tam's brother, you'll be very popular around here."

"Well, the business thing has nothing to do with me," Tunney asserted, somewhat irritated. "And I want nothing to do with it. I've seen what it's done to Tam, to you, Molly, and Cissy, you as well. It just takes so much of your time and energy. It's like there's nothing left for just you. No thanks. The corporate thing's for you guys.

"Anyway, no one here knows I'm Tam's brother, and I'd like to keep it that way."

"Uh, Tun, the entire building knows you're Tam's brother," Molly informed him with a smile.

Tunney looked shocked. "What?" He turned to Cissy and then Molly as they nodded. "You mean they all know?" he asked incredulously.

"'Fraid so," Molly confirmed. "Once security saw your name and Tam's real name in the newspaper, they connected the dots. And once security knows who you are, everyone in the building knows. To be honest, I think you've advanced Tam's reputation, because the staff like that their new CEO has this cool musician-slash-cowboy brother who isn't 'corporate.' Believe me, Cissy and I never said a word." Molly giggled.

Cissy made a motion, crossing her heart. "It wasn't me, babe."

"Well, I'll be. Do you think I'll be in the next article?" Tunney asked, tongue-in-cheek.

"Tunney," Molly said with some concern. "You were in a few articles today. I tried not to look at all the stories. There's so much personal information on me, but I did see a few mention you by name and state you're the CEO's brother and a musician and always wear jeans, cowboy boots, and a hat. You come off as a real individual," she added, trying to be positive about the references to him.

"Damn," Tunney said with surprise. "I sure didn't expect that. Cissy, are you in some articles too?"

"No, none that I've seen." She laughed.

"Well," Molly said, "now that we've reviewed our press coverage, I need a few minutes with Cissy, and then we can all start our evenings. Tunney, you probably know I'm seeing Tam tonight."

"Yes, and thank God," he said with a chuckle. "He told me he was going to ask you to dinner. You two've been going a bit crazy being kept apart. It's high time you got together, I say.

"I'll take a seat right here while you ladies finish up." He plopped on a chair in the waiting area outside Molly's office. "Maybe I'll sign some autographs while I'm waiting," he called out to them as they went into her office.

Molly and Cissy went through a checklist of things for the next day before starting to close down their computers to get ready to go.

As they walked out, Molly whispered to Cissy, "Don't set up any early meetings for me tomorrow. I'll be in a bit later."

"Got it." Cissy smiled knowingly.

Molly rushed home to get a shower and change into something more casual and comfortable. There was no way she was wearing the standard navy-blue business suit she wore to work.

It was tough for her to decide what to wear because she wanted to look so fabulous for Tam. She racked her brain for the right thing and kept pushing aside hangers of clothes as she rejected outfit after outfit.

And then she saw it: the silk mint top she wore when she first met him. It was a bit faded but still in wonderful shape. Did she still have the scarf? She went to that hook where she kept her scarfs and found it buried underneath tons of others. Voilà. She grabbed her best pair of jeans and a really attractive pair of platform heels. Perfect.

Molly combed her hair and did her makeup, finishing just in time. The car was in her driveway to pick her up.

When she got into the car, the driver handed her a blanket. "Miss, my name is Bill, and I'll be driving you tonight. There's a possibility there will be photographers at Mr. Bart's building, so he advised you hide under the blanket when we enter the parking structure," Bill said very professionally.

"Thank you, Bill," Molly said, taking the blanket. "I appreciate that."

When they got close to the building, Bill asked her to hide under the blanket, crouching down very low in the backseat. Bill wasn't entirely sure, but it looked to him like there might have been cameras outside, so it was better to be safe than sorry.

Molly wasn't interested in seeing a tabloid shot of her entering the parking structure for Tam's condo. When did life get so complicated?

When she got out of the car, she thanked Bill and headed up to Tam's penthouse suite. She smoothed her clothes when she came out of the elevator but stopped in her tracks when she saw Tam hugging a very attractive blonde and kissing her good-bye.

Molly's brain raced a mile a minute. Talk about déjà vu! What was happening? Was everything between them a lie? Did he use her to get this takeover agreement?

She was frozen in her tracks as the woman walked right up to her.

"Molly?" the woman asked. "I'm Della, Tim's ex-wife. I had

to come by with some school forms that needed to be signed right away for the kids.

"He told me he'd planned a special evening with you. I'm so sorry to get in the way," she said very cordially.

Molly recovered herself immediately and put her hand out to shake Della's. "It's good to meet you. Tam has told me what a wonderful mother you are. The kids sound great, too, and I hope to meet them some day," she said warmly.

"He's a very good father, and I do hope you can meet the children," Della told Molly. "As your relationship with Tim has been in the media so much, I already feel like I know you, so I feel comfortable telling you the other reason for my visit. I told Tim I've met someone who is very special to me, John, one of our daughter's teachers.

"He's a fabulous man, and we like all the same things: literature, theater, and quiet evenings at home. Tim might have mentioned I wasn't the best corporate wife. The business environment was never a good fit for me," Della explained with a touch of sadness.

"No, Tam never said that, but I'm happy you can have a good relationship with him because of the children. And I thank you for letting me in on your news. I'll keep it to myself, as one relationship in the news is quite enough," Molly replied with an ironic smile.

"That's for sure. He and I have had to talk to the children about it. We've handled it the best we can," Della said.

"I'm sure you have." Molly nodded.

"Our divorce wasn't entirely Tim's fault. We both had a part to play in it," Della said a bit sadly. "Tim seems genuinely pleased that I've found happiness with John. That's why he gave me that hug and kiss," she added.

"Thanks for sharing that," Molly said, touching Della's arm. "It means a lot that you'd be so honest with me."

"Well, I felt it's important for you to know, particularly as your relationship with Tim, our divorce, and your husband's death have been featured in the media. Because of all that, I feel like I can talk to you about anything." Della laughed uncertainly. "I hope I haven't been too forward."

"Not at all," Molly assured her. "I'm so glad to meet you, even though I got a bit of a shock seeing you kiss Tam!"

"I'm so sorry about that," Della said with a smile. "I'm glad, really, to have this opportunity to share my good news in person. I need to let you go. I know Tim is anxious to see you.

"It was wonderful to meet you, Molly."

"You as well," Molly replied as Della walked away.

Life is full of surprises.

She'd fully calmed down by the time she knocked on Tam's door.

"Molly, I was getting worried," he said, opening the door wide.

"I ran into your wife—I mean ex-wife," Molly said, stepping into the condo. "I saw you hug and kiss her, and I kind of froze in place, but she explained everything. I think my heart stopped for a minute."

"Oh my God, Molly, I'm so sorry," Tam apologized, mortified. "The last thing you need is something else to upset you. I want to assure you that you can trust me."

"I know you needed to sign the school papers for the kids, and that's important.

"From now on, we need full disclosure—a term we've used a lot lately." Molly laughed. "We can never again have a misunderstanding like we had years ago."

"I totally agree." Tam swept her into his arms. "Total disclosure right now is if I don't kiss you, I'm going to burst."

She melted into him and they kissed tenderly. When they drew apart, Molly touched his face and stroked his hair.

"Do you recognize what I'm wearing?" she asked.

He pushed back from her and took in her outfit: the jeans, the mint top, the scarf.

"You're wearing the same outfit you wore when we first met," he said, pulling her close and kissing her neck. "Mol, you're so beautiful."

They heard distinct noises coming from the kitchen.

"Andrew, my chef friend, is in the kitchen making dinner for us, so we may need to keep our distance for a bit." He laughed. "Let me give you the tour of the condo." He took her hand, leading her to the main living area.

His suite was on the tenth floor, and it overlooked the Boston Common. It was stunning and contemporary in design, with wonderful views of downtown.

He took her into the kitchen to introduce her to Andrew. The kitchen was modern as well, with gleaming stainless steel appliances, quartz countertops, and sleek cabinets. Andrew handed them each a glass of white wine and asked them to take a seat in the dining room, as he was ready with the first course.

Tam pulled out her chair, and she sat at the table with one of the best views of Boston she'd ever seen. Molly looked out at the lights of the city and felt like she should pinch herself. Was she really here with Tam, her first love?

Andrew served soup as the first course, an asparagus puree. Molly tasted it and loved it from the first bite, as it was creamy and delicious, with a dollop of crème fraîche on top.

"I love having you here with me," Tam said, taking her hand. "This takeover process has been agony. I would find myself thinking of you during important meetings. I would get up and walk over to the window or get myself a cup of coffee to try and concentrate on the matters at hand…"

"It's been the same for me." Molly agreed, squeezing his

hand. "I've been so embarrassed with our relationship detailed in newspapers and television... even tabloids!"

"Incredible," Tam said, shaking his head.

Andrew brought out the next course, an arugula salad with shaved parmesan, and poured them more of the French white wine he'd served during the first course.

"This is delicious, just like the soup. Thanks, Andrew," Molly said. "You're a very good chef."

"I hope you'll like the next course, too," Andrew said, rushing back to the kitchen to get the main course ready.

Tam leaned over to whisper to Molly. "He'll leave after dessert so we can have some privacy."

Molly did like the next course, which was halibut piccata with a wonderful white wine sauce with lemon, butter, and capers, served with sautéed spinach.

Tam and Molly discussed the deal a bit during dinner, including the timing and the final approvals to come. As all this information was now public, they were now free to discuss it. They knew they would have plenty of time to have more personal conversations after Andrew departed.

It was during dessert, a perfect lemon tart, when Molly brought up her proposed new role. "There have been so many things that have surprised me over the last weeks, and today was no exception. Ken told me today about the role you've proposed for him and for me.

"While I wasn't sure at first, the more I thought about it, the more I liked it. I desperately need a change, and I have a real passion for corporate social responsibility. I think I can make a real difference." Her enthusiasm for the new role made her eyes sparkle.

"I agree," Tam said. "Your legal background will be very helpful as you set up the new foundation and assist Ken with all the board work. I put a lot of thought into the roles for you both."

"I believe Ken was genuinely touched that you asked him to mentor you. There's no question that you surprised him, but in a good way," Molly said, appreciatively taking Tam's hand.

"He's a fantastic leader, and he can help me and the company. I have no doubt he'll do a superb job pulling the companies together."

"He will, and I'm glad to continue to report to him. There's no way I could report to you. Isn't there a rule against someone sleeping with their boss?" Molly said with a mischievous twinkle in her eyes as Andrew came over to the table.

"I've cleaned up, so the two of you are on your own," Andrew said with a wink. "I hope you enjoyed it."

"Andrew, it was the best meal I've had in Boston for a long time. I'm afraid Tam and I—even though we couldn't eat together—haven't had much time for fine dining lately," Molly said.

"That is unfortunate," Andrew said, smiling. "Anyone who follows current events knows what you two have been doing lately. It's important you know I'm sworn to secrecy about this dinner tonight. No one will find out about this from me."

"Thanks for that, and thank you for a fabulous dinner." Tam stood, shaking his hand.

"It was wonderful, thank you," Molly repeated as Andrew headed out the door.

Tam pulled Molly's chair out and invited her to take her wine over to the living room, and they sat on the couch together. She kicked off her shoes, curled up under his arm, and hugged her knees to her chest, letting out a huge sigh.

"Can we finally relax and be together?" she asked. "It seems like years since we had a few moments by ourselves without any pressures."

"Can we get back to the comment you made about bosses and employees sleeping together?" Tam arched his eyebrow coyly. "Did I understand that you didn't want to report to me because you wanted to sleep with me?" He pulled her close.

"Mr. Bart," Molly chided, teasing him with his professional name, "I won't have you putting words in my mouth." She laughed.

With that joke, he pulled her to him and kissed her. She wrapped her arms around him and moved closer, and their kisses became more passionate.

She pushed herself back and looked into his eyes. "Tam, there are so many things I want to know about you, about your life... Are we moving too fast? Shouldn't we take more time to fill in the blanks of our lives? I'm a little scared. If I'm honest with you and myself, I don't want to be hurt again..." Molly said, her voice trailing off.

Tam pulled back and looked her straight in the eyes. "Molly, we can do whatever you want to do. We can talk all night. We can make love all night. I can answer any question you have for me.

"I feel like we'll have plenty of time now to fill in all the blanks for each other. Part of me just doesn't want to wait anymore. We've known each other for over seventeen years.

"Yes, there was a big gap, but we know each other so well. We know each other's likes and dislikes. We know each other's families. I hope by now, you know my true character," Tam said, gazing deep into Molly's eyes. "I understand the last year has been the worst of your life, and you don't need any more heartache. I want to be part of the joy in your life, to help alleviate the pain. I can't imagine the loss you must have felt when Jim died. It must have been terrible..."

"It was, but I did make it through somehow," she said softly. "I had the most incredible dream about Jim the other night. He came to me. He told me he loved me and that he wanted me to be happy. It was like he was giving me the okay to be with you, to love you again." Molly stared into Tam's rapt eyes.

"I'm glad, Mol, because I sure want to love someone who loves me back."

"I fell in love with the young musician in the torn jeans. Now I have to get to know you in a whole new way. You're this impressive and imposing CEO who's taking over my company, not the young man I knew who was just starting out." She shrugged. "We're both different people now. How do we know we can recapture what we once had?"

"I don't question that we can," Tam answered. "I agree that we're different people, but there's something so special about our initial connection and love…

"As an executive and CEO, there are all kinds of folks who want things from me. It's difficult to know who to trust. With the acquisition of your company and the celebrity status we've both unfortunately attained, the demands will become more intense." He continued after a short pause. "You knew me way back when and want to be with me for me, not what I've achieved or become."

"True," Molly said. "Our love has a long history, going back to the first night by the pool at the party…"

Tam touched Molly's hair gently and kissed her neck and throat. Molly stroked his hair and cheek as he kissed her. As he moved up to kiss her lips, she wrapped her arms around his neck and pulled him to her. Their kisses became more passionate, and she could taste him, still the same as all those years ago.

She pulled him close to whisper in his ear. "The first time we made love, you touched me and it tingled in such a sensational way. I've longed for your touch so much."

Tam gasped and lifted her from the couch, and they headed

for his bedroom. When they sat on the bed, Molly just wanted to touch him all over. She stroked his arms, his legs, his taut chest, and then took his face in her hands and kissed him gently, then more urgently.

They fell back on the bed, and she could feel his arousal matched hers. His hands floated over her breasts outside her blouse, and his touch felt wonderful and familiar. She pulled her top over her head and began unbuttoning his shirt and running her hands all over his body as he groaned in pleasure.

Molly removed his shirt and ran her fingers inside the waistband of his jeans, reaching down farther each time. By the time she unbuckled his belt and touched him fully, he was ready to jump out of his skin.

Molly and Tam quickly removed the rest of their clothes, and their bodies merged together, as they had years ago. As their passion grew, Molly told him how much she wanted him, to feel him inside her again. When Tam finally entered her, she screamed her delight and moved with him in rhythm, in total sync. When they couldn't contain themselves any longer, they both climaxed.

Tam and Molly stayed entwined for a long time, holding each other, wishing this night could last just a bit longer.

When Molly woke very early in the morning, she just watched Tam sleeping next to her. He was beautiful; he was her Tam, and he was with her again. The love she felt for him almost overwhelmed her at that moment—and frightened her as well. Were they moving too fast?

Molly didn't want to wake Tam, but she had to touch him, so she started stroking his hair. He woke up and smiled at her, pulling her over for a good morning kiss.

"What were you thinking just then?" he asked.

"How much I love you and how wonderful it is to be with you again," Molly answered honestly. "But scary, too."

"There's nothing to be scared about, Mol. I'm not sure I could love you any more than I do at this minute," he said, smiling and cradling her to his chest.

"I suppose if we become an old married couple, we would always recall this night fondly, just like the first time we made love."

Tam pulled back and looked straight at her. "Did you just ask me to marry you?" he asked, wide-eyed.

"Technically, no, but I certainly could ask you to marry me," she said a bit mischievously. "You know how much I don't really respect traditional gender roles." Molly grabbed a blanket and wrapped it around her, jumping to the floor and walking over to his side of the bed.

She knelt next to Tam as he turned to face her, propping himself up on his elbow. Next, she took his hand.

"Tam Rozomolski, you were my first love, and you are always with me and will be forever. We were lost to each other once, but never again. The first time I looked into your beautiful steel-blue eyes, I fell in love. And each time we've been together since, I yearned to see you again. Can you see our future as we grow old together? Will you make me a very happy woman? Will you marry me?"

Tam grabbed Molly and pulled her up onto the bed and into his arms. "Yes, I will marry you, Molly. You were always the one who was better with words, but I've thought about asking you to marry me so many times, so please let me do it."

Tam got out of bed, stark naked, and knelt, taking Molly's hand.

"Molly, you are the love of my life. Will you be the stepmother to my children? Maybe have one of our own? I love you so much. Will you marry me?"

"Yes," Molly said, pulling him back into bed with her, and she continued to whisper yes in his ear over and over as they made love again while the morning light filtered in through the blinds.

They had fallen asleep again for a short time, and when Molly woke up, she could see the clock read 7:05 a.m.

Tam was next to her with his smart phone, reading something and chuckling. She smiled at him. "Good morning," she said. "What's so funny?"

He read out loud a headline and the start of a story: "'Hostile Takeover: a Love Consummated After Deal? With the agreement in principle for TBBM to take over WHK, speculation centers on how long it will take for TBBM CEO, Tim Bart, to bed his former love, Marjorie Parr, WHK's senior counsel...'"

Molly and Tam looked at each other and laughed, shouting at the same time, "Not that long!"

Molly scooted over to give Tam a hug and lie close to him, stroking his cheek. "Okay, Mr. Big Shot CEO, we both have to get to the office. I told them I would be in late, but, as you well know, there's a ton of work to do.

"I love you, but our personal plans will have to wait, if just for a bit. Let me get dressed, and you can call Bill to take me home so I can shower and get into work. I'll definitely be hiding under the blanket on the ride home." She laughed as she headed out of bed to get dressed and ready to go.

Tam watched her leave the bedroom and couldn't stop smiling.

chapter twenty-nine

Tam rushed into the office and picked up some notes on his desk from Gerrie on his schedule for the day.

"Well, how'd it go?" Tunney asked, sitting up on the couch.

Tam didn't even notice him there when he walked in and was startled. "Good morning to you, too!"

Gerrie walked in with two coffees. "Good morning, Tim. I thought you would be in any minute, so I got a coffee for each of you." She smiled at the two brothers as she handed them the hot drinks.

"I think Gerrie's one of my favorite women in the world, along with Molly and Cissy, of course," Tunney said with a tip of his cowboy hat to Gerrie.

"Thanks, Tunney, that is high praise," she said. "I'll leave you two to catch up for a minute. Tam has a jam-packed schedule today," she added, leaving the room and closing the door.

"So what happened with Molly?" Tunney asked, taking a swig of his latte. "Spill the beans."

"Tun, I'm one happy man. It was wonderful. We had a great dinner. Then we talked, and then…" His voice trailed off.

"Sealed the deal, as they say?" Tunney snorted.

"Yes, and *she* asked me to marry her!" Tam declared, slapping his hands on the table.

"Ha! Sounds like Molly." Tunney laughed. "And I assume you said yes."

"Of course, and then I asked her to marry me more formally... but I wasn't dressed formally... or really at all!" Tam chuckled, shaking his head at the memory.

"That's a lot of detail, even between brothers. What do the kids say—TMI?" Tunney said, laughing aloud. "Seriously, Tam, I'm so happy for y'all. When can we see her?"

"When can 'we' see her?" Tam asked, smiling. "You've had the opportunity to see her a lot more than me lately.

"Okay, here's an idea. We can set up a dinner tonight for the four of us so I can meet Cissy. Do you think she'll be excited about being the date of my best man?" Tam asked.

"If you're asking me to be your best man, I accept, and I think Cissy'll be thrilled. Dinner's a great idea. Don't worry about tonight. Leave everything to me," Tunney said, a sly grin splitting his face. "Congrats again, bro. I know it's hush-hush, so it'll just be the four of us for now, but I'm sure Molly will want to call Fred and Margaret. I assume you'll call Mom and Dad?"

"Will do," Tam confirmed, getting up from his chair to give his brother a big hug. "Now get outta here so I can get some work done."

Tunney smiled at Tam as he left, bowing deeply and removing his cowboy hat from his head in a broad sweep.

The takeover was the center of activity at both TBBM and WHK. Everyone was abuzz at Molly's company that morning with the announcement of the takeover the night before. She hurried into her office, greeted by everyone she saw in the hallway.

As Molly usually got in so much earlier than this, she wasn't used to seeing so many people when she arrived. Of course, she was very popular now, as everyone in the building knew of her relationship with the CEO of the acquiring company.

Molly was happy to see Cissy sitting at her desk, making some changes to the schedule for the day.

"Good morning," Cissy said, smiling broadly. "I assume you had a good evening." She cocked her head.

"I did." Molly beamed. "Perhaps we have a few minutes to chat before my day begins?"

"I'll grab the coffees," Cissy declared, running down the hall toward the cafeteria.

Molly turned on her computer and walked over to the window to gaze out at the beautiful New England spring day. She could see the flowers blooming and the birds active in their nests.

She thought about how her life was about to change, but she was excited about those changes, as she had no reservations about being with Tam and taking a different path with her career.

No one knows what's next in life, she thought. *It could be tragedy, like Jim's death, or joy, like finding Tam again.* She shook her head at her own recent luck.

Cissy returned her office with two lattes and put them down on Molly's desk. "Lost in thought?"

Molly came to sit at her desk and grabbed her drink. "Yes, I'm so excited about the next chapter in my life." She smiled. "Tam and I are getting married, and I have a new job."

"Well, that *is* a lot of news. Congratulations! I'm very happy for you both," Cissy said. "I suppose it was a very romantic proposal."

Molly laughed loudly. "It was. I asked him, but then he asked me. We both accepted."

"Excellent." Cissy clapped excitedly. "Can't wait to hear more about it when we're in a more relaxed atmosphere and can toast your good news."

The women sat and talked for a while, and Molly explained her new position and Ken's. "So you can see your role will change a bit, but you'll still work closely with Ken and me."

Cissy put her hands over her chest. "Thank God. You know I need this job and how much I enjoy working for you and with Ken. I'm really thrilled with all of your news.

"Oh, and speaking of Ken, you have a meeting with him in just a few minutes," Cissy said, getting up to go back to her desk.

"Perfect," Molly said. "I want to tell him the good news."

She rushed over to Ken's office, nodding to folks on the way, but not stopping to chat.

When she saw Nell, she instinctively gave her a hug.

"Well, that's a nice 'good morning' from you." Nell laughed. "You'll have to give me the update after you've chatted with our boss."

Molly went into Ken's office and sat in front of his desk. It was clear she was happy and relaxed, which was a change from the frantic and stressful times they'd shared most recently.

"Let me guess," Ken said. "You're in a very good mood that is driven by more personal interactions than professional ones."

"You are one very intelligent man, a brilliant man," Molly said, smiling ear to ear. "I suppose I have to come right out with it. Tam and I are getting married."

"Wow, that was fast, but I assume waiting seventeen years was long enough. Congratulations," Ken said, rising to give her a warm hug. "You may be surprised to hear this, but he told me he was going to ask you to marry him when we met the other morning. I knew then he was serious about his relationship with you, which made me relax a bit about his intentions."

"You sound like my father," Molly said, laughing. "Who, I just found out this morning, was asked by Tam for my hand in marriage when he saw my parents in Wisconsin! It seems Tam told everyone." She giggled. "Seriously, my mother and father were thrilled with the news as well. We obviously aren't ready for a public announcement yet, however."

"That's up to you and Tam," Ken said. "On a business note, we'll have to tell the board," he said more seriously.

"Absolutely. Perhaps we can make the announcement during our next meeting, and *Tim* can be there as well," Molly suggested, emphasizing the name Tam used for business. "We are keeping it just among the family and closest friends right now, as this will make the news, of course, and we just aren't ready for that."

"Got it. My lips are sealed," Ken said. "But we will have to make a formal announcement when you and Tim choose, as the interest in your relationship is intense inside and outside these walls."

"I'm going to think about all of that later. Right now, I just want to focus on Tam and me and, professionally, the combination of our companies in the best way possible. I have a narrow focus right now."

"I'm ecstatic with your personal happiness and, as I will continue to be your boss, look forward to working with you to achieve your professional goals," Ken said with great affection.

"Thanks, Ken. Now I need to get to work," Molly said, heading back to her office.

After she had settled in, Cissy stepped into her office to give her a quick update. "I am to tell you not to make any plans for this evening," she said, smiling. "Tunney's putting together a dinner for the four of us. He wants me to meet Tam, and we can discuss the wedding plans. He's the best man."

"Of course," Molly said. "I hope you'll be my maid of honor, as you've lived this relationship with me in the last few months."

Cissy came over to give Molly another hug. "I would be

honored," she said with a tear in her eye. "It's wonderful to see you so happy. Who would have thought, with the tragedy of just over a year ago, that you could be so happy today?"

Molly sat down with a serious look on her face. "I never dreamed I could love anyone again when Jim died. I felt so alone. My world was shattered. I certainly never would have guessed I would find love again with Tam. Life has so many twists and turns," she said quietly.

"Thank God for this latest turn in your life," Cissy said.

Molly smiled. "It is wonderful. I'm also thrilled about having Tunney back in my life, and in yours. You seem very happy together."

"Tunney has been such a surprise, a revelation, really," Cissy said thoughtfully. "To be honest, I'd given up on meeting anyone special, and he just waltzed into my life the same time he came back into yours. He gets on so well with my kids, too. I think I'll wait a bit before asking him to marry me, though." Cissy laughed.

"Oh, speaking of marriage, I need to make another call to share the good news," Molly said.

"Ruth," she said excitedly after Cissy returned to her desk and Molly dialed her friend's number, "it's Molly. I have some very big news..."

Molly hung up the phone after a wonderful conversation with Ruth. Her friend had been leery of Tam and their relationship all those years ago, but she seemed genuinely pleased for both of them today.

Ruth had been there for Molly after Jim died, and they shared many late-night conversations recently. Molly made a promise to herself to see more of Ruth in the future.

Ruth had married Bobby and they had two kids, a son and daughter, and lived in the Chicago area. It would be fun to spend some time with them.

Molly hadn't told Tam yet, but she really wanted the wedding in Wisconsin so they could celebrate with their families and friends.

Her job had kept her so busy that she didn't see her old friends or her parents as much as she should. As her life was changing drastically soon, she was resolved to make many changes for the better...

Just then, Molly looked at the clock and saw it was time for her next meeting. It was the usual grind for now, but things would be very different for her in the future.

chapter thirty

Tunney and Cissy arrived early at a private room at Bellini's for the special celebratory dinner with Tam and Molly.

They decorated the small room with flowers and funny wedding decorations. Tam's driver, Bill, was going to bring both Tam and Molly to the restaurant, carefully watching for any photographers.

"Those two deserve something special with what they've been through these last months," Tunney said, arranging the fluted glasses around the champagne bucket.

"I would have never guessed a guy like you would be good at party decorations." Cissy laughed as Tunney taped up a white streamer.

"You'd be surprised at what I'm good at, spending lots of years in bars, dance halls, and tons of different concert venues," he replied with a wink. "I've played plenty of special events, including a whole lot of weddings and bar mitzvahs, which always have nice decorations."

"There seems to be no end to the things you're good at," Cissy answered with some sass. With that, he came over and took her in his arms, kissing her senseless.

"I take your meaning," Tunney said, smiling and then kissing her again.

"Well," Cissy said, pulling away and smoothing her blouse. "It seems like we're getting carried away here when this party is about Tam and Molly."

"True," Tunney said. "We can continue our celebration a bit later," he added with a chuckle.

Tunney and Cissy finished the decorations and moved to the back of the small room to admire their handiwork: flowers on the table, streamers with wedding bells, champagne on ice, and a funny sculpture of a bride and groom.

They also got a small bride and groom to go on top of the dessert, Molly's favorite tiramisu. Tunney had planned a special surprise as well.

When Tam and Molly walked in, Tunney had his smart phone play the wedding march, and they both looked so surprised and pleased. Molly walked over to Tunney and gave him a huge hug; she was so touched she was speechless.

"Well, boss..." Tunney pulled halfway out of Molly's hug. "Now I'm going to have to call you sister as well," he said softly.

Molly just pulled him to her and continued to hug him. "I like the sound of that, and there's no one in the world I'd rather call brother than you, Tunney," she said, struggling with her flurry of emotions.

Tam looked on with great affection for two of the people he loved most in the world. When he glanced over at Cissy, he ran over to shake her hand.

"So good to meet you, Cissy," Tam told her before quickly enveloping her in a hug. "I need to give you a hug for everything you've done for Molly and for what you mean to my brother."

"It's so wonderful to finally meet you," she replied. "I can't tell you how much I've heard about you from Molly and Tunney... and the media," she added with a laugh.

"That's what's scaring me," Tam said, grimacing.

"Okay, folks, it's time for a toast," Tunney announced, popping the cork from the champagne and pouring four glasses. "To my little brother, Tam, and Molly, the love of his life. Congratulations on finding each other again and on your upcoming marriage.

"On behalf of Cissy and me, all the best for many years of happiness," Tunney said with great emotion. "And before I get too misty here, let's hope there will be a time very soon when you don't have to go out in disguise or under a blanket... and that every move you make isn't prime time news!" he added with a laugh.

"Cheers," they all said, clinking their glasses.

"By the way," Tunney said, "Cissy and I have sworn the restaurant staff to secrecy as well, so let's hope your great news doesn't leak out. You should get married very soon to beat all the media to the punch."

"Molly and I haven't had the chance to discuss it, but that's what I want as well." Tam agreed. "A small wedding in Wisconsin with just family and close friends makes sense. Of course, if that's what Molly wants." He spun around to see her reaction.

"That is *exactly* what I want. Looking around this room, I think we've found our wedding planners." Molly laughed.

"Sold," Tunney said. "Cissy, you in?" he asked.

"Absolutely," Cissy said. "The two of you are going to be so busy with finalizing the takeover that you will really need help to plan a wedding. Let us do the heavy lifting for you."

"Sounds like an offer we can't refuse," Molly said.

"We'll get a place lined up and come back to you with dates next week and will check those dates with the families so we're ready to roll," Tunney said.

Molly turned to look at Tunney and Cissy. "How lucky I feel to have you both in my life," she said and then turned to Tam.

"Despite all the drama that kept us apart, it is wonderful to be with you again, finally. I do love you so much—"

Before she could finish, Tam took Molly in his arms and rocked her back and forth. "Me, too, Mol, me, too."

The four of them laughed and talked through the dinner and planned for the future, which was unfolding right in front of them.

chapter thirty-one

Over the next few months, the work was grinding for Tam, Molly, and Ken as they pulled all the pieces together to plan for the combination of the two companies in the best way possible.

It was difficult, as they would have to say good-bye to some good people when the final regulatory approvals came through. Tough choices had to be made about leadership. Both Ken and Tam had already assembled very impressive teams.

As promised, Ken took the lead and went to Tam to hash out the final teams. Molly kept busy working with Bryne Tena, Tam's legal counsel, and her counterpart on all the regulatory reviews, including those with the Justice Department and the European Union. They also worked together on items of interest for both boards.

While there were detailed agreements that had to be assembled and bumps along the way, things seemed to be going as well as could be expected.

In the little spare time they had, Tam and Molly spent just about all their free moments together. It helped that they could discuss issues at work and then unwind, separating completely from the challenges of the workday.

Tam introduced Molly to his children, and they spent as much time as possible with them, particularly on the weekends.

The kids seemed to be adjusting well to Molly and John, their mother's new boyfriend.

There was no way to stop the press from knowing Molly and Tam were together, as it seemed like everyone in both companies knew of their relationship. They didn't try to hide it anymore, but they didn't let on about the wedding, which was top secret and coming up very soon.

True to their words, the couple kept the guest list small, Cissy, Ken, and Jen being the only work-related invitees. Ken and Tam had become very close through the merger, which was gratifying to Molly.

While they had some tough moments and disagreements, as was to be expected, they also forged a real bond, with Ken mentoring Tam in those areas where he was less experienced.

Molly and Tam told the members of the boards of directors for both companies the news about their upcoming marriage. They also explained that Tam wouldn't have any power over Molly's job status or compensation, as that would reside solely with Ken.

In the course of combining the boards, just like the leadership team process, some board members would have to depart. These were delicate conversations for both CEOs, and they took their responsibilities very seriously as they made decisions and had individual talks with board members.

Some conversations were easier than others in that some of the older board members chose to withdraw on their own; others were quite disappointed not to be chosen to continue to serve.

Molly loved her new role leading corporate citizenship, which involved creating a new function that would eventually bring together operations from WHK and TBBM. In this area, she found she really enjoyed working with the talented teams in both companies.

Another issue that took a great deal of her time and Bryne

Tena's was the combination of all the real estate of the two companies. There would have to be site closures and combinations and all the leases were being examined for timing, as a number of properties would be exited over time.

Eventually, the corporate headquarters for WHK would be closed and combined with TBBM, but that would take some time, as the corporate staffs would be needed for a period of time, even after the closing.

There was a lot to do, but it was handled efficiently, and Tam and Ken tried to remove the emotions from the business as much as possible.

For Molly and Tam, time whizzed by, and the wedding would be upon them in no time. They tried to be in as few meetings together as possible, but one day they found themselves in a long session in Tam's conference room, the exact same one where they'd reunited so dramatically after so many years apart.

Tam picked up the water pitcher to pour himself a glass of water and glanced over at Molly with a smile, one of the few times he addressed her personally at formal meetings.

"Don't worry, Molly. I have a firm hold of it this time." He laughed and poured himself a glass of water.

All the participants laughed at that comment, as a number of them were present for the infamous meeting between the two a number of months ago.

Molly smiled back at him from the end of the table. "I'm very glad there will be no serious accidents today," she called out.

"I echo that sentiment," Ken exclaimed, laughing.

When the meeting was over, Tam grabbed her elbow lightly and steered her to his office. He smiled at Gerrie as he closed the door behind him. Then he swept Molly into his arms and kissed her. As she laid her face against his chest, she wrapped her arms around him.

"I thought we agreed there would be no displays of affection at work," she said with a sly smile.

"Okay," Tam said, "I lied," bringing her face back to his for another kiss. "Also, remember what I told you about the company plane…" Tam said as he kissed her neck. "I lied about that, too."

"You are so naughty." Molly giggled.

"Not nearly as naughty as I want to be," he growled, pulling her to him for another kiss.

"We're in front of a window, you know," Molly pointed out and pulled away and affectionately stroked his cheek, laughing.

Tam's phone began ringing and Gerrie answered it, but she was an intelligent woman and wouldn't interrupt her boss, as she was pretty sure she knew what was happening in his office.

chapter thirty-two

It was the week of the wedding and all the plans had come together. Cissy and Tunney flew out a few days early to get things ready.

Molly really missed Cissy at the office but had another assistant from her department sitting in.

Tam and Molly had found a home close to work and had her place up for sale. The kids had their own rooms at the new house and were having fun decorating them in their own tastes and styles. Molly enjoyed helping the kids, learning a lot about what ten-year-old boys and twelve-year-old girls really liked. She found she was woefully behind the times.

Tam was paying personally for the company plane to take them to Wisconsin on Thursday night, along with his children. Molly had a special carrier for her wedding dress so it would be kept intact and hidden from Tam.

The kids would stay with their father at his mom and dad's and Molly with her parents. They didn't like being apart, but it made sense, particularly with the kids, and it meant the world to the parents.

The rehearsal dinner would be Friday night at Fred and Margaret's and include Tam's family.

How wonderful it will be to be all together again, Molly thought.

Margaret was handling all the cooking herself but had brought in a chef's assistant from town and another friend to help serve. It would be a real family affair, and of course the food would be fantastic.

When the plane arrived at the small, private airport, separate cars picked up Tam and the kids and Molly, as arranged by Cissy and Tunney, and took them to their respective parents' houses for the night.

Molly kissed the kids good-bye and then reached for Tam.

"All of a sudden, I'm not liking this idea of staying apart," Tam said, squeezing her in a possessive hug.

"It's the right thing. You should spend time with the kids and your family without me. It's just two nights." She sighed, looking into his eyes. "And we have waited seventeen years."

Tam nodded, kissed her good-bye, and reluctantly let her go into the other car, then joined his kids.

Molly melted into the backseat and closed her eyes for a moment. What a whirlwind the last six months had been and how different her life would be going forward. She didn't realize how exhausted she really was as she quickly went to sleep while the car whizzed through the gentle farmland of Wisconsin.

She woke just as the car stopped in front of her parents' farmhouse. They popped out of the screen door and came running down to see her. She grabbed her mom in a big hug and then her father joined them. Molly couldn't stop the tears from flowing, and she saw them in her parents' eyes as well.

"Welcome home, hon." Her dad greeted her. "It's so good to see you."

"Dad, Mom, it's fabulous to be home," Molly said. "I can't believe the wedding is almost here."

Once they grabbed her bags and moved inside, Molly laid her

wedding dress carrier over a chair in the living room, smoothing it to make sure the dress inside wouldn't get wrinkled.

"I cannot wait to see you in your dress," Molly's mother declared, draping her arm around her daughter. "We are just so happy for you."

Molly smiled at her parents. "This is the beginning of a new chapter for me. Tam and I want to spend more time in Wisconsin with his family and with you," she added as they went up the stairs, with Fred carrying her bags and Margaret carrying the dress.

Molly sent a text to Tam to let him know she arrived at her parents', and, as it was a bit late, Margaret asked them to sit down to dinner right away.

She made one of Molly's favorites: breaded chicken cutlets stuffed with garlicky cheese, spinach, and sun-dried tomatoes, and heirloom carrots baked with honey and balsamic vinegar, along with a salad made of fresh lettuce and vegetables from the garden. It all tasted wonderful.

Molly and her parents talked for hours, but Margaret made Molly get to bed at a decent hour, as she wanted her to get as much rest as possible before the wedding. Not surprisingly, it only took a few minutes for her to fall into a deep sleep.

The next day, Tam planned to come over in advance of the rest of his family to spend some time with Molly and greet her parents. He hadn't been able to spend much quality time with Fred and Margaret since his surprise visit, so he hoped to be able to enjoy time with them under less stressful circumstances.

He felt so content driving over to Molly's that afternoon. It was a wonderful late summer day and the drive was familiar and comforting. He'd really enjoyed seeing his whole family at his parents' house, and the kids had a blast with their grandparents, uncles, aunt, and cousins. Molly was right that they needed to spend more time with family.

When he pulled up in the driveway, Fred was outside doing some yard work. Tam popped out of the car and walked over to greet his father-in-law-to-be with a handshake. "Fred, it's so fantastic to see you. I'm so happy to finally be part of your family."

"Better late than never." Fred laughed. "Come on in. I know a couple women who are anxious to see you."

Margaret was in the kitchen, working on the night's dinner. The rehearsal dinner that evening would take over the whole dining room, living room, and front porch, and Tam could see everything coming together.

"Margaret, we're all looking forward to the feast tonight. Don't tell my mom. She's a very good cook, but I think I prefer your cooking. You could be a professional chef." Tam gave her a big hug hello.

"As my new son-in-law, you've gotten off to a great start," Margaret sang, returning his hug. "You look just like you did years ago, wearing those jeans and that shirt," she added.

Molly came down the stairs wearing her jeans and a blue T-shirt and joined them in the kitchen, sneaking up behind Tam and putting her arms around his waist and peeking around his back.

"Hello," she said, and he spun her around to give her a kiss and a hug.

"Hello," Tam replied. "This is your last day as a single woman. Tomorrow, you'll be Mrs. Bart."

"Hmm. That's something I wanted to talk to you about. Bart isn't your real name, so I don't want to take that. If it were Rozomolski, I would, but you don't use that anymore.

"I had hoped to revert to my maiden name, Greenly, so if we did have kids, my parents' name would be carried down." She paused a moment and worried her lip a bit. "Sorry to hit you with this at the last minute, but I'd just been thinking about it…"

"Oh, Molly, that is thoughtful," Fred said, "but it is really your decision, as well as Tam's."

Molly looked to Tam for his response. He was quiet for a moment. "I hadn't thought about it that way… but sure, if that's what you want," he said. "We aren't even married yet, and you're thinking about kids." He winked. "I want you all to myself for at least a little while, babe."

"Thanks," Molly said, putting her arms around him again. "I was just thinking ahead, as I always do."

"Fred, Margaret, if I can whisk your daughter off for a while, I'd love to have tea and your famous scones on the porch when we get back. Would that be okay?" Tam asked.

"Absolutely," Fred said. "You kids go off and have fun."

Tam smiled back at them as they headed out the door. "I sure love being a kid in my forties."

Molly looked at him quizzically. "Where are we going?"

He took her arm and steered her over to the car. "You'll like it. It's just for you and me."

Tam took off down the road, and Molly realized almost immediately where he was taking her. When they parked on the dirt shoulder and walked down to the side of the creek, Tam unrolled the blanket he'd brought and spread it on the ground next to Molly's tree.

The grass was warm and smelled like summer, and the water was flowing quickly, pushing along broken branches and leaves. Molly immediately popped up on the trunk of the tree that reached right over the creek.

Molly took off her shoes and threw them at Tam and then put her feet into the current, shrieking at how cold it was, even on this hot day. She touched the heart Tam had carved in the bark so many years ago and traced their initials with her finger.

"You're right. This is perfect," she said, splashing some water at him. "Remember when you carved this?"

"I do. How could I possibly forget?" Tam asked, smiling.

"So much has happened since then. There was a lot of pain, you know?"

"I do," Tam answered thoughtfully. "I believed you were gone forever when I saw you with Jim. I know it doesn't compare to the pain you felt when he died, but I was devastated when I lost you."

Molly kicked her feet in the water. "That's the part that's so hard for me. I had to lose you, find Jim, and lose him to find you again." She teared up, her voice thick with emotion. "That's what keeps me from feeling pure joy right now. I really can't thank you enough for letting me invite Jim's parents to the wedding. I had no idea how they would react to me remarrying, but they couldn't have been more gracious. I truly believe they want to be there. They told me Jim would want me to be happy.

"I had to call them when all those stories about us appeared. I wanted them to hear directly from me what was going on between us. They are wonderful people, and I'm glad they can attend. I hope you understand," Molly said.

Tam held out his arms to her, and she slipped off the branch and onto the shore next to him. She leaned against him and wiped away her tears.

"I'm glad they can attend. Honored, really," Tam stated. "Jim must have been quite a guy."

"He was. I'm still his wife in my head in many ways. I'm not saying I have any doubts about marrying you or that my love for you isn't sure and strong. It is. It's just so hard to explain when you love someone and then lose them…" She trailed off for a moment. "Thank God we found each again."

Tam put his arm around her, and they sat on the bank for a long time, just listening to the sound of the water flowing.

"Do you want to go back to your parents' house?" Tam asked gently.

"No, I want to be here with you. It helps to talk about the past. I'll have moments like this from time to time. Jim was such an important part of my life."

"I understand. You lived so much of your life with him. It's too be expected." Tam brushed a lock of hair behind her ear.

"The love I had with Jim feels so different than with you. With him, it was so solid and warm and loving…"

"How is our love different?" Tam asked with some concern.

"Other than being all over the news?" She laughed, breaking the tension. "Seriously, with you, our love is so intense, and there are so many surprises and certainly more risk and danger—"

"Do you mean passion?" Tam interjected playfully.

Molly smiled softly. "My love for you is so intense, so passionate… I ache for you when we aren't together… It scares me, as I've told you before."

"Mol, I've never felt for any woman what I feel for you." Tam pulled her close and kissed her with the passion they just discussed.

Molly grabbed him tight. "Oh, Tam, I don't want to lose you again."

"No chance," he said. "You're going to be stuck with me for a really long time."

As their kisses grew even more passionate, Molly pushed him back onto the blanket and sat next to him, unbuttoning his shirt. She pulled his shirt out from his pants and removed her T-shirt so she could lie on top of him, feeling his flesh next to hers.

As they removed the rest of their clothes and made love on

the blanket, they called out each other's names before collapsing and rolling over with the blanket over and under them, laughing and hugging, listening to the birds and the running water.

"You see?" Molly said. "This is exactly what I mean about our dangerous, risky, passionate love. You are the CEO of what will be a huge company, and I'm a high-level executive. We've just made love, outside, no less, and are naked on a blanket. Can you imagine what the tabloids would do with this?"

Tam laughed aloud as he gathered their clothes. "You're right, my most precious legal counsel, so let's get dressed fast!"

They tried to clean up the best they could and then went back to Molly's parents'. She sneaked in and called to her parents that she was going to take a quick shower before they had tea and scones.

Tam sat on the porch next to Fred in the old rockers that had been there for years.

"Tam, I would say if you weren't marrying my daughter tomorrow…" He laughed, cutting his sentence short.

"Sir, I haven't felt like a teenager for a number of years, but I sure do now." Tam laughed. "All I can say is guilty as charged! I love your daughter. What can I say?"

"Thank God for that, son. I haven't seen her this happy for a long time."

Tam just smiled as Margaret brought out the tea and scones.

It wouldn't be long until the whole gang arrived for dinner, so Tam excused himself to see if Molly was out of the shower, as he wanted to pop in.

She put her arms around his neck as she came down the stairs.

"You know, I would've loved to jump in the shower with you," he whispered in her ear.

Molly laughed and whispered back, "There is a limit to my

parents' tolerance, you know. Now go get clean."

When everyone arrived a bit later, the house was filled with so many sounds and lots of laughter. Molly looked around and smiled. As an only child, life had been quiet and still in this house. But with her new family, including her step-kids, it was going to be brimming with activity and noise.

She loved it already.

chapter thirty-three

On the day of the wedding, Molly was up early, unable to sleep. She read for some time and then showered, but didn't dry her hair, as her friend from high school, Barb, was coming over to do her makeup and hair.

Molly put on shorts and a T-shirt and went downstairs into the kitchen. Her mother was up, making coffee for her dad and tea for the two of them.

"Good morning," Molly chirped to her mom, giving her a tight hug. "Thanks for that fabulous dinner last night. Everyone had such a great time. I still feel full."

"It sure was fun, hon," Margaret replied with a big smile. "I'm glad everyone enjoyed it. It was wonderful to meet Tam's family and to spend time with his children. They're great kids. So excited for you today, baby."

"I'm a little nervous, Mom. My stomach is a bit unsettled," she admitted.

"Sit down here and have a cup of tea. Maybe that'll calm your nerves."

Just then, the doorbell rang, and it was Barb, ready to do Molly's makeup and hair. She came into the kitchen and got a cup of tea before heading upstairs with Molly to do her magic.

Cissy arrived just as Barb was leaving, and Margaret and Cissy took the off-white silk dress out of the bag. It was so beautiful and sleek, with long, clean lines and a plunging V-neck. Molly stepped into the dress, careful not to get any makeup or hair gel on it. Cissy helped her pull it on, and her mother zipped it up.

Margaret just stood there staring at her. "Well," she finally said, filled with emotion, "I am the mother of the bride again, and she looks so exquisite."

Molly twirled around. "Thanks, Mom."

"Tam is certainly a lucky man," Margaret said as Cissy nodded in agreement.

"When I first broke up with Tam, you kept me together. I don't even think I could have gotten out of bed without you. When Jim died, you both helped me so much," Molly said, looking at her mother and then Cissy. "The grief was so strong, so overwhelming… Every day I needed support to get through. My life had been so easy before Jim's death.

"I just wasn't prepared to deal with that kind of adversity. It hit me so hard, and I want to thank you both for everything you did for me," Molly told them, trying to keep her emotions in check. "When I saw Tam again, I had so many emotions running through me, and if I couldn't talk to both of you to help sort things out, I have no idea what I would have done.

"You helped me calm down, see reason, and think about the situation from my perspective as well as Tam's, which helped a lot. So you see, I wouldn't be standing here without you," she said.

Just then, Fred knocked on the door. "Ladies, are you about ready to go to the church?"

Margaret opened the door, and Fred gasped when he saw his daughter. "Is that the same girl who had on jeans and a T-shirt this morning, with all that stringy wet hair in her face?" he asked lightheartedly. "Molly, you look stunning." He took Molly's hand and led her out the door.

"You look pretty handsome yourself, Dad," Molly said, smiling brightly at him. "I think this is only the second time I've seen you in a tux."

"There are only two people who can get me into a tux." Fred smiled. "You and your mother."

The four of them descended the stairs almost regally, with Cissy grabbing the train of Molly's beautiful dress.

The limo was outside to bring them over to the church, and their flowers were inside. It was a short ride, and Molly knew the scenery well, as she'd traveled this road from early memory to attend Sunday services.

When they arrived at the church, there was a small room in the back in which Molly could wait until all the guests had arrived. While her parents and Cissy went to check on everything in the church, Molly had a few minutes to herself.

She'd been in this room one other time, when she married Jim. She remembered how she felt then: so nervous and jumpy, perhaps because she was never one of those women who dreamed of marriage.

In fact, marriage scared her, and that's why she felt so nervous when she married Jim. Molly knew he was the right person to marry, but she didn't feel ready for marriage at that time. So much of her life was still in front of her then.

Perhaps it was her life experience and age, because as she stood in the room, preparing to marry again, Molly was so calm. She knew she and Tam belonged together, that part of her had always loved him.

Wasn't that how it was with your first love? You might not be together, but you always wanted the best for him or her. As angry as she was with Tam all those years ago, she always wanted him to be okay, even though they were apart.

Molly looked in the mirror once more and admired what she

saw. The hair and makeup were perfect and the dress fit exactly right. But what about inside? How was she different than the woman who married Jim fifteen years ago, who stood right here, gazing in this same mirror?

Well, she was older, wiser, had many life experiences that added to her maturity. Molly had traveled so much internationally that she had a much more global view of world events. She had endured unbearable loss and grief and survived. Achieved career success. Had two deep, true loves.

Most profoundly, she learned that working sixty hours a week sucked too much of the life out of her and took her away from the people she loved. Molly knew now that she wanted to do something that was about others, and her new work around philanthropy and corporate social responsibility would give her that platform.

Molly also made more money than she ever thought she would, and Tam made millions every year as a CEO. They would give back and help others, teaching the children to do the same. The kids needed to understand that most people in the world didn't have the advantages they did. Tam and Molly came from nothing and worked very hard to get where they were today; the children would have to do the same. Nothing should be simply handed to them.

When this merger was complete, Molly vowed to make changes and influence Tam to ensure his work wouldn't overwhelm his life. *Hard to do as a CEO*, Molly thought, but she felt their love and life together would persuade him.

Molly surprised herself with all these thoughts just before she walked down the aisle. That was exactly the problem with her life; she had no time to truly think.

She'd never felt more ready for the next phase. And as it was time for her to begin the walk down the aisle, that was a good thing.

When she saw Tam standing there with Tunney, her stomach did flip-flops and she held on to her father's arm more tightly.

She loved her parents so much that she wanted them to have the total wedding experience again. It was important to them to have the wedding in the church, along with the tradition of her father walking her down the aisle. If it were up to Molly, she would have been content marching out into a field to marry Tam in her jeans and rubber boots!

It just didn't matter to her, but it mattered to her parents and to Tam's, so they decided to go the traditional route again. Tam and Molly had already given themselves to each other; her father wasn't really giving her away, particularly since she'd been married before. But as she stood next to Tam and looked into his beautiful, steel-blue eyes, this kind of wedding felt right to her.

After the ceremony and a whole lot of photos, Tunney grabbed her just before she got into the limo to ride over the reception. "Hey, boss—I mean, sis—are you ready for some fun?" he asked, giving her a quick hug.

"I'm not sure what you have planned, but I'm ready," Molly said, laughing.

After Tam and Cissy helped her into the back of the limo, the procession headed to the reception. Molly kept hold of Tam's hand as he slid over closer to her in the backseat. She took his hand in both of hers and then held it up to her cheek, and he used the back of his fingers to stroke her face.

"We certainly waited a long time for this day," she said, looking straight into Tam's eyes.

"Too long." He agreed, gathering her into his arms and kissing her gently, but trying not to wrinkle her beautiful dress. "Hey, this is hard with you wearing this thing." He laughed.

"It'll get a lot easier later," Molly whispered in his ear, and he responded with a knowing chuckle.

He pulled back and stared at her seriously. "I never explained my and Tunney's real names to you, and I suppose I should now that we're married."

Molly looked at him quizzically.

"Tam stands for Tymoteusz, the Polish version of Timothy, which, of course, was derived from Greek, meaning honor and respect."

"Very fitting," Molly responded seriously.

"Tunney is short for Bartlomiej, which is Bartholomew in English and means hills, mounds, or furrows. Not really sure how Dad got Tunney out of Bartlomiej." Tam laughed as he explained.

"I had no idea," Molly said.

"So when I decided to change my name, I took Tim as my first name, well, Timothy, legally, and then Bart, as that was the short version of Tunney's real name. Now you know our secret."

"When you guys told me I needed to know you a lot better before you explained your names, you really weren't kidding," Molly said, laughing. "It took more than seventeen years and a wedding."

"Now I expect you to keep our secret. No one knows outside of the family," Tam said seriously.

"Well, I am family now, so the secret is safe with me," Molly answered.

"One other thing… Under no circumstances, even when joking, should you call Tunney Bartlomiej. Got it?" Tam asked rather ominously.

"Yes, sir." Molly mock saluted.

The car stopped in front of an old barn that was beautifully set against a field, and the photographer was there to take photos of just the two of them.

Molly had driven by this farmhouse for years and always

admired it. The barn had started out red but had faded to almost a dark pink over the years. Molly had never thought she would be taking her wedding photos in front of it, but here they were. The light was perfect, so the portraits should be wonderful. She loved the fact that memories of this day would be captured in front of an old barn in Wisconsin.

As they were leaving, Tam grabbed Molly to kiss her, and the photographer snapped the shot. That photo would be her favorite.

By the time they got to the reception hall, everyone was outside waiting for them, clapping and cheering.

Inside, Molly could see a stand had been set up for the band at the back of the hall. Tunney and Cissy had told them they would just use recorded music, but she could now see it was going to be Tunney's band. Now she understood his comment about the fun.

Once inside, Tunney asked the guests to take their seats and grab a glass of champagne for the toast, and then dinner would be served.

Margaret had worked with the caterers on the menu, so Molly knew it was going to be delicious. As she looked around and saw all the people she loved so much, she felt warm inside.

Nothing really matters like your family and your dearest friends and how wonderful it is to have them all together. She would make sure the photographer got shots of everyone.

Molly observed both sets of parents at the front table and thought she and Tam were so lucky that their parents were aging well and were healthy and active. What a blessing.

Tunney tapped on his glass with a spoon to get everyone's attention. "Thanks, everyone, for your attention. First, on behalf of Tam and Molly, thank you for coming to this joyous occasion. Better late than never, I say.

"Now, as best man, I have to make a toast. I won't have much to say now, but I'll have a whole lot to say later. For now, please raise your glasses to toast my brother, Tam, and his beautiful bride, Molly. Congratulations, you two," Tunney said, lifting his glass to them. "We love you both."

After the applause settled down, Tunney got back up to speak. "We aren't going to do things traditionally tonight. You'll hear from my brother and me later, once we get the music going. For now, we're going to hear from the bride. Molly?" Tunney said, taking her hand as she rose from her seat.

"As Tunney knows," Molly began, "I've never been one to do things traditionally. Tam is used to that as well, as I asked him to marry me first," she said, turning to Tam to share a laugh.

"I wanted to thank all of you for coming to our wedding. As Tunney said, it's taken us a long time to get here. Every one of you is special to Tam and me, and we are so excited you could share this happy day with us. To get to this point, we both had to endure heartache, going back to when we broke apart.

"If we didn't go through that heartache, I would have never married Jim, a most wonderful man who died too soon. I am so grateful to his parents, Amanda and Hugh, for traveling to be here with us today. Their love and support of Jim and me was extraordinary, and they will always be a part of our family," Molly said, wiping away a tear and blowing a kiss to them, which they returned to her.

"Our parents are incredibly special to us, and Tam and I cannot thank them enough for their love and for everything they have done for us. We are who we are because of you, and I want you to know we will be seeing more of you in the future," she vowed, nodding to Fred and Margaret on one side of the table and Tam's parents on the other.

"I was an only child, as you all know, but not anymore. Tam's family is my family now, and I feel truly blessed to be part of it." Molly continued, looking at Tam's brothers and sister and their families. "How lucky I am to be stepmother to two great kids." She smiled warmly at Chad and Marnie.

"Tam and I are indebted to Cissy and Tunney for their support and encouragement and for handling the arrangements for our wedding. Tunney introduced me to Tam years ago, so we literally would not be here without him. Thank you so much, Cissy and Tunney!"

There was a lot of hooting and hollering and laughter, and Molly waited for it to die down before continuing the most emotionally challenging part of her speech.

"Now, I would like to toast Tam, my husband," Molly said, smiling broadly as the cheers started again and Tam stood next to her.

"I fell in love with you seventeen years ago when I looked into those beautiful, steel-blue eyes as we stood next to the pool at Ruth's parents' house. I was a goner at that point, and Ruth and the whole band knew it. My feelings for Tam were very clear to me after we shared our first kiss, shut away in the pantry!"

Tam blushed, and the whole room was filled with laughter and few hoots, including from Ruth and Bobby.

"I'm beyond happy we found our way back to each other, as difficult as it has been at times. So, Tam, my husband, I am honored to be a stepmother to your wonderful children and to be your wife. I love you."

Tam took her in his arms and kissed her to thunderous applause.

"Now, let's eat!" Molly shouted.

She picked at her food, and, as soon as they could, the couple went over to say hello to all their guests and take photos at each table. They kept true to their word about a small wedding, and there were only about eighty guests. Every table had a toast and kind words for them, and they relished the opportunity to chat with all of them.

Out of the corner of her eye, Molly could see Tunney, Brett, and Murph were setting up on the band riser to get ready to play. She wasn't surprised Tunney had discarded his tux in favor of his jeans and cowboy hat, shirt, and boots. She laughed thinking about how uncomfortable he was in the formal outfit. It was so not him.

As Tam and Molly were strolling around hand in hand, chatting with everyone, Tunney called attention to the stage. "If I could get your attention again," he said with the same authority he did when trying to talk over everyone at a nightclub. "Now that I've gotten out of that monkey suit, the party can begin," he declared to much cheering.

"I need to tell you a few things about my brother and Molly." Tunney continued. "Yes, they wouldn't be together without me, 'cause I met Molly first and introduced them. She set up a 'meeting' before she would hire our band for their graduation party. What college senior sets up a meeting? Well, that's our Molly.

"That's why I call her 'boss.' You know, I loved her from the first time I met her as well. I'm so glad she's my sister now.

"When Tam and Molly broke up all those years ago, I didn't see Molly, but I saw Tam. He was a broken man. He loved Molly with all his heart. I know now that Molly was devastated too. It was a true misunderstanding that kept them apart.

"When Tam went to tell Molly what really happened, he saw her with Jim and could see the love they had. I couldn't do much to help my brother. He knew he'd lost Molly. Tam could tell what a fine man Jim was and how he loved her," Tunney said with a touch of sadness. "I just tried to be there for my brother back then." His words held such emotion that you could hear a pin drop in the hall.

257

"When Molly and Tam found each other again at that stupid corporate meeting, they started a whole new chapter in their lives.

"Unfortunately, because of crazy legal rules and regulations around mergers and acquisitions and all that crap, they couldn't really talk to each other. I know for a fact it was agony for both of them, and I went back and forth between the two," Tunney said, scanning the crowd.

"I know Ken, Molly's boss, and Jen, his wife, have been very supportive of her over the years and helped her through very difficult times." He tipped his hat to Ken and Jen. "And now they're very important to both Molly and Tam.

"What I saw between Tam and Molly, then and now, is two people who have this incredible love for each other that's so strong. There are a lot of people looking for love in bars, nightclubs, dance halls, and what they find, maybe, is lust rather than love.

"Those folks don't look at each other the way Tam and Molly do. It's real love, true love, and I'm so happy for both of them and proud to call Tam my brother, not because he's some big CEO, but because he's a genuinely good man, and to call Molly, one of my favorite women in the world, my sister," Tunney said, to great applause.

"One of the things Molly always wished for when Tam and I played in the band together was to dance with him. Well, babe, it's your wedding day, so I want to invite you up here to have the first dance with your husband."

With that, Molly and Tam made their way to the space that was cleared for the dance floor, with tremendous applause and cheers from the crowd. They kissed as they started dancing, and the cheering continued.

"Oh, Tam, I'm speechless. I'm so happy," Molly said, smiling up at him. "You probably don't know how much I wished I could dance with you when I used to come to all your gigs.

"It's wonderful to be in your arms, dancing. It's perfect. And to have all these people here with us…"

"I agree," he said, nuzzling her hair. "The kids seem to be having a great time too. I was kinda worried about them, but they're running around with all those cousins."

"You mention the kids… I think I should tell you I'm a bit… late."

"Late for what, their birthdays?" Tam was confused.

"No, late in that I think I might be…"

"Pregnant," he said, wide-eyed. "Oh my God, Molly," Tam said as quietly as he could so others couldn't hear.

"Now, don't say anything." Molly shushed him, concerned. "I haven't taken a pregnancy test or gone to the doctor. It could be just stress."

"Hmm." His wheels were turning. "I have an idea."

Just then, the dance ended to great applause, and Tam handed Molly over to her father for the next song. As she moved around the dance floor with Fred, she could see Tam having a conversation with Ruth and then Bobby, and Ruth left the hall.

After all the dances with the parents and wedding party were over, Tam and Ruth cornered Molly, away from the noise of the band.

"Listen, I told Ruth what was going on, and she's not going to tell anyone. She ran next door to the pharmacy and got a pregnancy test, and I want you to take it. If we're going to be parents, I need to know right away," Tam said urgently.

"Oh, Tam. You know all the stress and everything could be causing me to be late. My system could be off. There's no guarantee I'm pregnant. Please don't get your hopes up," Molly pleaded, keeping her voice down. "To be honest, we've been so busy that I really didn't think about it until you mentioned the children."

Ruth grabbed Molly's arm and guided her into the ladies' room. "I'll go into the stall next to you and hand you the pregnancy kit. I have a bag as well, if you need to hide it. Plus is pregnant; minus is not."

Tam watched as they went inside the restroom. He ran over to the bar to get a drink. The next couple minutes were agonizing. Could he become a husband and father-to-be in the same day? Incredible.

He just needed to remember what Molly said; it could just be the stress. *Calm down*, he told himself over and over.

Thank God Tunney was onstage. He would see Tam was a wreck in two seconds.

If Molly were pregnant, that would be wonderful. If she wasn't, that was fine, too.

There were a few women in the ladies' room when Ruth and Molly first came in, and they greeted her with words of congratulations before she could go into the stall. Then Ruth slid into the stall next to her.

Ruth handed Molly the pregnancy test kit under divider. Molly opened it and, with some effort in her wedding dress, followed the instructions on the package.

"It says to wait three minutes," Molly whispered. "I can't believe we're doing this! Can you time it?"

"Yes, of course," Ruth said.

Just then, another woman came into the restroom and used the stall next to them. After she washed her hands and left, Molly asked how much time was left.

"I think we should give it one more minute," Ruth whispered. "Hey, if it's positive, no more champagne for you!" She giggled.

"And no wine on our honeymoon in the south of France," Molly whispered, groaning. "Well, the result will be definitely worth it," she said with a laugh, still trying to keep her voice down.

They both waited, trying to be patient. "Okay," Ruth said. "Now."

Molly looked at the stick. "Oh my God, it's positive. I'm pregnant!" Molly said in an excited whisper.

At that moment, another woman came into the bathroom.

Molly put the test back in the bag, came out of the stall, and discretely threw the bag into the trash bin.

As both Ruth and Molly washed their hands, the wedding guest offered her congratulations to Molly and told her how beautiful she looked. "You are absolutely glowing."

It took all of Molly's will not to laugh out loud.

"Thank you so much," she replied. "I'm so happy at this moment, on this day."

With that, all three women left the ladies' room, and Ruth whispered in Molly's ear, "I'll let you tell Tam," and she wandered over to rejoin Bobby.

She smiled at Ruth and hurried over to Tam, who was talking to his cousins, or making a valiant effort to do so.

"Can I steal him for a minute?" Molly asked the group, grabbing Tam by the arm.

She steered him to as quiet a corner as she could find and looked up at him, smiling coyly.

"What! Tell me. Are you pregnant?"

"It looks like our lives are about to change in more ways than one," she said, laughing. "Yes, the test says I'm pregnant. Can you believe it?"

Tam enveloped her in his arms.

"Now, I'll need to go to the doctor to confirm it, so we shouldn't announce it here," Molly said urgently. "Tam?"

"Mol, we've got to tell our parents," Tam pleaded. "Fred and Margaret are going to be grandparents for the first time."

Ruth watched from across the room as Tam and Molly pulled Fred and Margaret aside and talked to them with their heads close together. She could see they were overjoyed with the news. *What a day*, Ruth thought. She also saw Molly and Tam walk over to his parents to tell them the news. Tam's mother began crying.

Uh-oh, Ruth thought as she saw Tam making his way to the stage. As the band ended a song, he jumped up and grabbed the mic from Tunney.

"My brother has had the mic tonight, and so has my beautiful wife, so it's now my turn," he said, smiling broadly at the crowd. Molly rushed over to the head of the stage to try and remind him of his promise not to announce her pregnancy.

"Family and friends, it means so much to Molly and me that you're here with us to celebrate this fabulous day, this glorious day." Tam began, winking at Molly. "I would like to address my children," he said, staring at Molly and her stomach before looking at his son and daughter, who moved to the front of the stage. "Today, we have a whole new family to celebrate, and Molly and I want you to know how much we love you and how special it is that we'll be a family.

"While we are looking forward to our honeymoon in France, we can't wait to get back to you, our family," he added. "And for all the people here who don't have a spouse or partner, I wish you could find someone as special as I have. The first night I met her seventeen years ago, I played the guitar and sang in my brother's band. When I looked at her that night, I knew I never wanted to be apart from her.

"When she would come to hear the band, I always looked for her in the crowd. When I saw her, I knew everything was going to be all right. So this song is for Molly," he said, smiling at her.

Molly marveled at what was happening. Her husband was going to sing to her. How did a woman so hell-bent against traditional roles find herself married, pregnant, and being serenaded by said husband? She laughed to herself. Today's events seemed unreal.

As Tam strapped on his guitar, Molly moved even closer to the stage. When she looked into his steel-blue eyes and listened to him singing, Molly silently said her promises to him, which were as sacred to her as the vows they took in the church.

We will get a house here in Wisconsin, so our children will really know our families.

After the merger is complete and I finish building the new corporate social responsibility organization, I'm leaving my job to focus on our family and philanthropy. We have more money than we could ever need, and we must focus on us, our family, and helping others.

Our children will work for everything and make their own futures, and we will teach them to volunteer to help others.

We will do whatever we can to support Tunney and Cissy in their relationship, as we want them to feel the kind of happiness we do right now.

I will never let you drown in your job, Tam, and will help calm and cheer you when the stress and demands are overwhelming; I know you'll do the same for me.

I will encourage you and Ken to work together to teach others how to be the best CEOs and leaders possible, sharing your formulas for leadership development and integrity and ethics, as you are both rare leaders.

We will stop by and see our tree every year to remind us of the love we had, lost, and found again and never, ever take it for granted.

I will do my best to keep our passion alive, even when we're buried in diapers and late-night feedings.

I will look in those same beautiful, steel-blue eyes decades from now, and, despite any grey hair, wrinkles, and extra pounds, will still see my Tam, the man I loved from the first moment we met.

We will fight through any adversity that is thrown at us, and it will come, as we can never lose each other again...

Molly smiled at Tam when she finished thinking through her vows. They had a way of communicating without talking that started on the first night they met, so he understood she was telling him something.

When Tam finished his song, Molly did something she'd never done before. She went onstage and hugged and kissed him. He seemed a bit surprised, too, but certainly pleased.

After they kissed, the applause and hooting was so loud Tam had to almost shout in her ear, "What were you saying to me during the song? I could tell you were thinking about something serious."

Molly smiled and stroked his face. "We'll have plenty of time to talk about it. A lifetime, really." She wrapped her arms around him as their family and friends cheered.

It is so great to be home.

acknowledgements

Thanks to all of my friends and family who believed I could achieve my dream and write this book. I loved writing it and living with these characters. Perhaps I am not entirely done writing about them yet!

I would be lost without the support of family and friends in Milwaukee, Wisconsin, my hometown, and in Liverpool, England, my husband Roy's birthplace and home to many family members and dear friends. While we live in California, we spend a great deal of time in England and Milwaukee, and I am grateful to my friends and family from all over for their unwavering encouragement and support. It sure helps when you are writing your first book to hear people say, "I can't wait to read it."

A big thank you to my editor, Cassie McCown, for being an honest critic and helping this book flow easily. She's a real talent and great sounding board for ideas. Kris Radish, best-selling author and college friend, provided invaluable advice, direction, friendship, and support. Kris is, and has been, an inspiration to me, and I am indebted to her for everything she has done to support my writing.

Thanks to you, the reader, for taking the time to read *Hostile Takeover: A Love Story*. Without you, the writing doesn't matter. I have a long list of writing projects I want to complete, and I hope with your support, I will do it. Thanks for your encouragement so far.

about the author

Phyllis J. Piano spent more than 30 years as an award-winning corporate communications expert for some of the world's largest companies. She has somehow managed to maintain her sense of humor, love of writing, and her passion for life and the people she loves and cares about.

A world traveler, Piano has left the corporate world and has fallen back into the arms of her own first love...writing. She and her husband split their time between, California, England and the Midwest. When she is not packing a bag, making artisan sourdough bread or cooking with lots of garlic, Piano is working on a screenplay and her next novel.

Selected Titles from SparkPress

SparkPress is an independent boutique publisher delivering high-quality, entertaining, and engaging content that enhances readers' lives, with a special focus on female-driven work.

Visit us at www.gosparkpress.com

The Balance Project, by Susie Orman Schnall. $16, 978-1-94071-667-1. With the release of her book on work/life balance, Katherine Whitney has become a media darling and hero to working women everywhere. In reality though, her life is starting to fall apart, and her assistant Lucy is the one holding it all together. When Katherine does something unthinkable to her, Lucy must decide whether to change Katherine's life forever, or continue being her main champion.

So Close, by Emma McLaughlin and Nicola Kraus. $17, 978-1-940716-76-3. A story about a girl from the trailer parks of Florida and the two powerful men who shape her life—one of whom will raise her up to places she never imagined, the other who will threaten to destroy her. Can a girl like her make it to the White House? When her loyalty is tested will she save the only family member she's ever known—even if it means keeping a terrible secret from the American people?

Learning to Fall, by Anne Clermont. $16.95, 978-1940716787. Raised amidst the chaos and financial insecurity of her father's California horse training business, Brynn Seymour wants little more than to leave the world of competitive riding behind. But when her father is trampled in a tragic accident, she struggles to save the business—and her family—and is forced to reckon with the possibility that only the competitive riding world she's tried to turn away from can heal the broken places inside of her.

Found, by Emily Brett, $16.95, 978-1940716800. ICU nurse Natalie Ulster has a desire to see the world and a need to heal, which is compensation for her own damaged heart. Natalie grabs life by the globe and accepts successive assignments in Belize, Australia, and Arizona. When Natalie meets Dr. Joel Lansfield she's not sure she's ready to make room in her heart for love. However, too many near-death coincidences force her to ask herself a frightening question: Is someone trying to kill her?

About SparkPress

SparkPress is an independent, hybrid imprint focused on merging the best of the traditional publishing model with new and innovative strategies. We deliver high-quality, entertaining, and engaging content that enhances readers' lives. We are proud to bring to market a list of *New York Times* best-selling, award-winning, and debut authors who represent a wide array of genres, as well as our established, industry-wide reputation for creative, results-driven success in working with authors. Spark-Press, a BookSparks imprint, is a division of SparkPoint Studio LLC.

Learn more at GoSparkPress.com